The Miracle Terminus

Cenarth Fox

Book 1 *The Miracle Railway*
Book 2 *The Miracle Branch Line*
Book 3 *The Miracle Royal*
Book 4 *The Miracle Terminus*

Acknowledgements

With grateful thanks to

John McKay
Author World War Two novels

Trevor Viénet
World War Two Railway Posters

Andrew Watts
Norfolk Disused Railways

Front cover photograph

Lakeside and Haverthwaite Railway (L&HR)
Cumbria, England
(Photographer unknown)

Dedication

To all Heritage Railway volunteers everywhere

Chapter 1

George ran. Talk about a rare sight. He hurried home desperate for news of his missing daughter, Victoria. His shrapnel-tinged hip screamed but the station master didn't care. As he departed, the body of King George V arrived in the yard alongside the Up platform.

Over the last 12 years, the two Georges, King and station master, enjoyed a friendly, respectful relationship. The Monarch admired the SM for his sacrifice during the Great War and his courtesy in dealing with members of the Royal Family. The SM admired the King for his support of the little people, the hundreds who worked on the Sandringham estate and those in the village and on the Royal Station.

As he ran, George didn't think about the late King, only the health and location of his precious darling daughter. The fear in his wife's voice was palpable. The memory of his mother being abducted years ago at Whittleton station exploded inside his head. Connie survived but this was different. Ma was safe but not his daughter.

Where is she?

Victoria's a child and if she's been taken, the man or men involved —it couldn't possibly be a woman—were desperate for a ransom. Any delay, any wrong move from George or the police could mean the child might be killed, even die a horrible death. What could be worse?

He burst into the kitchen and embraced his wife. Housekeeper Miss Halfpenny looked distraught. Mrs Galbraith, former teacher of son James and daughter Victoria, returned when Louisa telephoned with news of the possible abduction.

George spoke first. 'The police are on their way. Now tell me again where have you looked?'

'Everywhere,' said Louisa and broke down.

Mrs Galbraith was the last person to see Victoria. 'I came to give her a few books as school was closed due to the King's funeral. She was fine, we chatted and she followed me to the front gate. I set off back to the village, turned and waved and she waved back.'

'Did you see her go into the house?' asked George.

'No, at least, oh I'm so sorry, I'm not sure.'

'Please don't distress yourself, Mrs Galbraith,' said George.

'All I can remember was a car parked on the road towards the church. I didn't think anything of it. I only remembered it when Mrs Miracle rang to tell me Victoria was missing.'

Another sob from Louisa and George knew he must remain outwardly calm. A surge of relief washed over him knowing his son was staying with the boy's grandmother in Cambridgeshire.

'Who have you told about this?'

Louisa struggled. 'Only you and Mrs Galbraith; oh George, where is she? She would never go off on her own. Someone has taken her.'

'I'll go and look. I'll return as soon as the police arrive. Stay here by the phone. Be brave, she's a clever little girl. We'll find her.'

He kissed his wife, gave a forced smile to the others and left.

Across the road at the station, the officer in charge of the King's coffin walked onto the platform looking for railway officials, in particular the man in charge, the station master. He even knew the SM's name.

The Royal Train with a locker section in one of the carriages as part of the formation rested ready to accept the VIP passenger. The locomotive hissed gently with the occasional metallic clang. The footplate crew stood ready not speaking.

Touching his cap, Sam Mason approached the visitor. 'I'm Mason, sir, senior porter.'

'Porter? Where's the station master?'

'There's an emergency, sir. Mr Miracle has been unexpectedly called away to attend to a possible kidnapping.'

'Then I'll speak with the Assistant Station Master.'

'There is no ASM, sir.'

'What? This is the Royal Station!'

'Yes sir but we're small. Only bigger stations have an ASM.'

The uniformed gent fumed. 'Look here my man; I have the body of the King outside ready to be transferred to this train.'

'And we're ready to receive His Majesty, sir.'

'The paperwork must be completed and in duplicate.' He turned back to his assistant who offered up the form. The officer pointed to the relevant section. 'Here, it states I require the signature of the station master from Wolferton station.'

Sam kept his responses soft and humble. 'When the station master is absent, sir, I am able to sign documents on his behalf.'

The visitor's dander kept climbing. He was a perfect example of a by-the-book man. If he submitted paperwork with any details not perfect, he'd cop it in the neck. He was born subservient. He wanted, no demanded the SM to sign.

Outside in the hearse, the King couldn't care less. He once proposed a toast to George and his bride on their wedding day at this very station, but right now his thoughts were elsewhere.

Sam Mason humbly accepted the paperwork shoved at him, signed on behalf of his boss and returned said material.

Fuming, the officer in charge tore off a copy and thrust it at Sam before snarling a threat. 'Heads will roll for this.'

He turned and nodded to the officer in charge of the bearer party waiting at the station entrance. In turn, he gave the signal to the soldiers waiting by the hearse. Under the watchful eye of the undertaker and Royal officials, the King made his final journey into the station he came to love.

The doors of the carriage were guarded by senior members of the Royal Family and senior staff of the Royal Household. The pallbearers entered the platform stepping the short distance to the relevant carriage perfectly in line with the station entrance.

As you would expect, the soldiers as pallbearers moved with military precision, their steps short and perfectly in unison. Villagers gathered on the platforms, more on the Down, removing their headgear. There would be many of the Monarch's subjects on the stations from Wolferton to King's Lynn and then thousands along the route all the way to London.

With the coffin resting safely and securely, the bearer party disembarked whilst those accompanying the Late King boarded the Royal Train.

The officer-in-charge nodded permission for Sam to give the 'right-away'. The guard's green flag was waved, and slowly and steadily the locomotive crew drew the Royal Train forward, and the Late King departed Wolferton station for the very last time.

Fare thee well, Your Majesty.

George didn't know what to do, where to look. He made a quick trip around the garden wanting to call out. His throat wouldn't co-operate. Victoria loved playing games and her father teased her time and again but always with love. She adored hiding to tease him back.

He knew she wouldn't hide for this amount of time and with her mother and the other ladies calling for her with desperation in their voices. Besides they'd looked in every possible hiding-place.

George hurried to the signal-box and climbed the steps. Cluffie met him at the door.

'I just heard, Mr Miracle but I told Sam I ain't seen your little girl.'

'What about any cars?' asked George desperate for anything.

'I ain't looking for cars but I heard one coming back from the church. I think it stopped before turning and driving back towards St Peter's. I can't see so well once they move away from your house.'

George looked out of the signal-box windows. Cluffie was right. The front gate of the station master's house was hidden around the corner of the property. If Victoria came from the front gate, she would not be seen from the station or signal-box.

'Thanks Cluffie. I'll get on,' said George departing down the stairs.

'Good luck,' called the signalman. 'I'm sure she'll turn up.' He wasn't sure at all but that's what people say to those in distress.

From across the road, Sam and the other porters watched their boss head home. He looked a shattered man.

As George reached his property, a police car approached. He stepped forward, waved and the car pulled in with two officers alighting.

'Mr Miracle?' asked the first. George nodded. 'Sergeant Brighton, sir and Constable Rock.'

George shook hands with both and invited them inside. The three women were both pleased to see action but despairing they may already have bad news. They didn't.

The police were told the story and the senior officer spoke. 'We'll arrange for officers from the region to come and search. Could you gather a group from the village, sir?'

'Of course,' said George.

'Only one person to co-ordinate and I suggest Constable Rock, so we can conduct an efficient search. May we use your phone, sir?'

'Of course,' said George again, 'but it might be easier to meet at the station. Plenty of room in the yards and you can use my office and phone as your HQ.'

Louisa loved the way her husband showed leadership but she couldn't shake the ache of despair.

Sergeant Brighton looked at the parents. 'We'll need someone to remain by the phone. If your daughter has been taken, you might get a call. I'll have an officer with experience in dealing with these matters come and stay if that's all right.'

Of course,' said George, 'we have plenty of room.' He spoke to Louisa. 'You'll be okay, my dear. I'll gather searchers from the village.'

'What about the estate?' asked Mrs Galbraith. 'I'm sure many of the tenant farmers would be only too glad to assist.'

'Great idea, Mrs Galbraith; I'll make a call from the station.'

Within the hour, close to a hundred men and a good sprinkling of women gathered in the yard beside the station. Several were on horseback. Two cars with police officers arrived. Earlier that day, the deceased and now former King rested in this same yard.

Sergeant Brighton introduced himself to the volunteers explaining the situation. They were to concentrate on two areas in and around the station master's house and further afield in the direction where the suspect vehicle headed.

They set off and being late January, daylight hours were restricted. Looking for the child in the dark was next to useless.

George was introduced to the officer who was to stay at the SM's home in case any kidnappers made contact. Constable Hatt was a senior officer in terms of years of service but still of lowly rank. The friendly, rotund chap moved slowly and George wondered if the officer was ever called upon to chase a suspect, how on Earth he could even get close to the criminal let alone make an arrest.

Inside, George introduced him to the ladies where Miss Halfpenny provided tea and biscuits and George returned to work. The porters eyed him wondering how best to approach their superior.

Typical George wanted all details of the station's operations in his absence. Sam held back.

'Did the Late King get away all right?' asked the boss.

'Yes sir,' replied the porter thinking now was not the time to explain the bumptious official demanding to see the station master.

'I'll be back and forth between my office and home, Sam. The police have someone stationed across the road so we're well placed to deal with any news when we find Victoria.'

When or if? Sam watched his boss struggle. What could the porter say? Having your child disappear, probably abducted, must be soul-destroying. Having no leads or news would compound their misery. Thinking positive must be everyone's response.

'We've had a chat, Mr Miracle. The lads have offered to work extra shifts allowing you to do whatever needs doing. We want you to not even think about station duties for now. All your shifts have been covered and will continue to be so for as long as it takes.'

George looked at the man he'd worked with for 12 years. The SM couldn't speak. The lump in his throat sat firm and kept growing. He nodded his gratitude, dropped his head and entered his office.

By late afternoon as darkness rolled in, the searchers had found nothing and no-one so disbanded keen to resume at first light. Victoria Miracle simply vanished into thin air.

Sleeping was impossible. Miss Halfpenny and Constable Hatt retired. George and Louisa were alone. The phone remained silent.

'You should get some sleep, my dear,' said George.

'I was about to say the same thing,' replied Louisa.

'Yes but I'm an old soldier. I can go without sleep.'

'We should have telephoned our mothers.'

'Why make them suffer? If Vicky is found soon we'll have saved them the grief and worry we're suffering now.'

Louisa broke down and George embraced her. They sat on the settee in front of a dying fire in the sitting-room.

She whispered between sobs. 'What is happening to us? Who has done this? Where is our darling girl?'

He didn't speak. He dare not raise the issue of their inheritance as a magnet for criminals. The Miracles never flaunted their wealth but it was no secret. Right now they would happily give away everything, every last penny to have their child returned safe and sound.

Chapter 2

The King is dead. Long live the King! As George and Louisa suffered unimaginable pain and dozens of people searched high and low for the young and missing Victoria Miracle, George V arrived at and then departed Wolferton station in a somewhat palatial box, and from there travelled up to London. The station master, with more pressing business to attend to, was absent.

Of course the Monarchy would continue and the late King's first born, Edward the Prince of Wales became King Edward VIII.

With enough given names to field about half a rugby XV, Edward, known within his family as David, broke with tradition and watched the proclamation of his ascension from a window at St James Palace in London with a certain Mrs Bessie Wallis Simpson by his side.

This was the first sign the new King would not be easy to deal with. Becoming King was the simple part; his coronation and choice of bride were other matters entirely.

Edward didn't fancy all that ceremonial carry on, had little time for history and tradition and worse, had chosen a possible wife whose behaviour and status was likely to upset the world and its mother.

He was not unlike his namesake, his grandfather Edward VII in that both men found the company of women much to their liking and due to this predilection, found themselves in hot water.

The grandfather engaged in liaisons at home and abroad and must have left a notebook with seduction instructions for his grandson.

Officials responsible for arranging the coronation could not have foreseen the problems the new King would create. Edward was the perfect Royal nightmare.

His failure to seriously and sincerely engage with those planning the big event in the Abbey caused many chaps to lose large chunks of their own hair.

Edward wanted change. Take the issue of money. When it came to the Royal image on coins, each new Monarch swapped position, i.e. if your predecessor faced left you faced right and vice versa. Edward ignored tradition.

On coins his father faced left and so Edward by tradition would face right. But no, the new King insisted he too face left. Why? Because facing left, Edward could display his immaculate hairstyle.

Being a bachelor, naturally thoughts turned to a bride for His Majesty. A pretty, pristine English rose from an impeccable old English family was hands down the ideal choice.

Edward had other ideas.

He chose an American divorcee currently seeking a formal split from her second husband. At this time, the British public knew little of the King's latest mistress.

The late King could not abide his son's lover, and the Prime Minister thought it totally unsuitable for a soon-to-be twice divorced woman with both ex-husbands still alive to even be considered as the Queen Consort. And as the new King was the titular head of the Church of England, you can imagine what the Archbishop of Canterbury, the Primate of All England, the Scotsman Cosmo Lang thought of the status of the lady in question.

'She's divorced? Say that again. Twice!'

Now because of his controversial actions, one didn't need a crystal ball to predict trouble ahead for Edward VIII. Thumbing his nose towards those at court, in Lambeth Palace and in the Palace of Westminster, he offered his arm to his sweetheart, Bessie, the smiling divorcee from Pennsylvania.

Edward's plan was simple. Get crowned, have Wallis obtain her latest divorce, marry his lover and reign happily evermore.

That was never going to happen and it's doubtful if even Edward believed it would. He was known to jokingly refer to his sister-in-law, the Duchess of York, as the Queen Mother. Did the new King show prescience sensing his younger brother, the Duke of York, would one day be King causing Elizabeth Windsor nee Bowes-Lyon to make Edward's prediction come true?

Chapter 3

In Wolferton, George and Louisa were unable to sleep. Anyone in their situation would likely pace the room, toss and turn or quietly cry the night away.

George slipped out of bed at 4am. His one sliver of pleasure came from seeing and hearing his wife actually asleep. She'd been awake for hours. He knew because *he* couldn't sleep. Outside the weather demanded boots, scarf, coat and gloves.

He opened the front door, the biting January air slapped his cheeks and he blinked in response. No moon meant an inky sky. Stepping on the doormat he stood on something. It didn't squish or crackle. He knelt and picked up a plain, unaddressed envelope.

Cue a rapid heart rate. Mail was never delivered to the front doormat and never in the wee small hours. Only one thought bounced around George's head. *This is from the person who took Victoria.*

Clutching the object, he moved quickly and quietly along the garden path. *When did the envelope arrive? Even now might the postman be in the garden or outside in the street?*

George scanned the property making out only plants. At the gate he looked into the street; again nothing. Opening the gate, he stepped onto the road. No human sounds or movement. The trees copped a buffeting as did George's heart.

Upstairs, Louisa woke, found her husband missing and went downstairs. Pulling her dressing gown tight she saw the partly opened front door and called from there in a loud and frightened whisper. 'George!'

He hurried back. 'Inside, you'll catch your death,' he said closing the door and guiding her to the kitchen where the stove still gave off a little heat. George switched on a light and produced the envelope.

'This was on the doorstep.'

They looked at one another with both their stomachs in freefall.

'It must be from the kidnapper,' she gasped and watched as he withdrew the page. Struggling to breathe, they studied the contents. The words were printed.

YOUR GIRL IS SAFE.
PAY THE RANSOM AND SHE WILL BE RELEASED UNHARMED.
GET £5000 IN USED NOTES.
DELIVERY DETAILS GIVEN LATER.
IF YOU AGREE, PUT VASE OF FLOWERS IN FRONT UPSTAIRS WINDOW.
NO FLOWERS, NO DAUGHTER.
WE WILL CONTACT YOU SOON.
CONTACT POLICE AND THE GIRL DIES.

The parents hugged one another. Louisa cried although her supply of tears was now close to empty. George comforted her. 'This is wonderful news my darling. She's alive and we can bring her home.'

They were interrupted by Constable Hatt who appeared half asleep and wearing the most colourful pyjamas in England.

'What's happened?' he asked and was shown the ransom note.

'This means she's alive,' said Louisa making a statement.

Hatt nodded. 'When and how did this arrive?' George explained.

'This means she's somewhere close,' added the SM. 'To hand deliver the note means at least one of them is nearby.'

More nodding from the officer but Louisa panicked. 'But if we involve the police, they say they'll kill Victoria.'

'Let's sit down,' said George. 'Tea please, my dear,' he asked mainly to give Louisa something to do, to take her mind off the situation. She made tea.

'This is the usual practice,' said Hatt. 'The police stay out of sight but stand ready to give advice and show ourselves only if necessary.'

'So does that mean the searching will stop?' asked George struggling to stay calm.

'No, but any police involved will not be in uniform. If we stop searching, you will be further depressed and the kidnappers will be suspicious wondering why the search has stopped.'

Both parents were uneasy. The thought Victoria would die because the police were involved turned their fear to horror. Hatt tried to get them dealing with practical issues.

'Tell me again sir, about raising the money.'

George nodded. 'I have a plan using our agent in London.'

'I'm guessing the people involved know you have the finances.'

Another nod from George who asked, 'What do we do next?'

'Keep calm and arrange to collect the cash.'

Louisa brought steaming mugs of tea to the table. 'As we agreed, George, we leave all this with Crispin Webb. He will understand and keep the matter hush-hush.'

'You're right, my dear,' said George who focused on the policeman. 'So we raise the money then wait for them to contact us?'

'That's about it. You want to be able to move immediately. Delays run the risk of angering the kidnappers. I know it sounds outrageous but we need to keep them as relaxed and as confident as possible. We are guided by one priority—the safe return of your daughter.'

The parents enjoyed a minor surge of confidence. Constable Hatt gave off an air of calm professionalism even if in those pyjamas he looked ridiculous.

Louisa startled the men by suddenly racing from the room and calling. 'I need to put flowers in the front upstairs window.'

'I was about to suggest that,' said Hatt. 'Kidnappers try to exert control by making demands. They issue an order and you comply as quickly as possible helping them to believe they're in charge.' George looked depressed. 'But we play our own game, Mr Miracle and we have right on our side.'

George wanted to be convinced and kept thinking aloud. 'Well they won't hand deliver their next instructions. They won't risk being caught walking up our garden path again.'

'You've missed your calling, Mr Miracle. You would have made a first-class detective.' He looked around. 'You wouldn't have a biscuit I suppose?'

George invaded foreign territory searching for food, failed and was saved by a returning spouse. The heavy-breathing and heart-pounding parents looked at one another as the visiting copper dipped two of Miss Halfpenny's Lemon Sour Cream biscuits in his tea.

As the Miracles watched the constable add to his substantial waistline, they didn't know if he was always calm or acting as per instructions. He chatted away treading that fine line between giving hope and hinting at the possibility of a long process.

'In my experience, Mr and Mrs Miracle, there is no set routine for kidnappers. Some plan thoroughly and others make a spur of the moment decision to commit the crime.'

'This must have been planned,' said George. 'Victoria would never get into a car with a stranger.'

'Never,' repeated Louisa.

'They may have used the King's funeral as a distraction,' said George.

Constable Hatt reckoned the SM was in the wrong job. Having explained the next steps, the policeman went for distraction.

'I was going to suggest, sir that you go back to work. The searchers will return at first light and if you're in your office, we can contact you with any developments. I'll be surprised if you hear from them today.'

George didn't want to argue. 'I'll contact our accountant and make sure everything is in order with raising the money.'

'But go back to work, sir and leave everything to us.'

Louisa panicked. 'But you'll make sure the kidnappers can't see any police. If they see police they said they'll kill Victoria.'

'I think we can be fairly certain the kidnappers are in a secure hiding place, Mrs Miracle. Local people and police in plain clothes will search the woods, fields, river banks and the like. Based on their note, I reckon the kidnappers have planned this well. They'll be hidden and believe me, they want that money.'

All three retired although sleep was a stranger to the parents.

After dawn the pressure kept building. Shaved and dressed, George came downstairs ready for work. Louisa tugged his coat.

'What do I do, George, if my mother telephones to tell us about James? I'll have to tell her. Or what if James telephones with all his news? The boy's clever and will know we're hiding something.'

This was a real problem. To lie about a granddaughter or a sister being kidnapped seemed unforgiveable. To say nothing was worse. George sighed.

'I'll leave it to you, my darling but if you do tell anyone, please stress we're hoping she'll return today or very soon.' He hugged her, kissed her forehead and crossed the road to the station.

His arrival caused a serious reaction. The porters were confused. *Why is he here?* Surely trying to help rescue his daughter would be his only priority. Besides we told him his shifts were covered.

Cluffie looked out from his signal-box and scratched his head. *What's the boss doing here?* The first train to arrive saw the guard and footplate crew stare in surprise.

Everyone knew about the missing girl and the assumption was she'd been kidnapped. The news spread and the massive inheritance from Louisa's father prompted people to put two and two together. *Although they never flaunt it, the Miracles have money.*

Up and down the line from Hunstanton to King's Lynn, station staff discussed the frightening incident. News reached London and in Liverpool Street, when told the news, Jack Rogers reacted with fury.

George Miracle was like a son to him. Alone in his office, the soon-to-retire SM lost control and slammed his fist into the wall causing equal amounts of damage to the building and his hand.

A secretary entered and stopped in shock at the sight.

'I do apologize, Miss Rickard. I've just received terribly sad news involving a young girl.'

Back at Wolferton, driver Ernie Cruickshank driving the first Down saw the SM on the platform. The driver stopped the train correctly, placed his fireman in temporary charge, stepped out of the cab and headed towards George. Ernie's thinking being that if the SM was back on deck his girl must have been found safe and sound.

George looked shocked. 'Problem, Mr Cruickshank?' he asked of the approaching driver.

'Not with the loco, Mr Miracle. I'm hoping you have good news about your wee girl.'

George lost any anger about a train being delayed. 'Alas no, Ernie,' he replied using the man's Christian name which he rarely did. 'But we live in hope. The police and local folk are doing a grand job and I'm ready to help at a moment's notice.'

There wasn't much more Ernie could say. He held out his hand which George shook. 'Everyone's got their fingers crossed, sir,' he said, returned to his cab and prepared to send the loco on its way.

George was in a quandary. At the station everyone wanted to wish him well which meant he was being worn down with kindness. If he stayed home, his mind was locked in the misery of his missing precious daughter and his inability to find her.

He decided to go home when Sergeant Brighton walked through the platform gate. Fear gripped George as the policeman's uniform shouted to the world that here was a copper.

They adjourned to George's office and closed the door.

'I've seen the ransom note, Mr Miracle and rest assured we'll keep any police presence to an absolute minimum.'

George looked ready to collapse. 'I don't know what to do.'

'You've done everything you can. The search parties will continue, detectives will keep looking for the kidnappers and we're ready to respond as soon as they make contact.'

George did and didn't want to ask questions. 'If Victoria's being kept in a building, why are we searching the fields and the woods?'

Brighton chose his words carefully. The police believed the girl was well hidden. If she'd been killed or escaped and died, her body might be found in the woods or where the searchers were looking. He didn't want to say as much. George did it for him.

'Is it because if she's dead, they'll dump her in a river or wood?'

The police officer's eyes spoke answering in the affirmative.

'Whatever you say or do, Sergeant, do not raise that situation with my wife.'

Chapter 4

That night, eating didn't appeal. George and Louisa lost their appetite picking at their food. Misery filled the room. The search turned up nothing and the kidnappers said nothing. Constable Hatt ate well removing the pattern on his plate. Miss Halfpenny collected the uneaten meals and with Socks the cat missing his mistress, the housekeeper fed the feline. Even the cat seemed miserable. The bleak mood depressed everyone. Was it worse than grief? Another layer of sadness occurred with the secrecy as no other family member knew anything. The telephone rang. George stood.

'I'll answer it.' He knew Louisa was close to collapsing and didn't want her speaking to a loved one, to anyone in her state. Not that he was feeling much better. Hatt observed from the corner of the room.

'Hello Dad, it's James,' said his son full of his usual excitement and joy. 'Have a guess what I learnt today?'

'Hello my boy,' said George. 'How are you and Grannie Mac?'

'We're both well, thank you and don't forget I'm coming home on Saturday morning on the 10:29.' Off he went with talking being his second favourite pastime. 'Mr Attwood is teaching me astrology.'

The former Wolferton Rector, Kenneth Attwood, now married and living in Cambridge, spent three half days a week at Hamilton-Weir House teaching his favourite pupil James Miracle.

Even in his misery George was thinking clearly. 'Astrology? Are you sure?'

'No, no I meant astronomy.' The bright boy explained the difference. 'We began with our solar system and next we'll study the cosmos, the whole universe. Did you know it's absolutely huge?'

'So I believe.'

'How are you, Ma and my baby sister?'

George froze. 'We're all looking forward to seeing you on the weekend, my boy. May I have a word with Grannie please?'

James did the right thing and fetched Rowena. She sounded wary.

'This is a first, the station master wanting a word.'
'Hello, mother-in-law. I'm afraid I have sad news.'
Rowena's heartbeat took off. 'What's happened?'
'Please don't distress James. Are you sitting down?'
'George,' she snapped in a sharp whisper. 'Tell me.'
'Victoria's missing, she's been kidnapped.'
A strangled cry came down the line.
'I knew this would happen,' she said. 'All that money from Louisa's father; it was bound to come back and haunt us.'

George begged in a whisper. 'Please don't tell James. We're working with the police and dealing with the people who took her. With any luck, she'll soon be home safe and well.'

'Should I keep James here until she's found?'

George didn't know what to say. How many parents get to deal with their child being kidnapped? His mind was a mess and making decisions right now became too difficult.

'Let me talk to Louisa and we'll telephone you tomorrow.'

He hung up feeling better that at least one family member now knew the situation. He told Louisa and she too improved; just. It may well be true; a troubled shared *is* a trouble halved.

Regular sleep disappeared. Several times in the wee small hours George reckoned he heard a sound. Was this the kidnapper returning with another letter? Were these the final instructions?

Twice he crept downstairs, opened the front door only to find an empty doormat. The second time, back inside, he switched on a lamp and put the kettle on the stove to be interrupted by Constable Hatt.

'Tea, officer?' asked George and the policeman happily agreed. George remembered the officer's habit and found Miss Halfpenny's latest batch of biscuits.

'There was nothing on the doormat, Constable. I've looked twice.'
'What about under it?'

George's face turned ghost-like. *He can't be serious.* The SM hurried to the front door. Lifting the doormat, he saw another ghost; another unaddressed envelope.

He looked into the pre-dawn darkness, saw and heard nothing and as he returned with the delivered item, Hatt dunked a biscuit.

'How did you know?' asked George handing the envelope to the police officer.

'An educated guess and a lot of experience,' he said spilling crumbs as he withdrew the letter.

ON EVENING JAN 31 PLACE BAGS OF MONEY INSIDE PLATELAYER'S HUT HALF MILE SOUTH OF HEACHAM STATION.

IF NO MONEY, WRONG MONEY OR POLICE, THE GIRL DISAPPEARS FOREVER.

IF YOU AGREE, REMOVE FLOWERS FROM UPSTAIRS WINDOW.

THIS WILL END WELL IF YOU DO AS TOLD.

George and the constable read and re-read the note. 'Will they keep their word?' asked the station master.

'For five thousand pounds I'm pretty sure they will.'

'But once they have the money what's their incentive to release my daughter?'

'They know they'll be hunted whatever happens but if your girl is returned safe and well, they probably believe the hunt won't be as intense, that the police won't go as hard if your daughter is ...'

'Is killed,' said George in a whisper. Hatt's face answered.

George's brain slipped into overload. 'What should I do now?'

'You've arranged the money. It needs to be brought to a secure place nearby and with a police escort. Let the police stay in control.'

'I would like to have a person I know working with the police.'

'That depends on the person.'

The SM thought of his friend George Carruthers. It was time for a difficult phone call which was made at 6am.

His Lordship was stunned but never more willing to help. The police would be in charge but Carruthers would represent the station master in the collection and transfer of the money. After all, it was George Carruthers who introduced the Miracles to Crispin Webb their financial adviser.

Hatt contacted his superiors and the police drew up a plan. Louisa came downstairs and needed to sit as the second note and latest news were explained.

'Can this possibly be true?' she asked. 'Will this actually happen? Will our girl finally be safe?' Without waiting for an answer, she ran upstairs to remove the flowers from the upstairs window.

Thanks to Crispin Webb, the notes—more like a king's than a station master's daughter's ransom—were cleared ready for collection. George wanted as few people involved as possible but naturally accepted the police being in charge albeit in a low-key, unseen role.

'Sergeant Brighton and more likely an Inspector will be here as soon as possible, sir,' said Hatt. 'Everything will be explained.'

Louisa's fear bubbled. 'But they say in their note if the police are involved, Victoria will disappear.'

Hatt reassured her the police would remain in the background.

George put his arm around his wife and spoke quietly, intimately. He tried to transfer his hope to her. She sensed his love and steely determination. He genuinely believed Victoria would be safe.

Louisa joined the faith movement and their expectations climbed although fear refused to go away, crouching silently in the shadows.

One topic dogged George; the subject of more kidnappings. He chose not to mention it to Louisa but his mind filled with fear for the future. If these kidnappers know about the Miracle wealth, what's to stop others from planning and trying the same?

And if this kidnap nets the criminals the massive amount of £5,000, how many others will try a copycat crime? Instead of a housekeeper, George reckoned they might have to employ a security guard. What sort of life would that be?

Despair whacked him as he thought of any damage Victoria may have suffered. Would she be physically harmed? Did they interfere with her? His insides strangled themselves. What about mental scars? Will she ever be able to sleep alone? Will she require the lights on every night? Will the trauma haunt her forever?

A sombre routine settled in the station master's house. Miss Halfpenny provided sustenance as George, Louisa and Hatt tried to find something to do. Any phone call sent nerves jangling.

George walked across the road to work. Senior police were due soon and waiting became torture.

Again the porters were super sensitive. Sam Mason wanted to shoo away his boss but knew the man was walking on eggshells. The porter talked about any trivial railway matter to distract the SM.

Every Up and Down train arriving at Wolferton saw George out and looking at what he wasn't sure and when driver Ernie Cruikshank pulled in, again he hopped down and walked to George.

'No news, Mr Cruikshank, but thank you for asking.'

'Just a thought, Mr Miracle,' said the driver. 'On the final Up last night, I saw a small light in the Ramsay barn t'other side of Snettisham. Could be nothing but it struck me as odd.'

George didn't understand. 'I don't follow.'

'Old Tom and his missus are abed early, 'specially this time of year. It could be me old eyes playing tricks. I'll leave it with you.'

Ernie hopped back on the footplate and away went the train.

George turned and saw three gentlemen approaching. They weren't train passengers and the SM felt a surge of relief. In his office the policemen led by Inspector Rolf Carstairs gave George the details involving Scotland Yard and the LNER company police. It was a major undertaking collecting such a large amount of cash.

'We will transport the funds from London first thing tomorrow before placing them as instructed in the railway hut tomorrow night. We then expect to locate your daughter safe and well and have her returned to you and Mrs Miracle as soon thereafter as possible.'

Relief was one emotion, impatience another as George absorbed the details. He wanted January 31 to be today.

'Tell me, gentlemen,' asked George, 'why is the ransom £5,000?'

'Well sir,' said the Inspector, 'it's the same amount of work and risk so why not make it worth your while. £50,000 is a huge amount of physical cash, and "white fivers" are large and difficult to transport thus forcing a possible delay in raising the money. The kidnappers want a quick result. Not being greedy, if I may use so crude an expression, gives the kidnappers a greater chance of success. Five grand in the hand is better than fifty grand they never receive.'

George didn't want to ask the next question but couldn't help himself. 'If my daughter is returned safe and well and the kidnappers get away with the ransom, will that encourage them to try again? Will the criminal underworld hear about their success and be emboldened to have a go? Is my whole family now in permanent danger?'

The police officers hesitated, which only made George even more anxious. Carstairs remained calm. "Let's get past tomorrow night, Mr Miracle and hopefully rejoice in the safe return of your daughter. Sufficient unto the day is the evil thereof.'

Not being a biblical scholar or any type of philosopher, George lacked any understanding and took no comfort from that answer. He and the police finished their meeting. The officers left and George went home. He told his wife and Constable Hatt a truncated version of the plan knowing she would question anything and everything.

The hours dragged with George looking at his watch every time a train arrived at Wolferton. Daylight faded. There was this slow but inexorable increase in tension with the parents close to breaking. Stuck at home, George struggled to dampen his fear and desperation.

All four adults jumped when someone knocked on the back door. It would have to be a local. Any official or stranger would use the front door. Surely it couldn't be the kidnapper.

It was dark outside and George held up a hand wanting Louisa and Constable Hatt to remain where they were. Hatt was having none of that and followed the SM out of the kitchen.

Chapter 5

Christopher Collins, born 1928, was a happy lad despite his many ailments. At the time, people with learning difficulties were referred to as mentally deficient. People with physical difficulties were called cripples. Poor families with disabled children struggled to pay for medical services. There were few vaccinations. Christopher suffered twice over being a retarded cripple; yet still he smiled.

His father died before the boy was born and his mother, Clemmie, hated having to rely on charity from friends, family and her church.

She fell on her feet when told about Hamilton-Weir House in Cambridgeshire. She was offered a week for herself and her boy and what a week it was. A nurse on hand, volunteers including one Rowena McClaren to mind Christopher, and lashings of healthy grub in a setting where the birds squabbled over who would be chief chorister in the beautiful grounds.

Back home happily reminiscing about their holiday, and delighting in the offer to return later in the year, Clemmie told her sister Hazel about the wonderful respite home and the marvellous experience she and Christopher enjoyed. Hazel became curious and wanted details. Who provides this service? Is it really free? Who pays for it?

It turns out Clemmie asked the same questions and one evening when most residents were tucked up in bed, the woman who did so much to get the whole venue up and running, explained how the wealthy philanthropist, Sir Jerome Hamilton-Weir bequeathed his fortune to his daughter who in turn used the funds to establish the charity. No intimate details, only a broad explanation.

Clemmie's news went from Hazel to Victor Crump, Hazel's hubby. He and his brother Edgar were a couple of bad 'uns always out for an easy quid; minor London East End villains, more mug than thug.

They investigated the background of the Cambridgeshire charity and discovered Rowena's daughter was married to a chap called George Miracle, the station master at Wolferton station in sunny

Norfolk. He and his wealthy wife produced a couple of kids including a bright bubbly daughter, Victoria. There was wealth in the family, a lot of it. The kidnapping seed was sown.

The knock on the Miracle kitchen door sounded friendly, neither official nor officious. George opened it and grinned. If he'd been a singer, he might have burst into song such was his delight in seeing the former Rector at St Peter's Wolferton, Kenneth Attwood.

'Kenneth,' exclaimed George and inside, Louisa's spirits soared. The men embraced, Constable Hatt was introduced and the former local Rector greeted the lady of the house and the housekeeper.

He was a familiar face having spent many hours teaching James Miracle here in Wolferton. He continued that role although now at Hamilton-Weir House. Kenneth was married, loving life and teaching religious education part-time at a junior Prep school in Cambridge.

This was a tricky situation. The Miracles and their visitor were delighted to see one another but a pall of sadness and fear filled the house. Everyone knew the facts.

'Mrs McClaren told me your terrible news and I decided to come straight away to do whatever I can to help.'

'Thank you, Mr Attwood,' said Louisa her heart full of gratitude.

'I referred to my list of former parishioners and Mr and Mrs Delbridge insisted I stay with them so I'm here for as long as it takes to bring your dear girl back home safe and well.'

In the midst of their sorrow, love squeezed itself inside the station master's house.

Victor Crump was meticulous. Rather than intelligence, he possessed rat cunning and knew planning to kidnap the daughter of the wealthy woman and her railwayman husband needed time and attention to detail. His brother, Ed, would do whatever big brother said and with delight. His wife, Hazel, would do whatever her husband said but out of fear. Victor never held back in giving his woman a slap, his middle name being Brute.

The trio needed a plan to kidnap the child, a simple ransom note describing the exchange, and a means of escape. Getting the money was no good unless they could flee with the dosh. Hiring a car was tricky and checking the village and station needed guile. But they did so and when His Majesty George V died, Victor knew the pomp and circumstance of the funeral was a perfect cover to snatch the child. Having a woman play the lead kidnapping role was vital. Females are friendly and can plead ignorance and helplessness.

'Excuse me, Miss, have you seen my puppy?' was the perfect hook to have the station master's daughter leave her family home being desperate to help. Outside the front gate, she was grabbed, drugged, bundled into the back of the car and whisked away without her mother or former teacher seeing a thing.

That night, it was like old times. Kenneth and George sipped coffee in front of the fire. The last train left and it was a re-run of those Sunday evenings when the Rector and station master would relax and solve the worries of the world. The others retired leaving George to further explain the details.

'It all happens tomorrow, Kenneth. The money arrives under police escort with my friend George Carruthers.'

'Ah, the *best* best man and fill-in father of the bride.'

'The cash is delivered to the drop off point and, please God, we get our darling girl home with her body and mind in perfect condition.'

'What do you know of the drop-off point?'

George shrugged. 'It's a platelayer's hut by the line to Hunstanton. The police have the details and no doubt they'll have studied the area and be ready to move when Victoria is safe.'

Attwood hesitated and George worried even more.

'You don't sound confident, Kenneth. Have you reason to distrust the police?'

'No but I'm surprised you haven't investigated the scene yourself.'

George stared at his friend. 'But I can't. Well I can but isn't that dangerous? The police told me to stay well away.'

'Of course you must not interfere but being a railwayman living in this area for a decade or more, you might have something to add to help the police. If you were to carefully inspect this drop-off area, your intelligence could assist in rescuing Victoria.'

Neither man spoke. George desperately wanted to help but dreaded doing anything which might harm his adored daughter.

'My car's available if you'd like to make a discreet visit.'

George thought about the suggestion and stared at his friend. He decided, slipped upstairs telling Louisa he was escorting their visitor to his digs. The SM worried about how easily he lied.

The former clergyman asked George to help push his Austin Ten away from the house. They climbed in, the engine burst into life and away they went heading north towards Dersingham.

It was many years ago, in an Austin 7, that Kenneth drove George from the vicarage to Wolferton station en route to London for the birth of James Miracle. Their current excursion also involved the unknown with the risk of life and death sitting quietly in the rear seat.

Again the dark country Norfolk roads on a cloudy night added tension to their trip. George's heart complained. The men didn't talk. They knew the potential risks but both were desperate to help save the life of Miss Victoria Miracle.

Victor Crump done good. For a kid who left school with poor grades, he knew how to plan. Right now, he and his brother were tucked up in a small rented cottage in Hunstanton while working on a building project in the town for a week. They said they were casual labourers who come and go when farm work slows during the winter.

Their kidnap victim was well hidden and cared for by Mrs Crump. The hiding place was not obvious to the police or anyone. Hazel hated seeing the child tied and gagged and fought hard not to show any sympathy. Tomorrow night, once the cash exchanged hands, the victim would be set free. With the money collected, Hazel would be given the signal to leave a note revealing the child's whereabouts.

Once George and the former clergyman reached the village of Snettisham, the navigator gave detailed directions.

'This is the best road to take. The hut is before we get to Heacham. Let's hide the car and we'll find the line.'

Kenneth turned onto a farmer's track. They were unlikely to be blocking anyone or thing. They stepped out standing on fresh snow. Coats, gloves and scarves were essential. George wondered if his daughter was not only safe but warm.

'Railway's this way,' whispered George and set off.

They reached the line and turned left heading towards Hunstanton. Walking on the sleepers was the easiest way to progress and certainly the safest. George didn't use his torch wanting their presence to be as close to non-existent as possible.

Neither spoke. They sensed danger. The stillness of the night, the chill and the crunch as they trod on the snow kept them company.

George stopped without warning. Kenneth collided with him. 'What's up?' whispered the driver.

'Hut just ahead, on our right,' whispered his friend.

They stared through the gloom. This shape, this structure stared back. They waited. Was someone inside? Surely not a platelayer, not in the depths of winter. They stood there getting colder.

Kenneth reckoned standing still would achieve nothing. 'George, we either turn back or we investigate. You choose.'

George removed his torch as much as a weapon as a source of light and crept forward listening for any sounds. They reached the hut. It never won an award for architecture. In the middle of flat Norfolk fields, it stood with its flat roof, window, door and that's it.

They heard nothing and waited. Snoring or shuffling, anything—nothing. The kidnappers would hardly be inside.

Kenneth whispered. 'They're not here. This is where they want privacy. Try the door.'

George gripped the door knob, turned it and pushed. Snow fell from the roof. They saw or heard nothing so entered and closed the door. George shone his torch on the floor not wanting any light to be seen from outside. Once satisfied with the contents of the workman's tools, George killed his light.

'It's what you'd expect,' said Kenneth. 'It's an empty space leaving no clues for when they'll come to collect the money.'

'There's one thing missing,' said George.

'Trust a railwayman to notice.'

'There's no lamp.'

'So?' asked Kenneth.

'They've taken it so no-one can remove an essential part of their equipment.'

'I don't follow.'

'They plan to stop the train. They know the timetable. With the lamp and its red light, they'll stop the train, engage the crew while one of them sneaks aboard and uses the train to transport them and the money. The police will be watching the roads as the kidnappers and their cash sail past on the train. By the time they release Victoria, they'll be long gone, half way to London or at any spot along the line.'

Kenneth was impressed if not totally convinced. 'What next?'

'Let's tell the police. We'll ask them if they've considered the kidnappers using the trains.'

Not confident, Kenneth agreed. Instead of turning back to the car, George continued the way they came. 'Let's get to the next bend.'

They traipsed along the sleepers leaving a trail in the snow. If more fell, their visit would remain undetected. Reaching a curve in the line, George stopped. He'd seen or heard nothing.

'Let's go back.' He set off but stopped causing Kenneth to stumble. 'What's up?'

George pointed across the fields. 'Can you see that?'

Kenneth looked. 'See what?'

George didn't want to say but rather give his friend the freedom to reply without prompting. 'I could be imagining things.'

Kenneth squinted. 'Do you mean that tiny light?'

'That's it. One of the older drivers told me he saw a light in a barn where the farmer and his wife would be in bed. I want to investigate.'

Kenneth suggested this whole venture so didn't object. They walked across the snow-covered field. The light disappeared. They approached a barn and a farmhouse. The family dog slumbered inside. In canine years, it was older than its elderly owners.

The two men stepped over a fence and trod gingerly towards the barn. George grabbed his friend. 'Look!' he gasped.

The light appeared again. It was visible through a narrow crack in the barn wall. The men took the long way round, disturbed a few chickens before walking slowly along the barn approaching the crack. They stopped and listened hearing only their own breathing.

No sounds came from inside. George made signs about his direction afraid to even whisper. He bobbed down, crawled until level with the crack and inched his head up to the slim opening. Kenneth watched not daring to move. George crept back to his friend.

'What is it?' whispered the former priest.

'A woman,' said George. 'Middle-aged, looks weary, has a lantern which is turned down low.'

'No-one else?'

'I couldn't see. But she seemed to be preparing food.'

'You think it's food for a kidnapped girl?'

'It's a clever place to hide. The farm is occupied meaning the police and searchers are less likely to be as thorough but the farming couple are elderly and could have been fooled. They may not even know the woman is in there.'

'Be careful, George. There could be others inside or the woman may panic and do something ... terrible.'

'I'm not leaving until I know for certain my girl is not inside.'

He set off walking as quietly as possible moving back around the barn. Kenneth followed. They reached the entrance where two big doors appeared closed. In the darkness it was hard to see.

'Do you want me to fetch the police?' whispered Kenneth.

George struggled to make a decision. He shook his head desperate to think of a safe move.

Kenneth grabbed George's arm. 'Listen,' he hissed. They slipped back against a pile of logs. One of the barn doors creaked and moved outwards opening about a foot. The men held their breath.

A woman appeared holding a bucket. 'Slops,' murmured George.

It was heavy and she struggled to carry it away from the barn.

'You keep her busy,' said George. 'I'm going inside.'

He set off and Kenneth faced a problem. He crept after the woman and waited till she began emptying her foul smelling cargo. He moved closer using the noise of the slops hitting the ground to cover his footsteps. Just as the noise stopped, he poked his favourite fountain pen into the small of the woman's back and threatened with a growl.

'Move and I shoot.'

After days of hiding, she was exhausted, her nerves frayed and now the fear and possibility of death made her freeze.

George slipped inside the barn. The lamp cast an eerie glow. Half the straw-covered floor contained bales of hay stacked high. He saw no-one in the dim light. He shone his torch around and saw a hole where a missing bale once sat. He moved quickly, dropped to his knees, wiggled his way inside and shone his torch into the space.

Only when his light was pointed hard left did he see the blanket covering a person, a young girl he loved with all his heart. Her eyes reacted to the blinding beam but her heart caught fire when the person holding the torch spoke. Her Daddy was here to rescue her.

Kenneth marched the woman back to the barn. She hated her job of guarding and caring for the child. She reckoned being caught and imprisoned would be better than living with her vicious husband and doing his bidding under pain of torture and abuse. For her, resistance was never an option. She collapsed on the straw and quietly wept.

'George,' whispered the former priest.

'Here,' came the reply although no-one was visible. George's feet and posterior appeared. He gasped. 'I've found Victoria.'

Kenneth wanted to shout. George gently helped his daughter to depart her prison. She was untied and her gag removed. Her father overdid the kissing.

'I knew you would come for me, Daddy,' she said hugging first her father and then Mr Attwood.

It was striking how normal Victoria appeared. Her terrible ordeal seemed not to have crushed her spirit.

'What's the plan, sir?' asked Kenneth.

'I'll carry Victoria and meet you on the road. If you miss us and finish up in Heacham, turn around and come back.'

'What about the prisoner?'

She spoke for them. 'I'll be no trouble. I'll come with you and wait for the police. I can tell them where the others are staying before coming for the money tomorrow night.'

The men looked at one another. The child spoke for her captor. 'She helped me. The men were horrible but this lady has been kind.'

George decided. 'You go, Kenneth. I'll bring the woman and carry Victoria.'

'I can walk, Daddy.'

'Victoria, if your mother finds out I didn't carry you, she will have Miss Halfpenny dismissed and make me the housekeeper as well as the station master.'

A smile or three appeared for the first time that night; for the first time in ages. Kenneth set off and George held his daughter's hand ready to pick her up if necessary. Hazel submitted, following with not even a whimper.

The rendezvous with the car was perfect. A silent Hazel sat in the front while George cradled his daughter in the back. She wanted to chat and relate her adventure in detail and it took some persuasion to convince her to sit still and relax. They reached Wolferton.

Kenneth couldn't help himself. The car pulled up outside the station master's house. It was late but the driver gave the horn a blast followed by a second. Being after 11.30pm it was against the law but who cared and who was going to complain?

People nearby woke and especially Louisa Miracle. With bare feet, she bounded downstairs pulling her nightgown around her. Carrying his daughter, George approached the kitchen door. Louisa opened it and broke down.

With tears in free fall, she attempted to kiss her daughter as George carried the child inside. Miss Halfpenny appeared and the celebrations took hold. Wearing his busy night attire, Constable Hatt entered, saw the young girl and immediately rang his superiors.

Kenneth escorted Hazel next door to the signalman's cottage and asked the sleepy Cluffie if he would keep the broken woman safe until further notice. As he watched Hazel being "secured", he asked her for details about her fellow conspirators.

When Kenneth returned to the Miracle's home, Victoria and her parents were recovering with Miss Halfpenny finding all sorts of goodies for the girl. Kenneth divulged Hazel's information and Constable Hatt made another phone call.

Sitting in their small rented Hunstanton cottage, nervously smoking and drinking, the Crump brothers were surprised by a silent and well-planned police raid. With no chance to fight or escape, the criminals were soon under lock and key. Hazel was collected from Wolferton.

George rang Lord Carruthers who advised the London money carriers to cancel their trip and return the cash to its former abode.

When certain folk such as George's mother and sister heard the news, their shock was even greater discovering they were not told about the kidnapping until it was all over.

It was hard to rejoice when the danger had never been revealed. But let's face it, all's well that ends well.

Chapter 6

Edward VIII was an odd fellow who became King when his father, the Monarch who proposed the bridal toast at George and Louisa Miracle's wedding at Wolferton station, died in 1936.

With the Church of England an integral part of the Monarchy, the new King needed to chat with the Archbishop of Canterbury.

Imagine The Most Reverend Primate's surprise, not to mention shock, when His Majesty told the churchman that all that palaver of bowing and scraping while wearing so much finery during a coronation didn't appeal to the King. In fact he didn't care for it at all.

'Must there be a coronation?' asked Edward. 'Can't you just wave one of your magic wand thingies and be done with it?'

Now that is not a verbatim report on the King's conversation but he certainly did try to have the whole thing called off or at least scaled down. Wiser heads prevailed and in the end the uncrowned King agreed to a ceremony with much less of the pomp and circus-stance.

So disinterested was the new King, several events tied to the coronation were abandoned. Dignitaries anticipating a slap-up dinner in London sadly popped their glad rags back in a wardrobe; choristers rehearsed in vain as the thanksgiving service was cut, as was the huge parade through the streets of London. At least the chaps following the horses with brooms, shovels and buckets were given the day off.

Remember Edward VIII was a bachelor at the time and so walked alone without a Queen Consort. He did have a lady friend although most of the British public was unaware of Bessie from Blue Ridge Summit in Pennsylvania.

So having persuaded the King to agree to a form of coronation, a committee of high-flying persons met to plan the big day. It was many months away but Royal coronations take plenty of planning.

You'd think it would help if the King deigned to attend such meetings. After all there's no show without Punch. But no, the odd Edward chose to go cruising on a luxury steam-powered yacht with his American lady friend by his side. The twice-married lady's current name was Bessie Wallis Simpson.

Edward asked his younger brother Albert, the Duke of York, to represent him on the Coronation Committee; stout fellow that Duke. He and his family had met George Miracle at Wolferton and George's disabled son James made a powerful impression on the Duke and Duchess and their two daughters.

The coronation date crept closer with Edward standing firm on his choice of third-hand bride. But the new Monarch's travails continued. His insistence on marrying his American sweetheart saw a fair swathe of the Empire oppose the union. The safety of the Monarchy was deemed so important, the government assigned detectives from Special Branch to spy on Mrs Simpson. They tapped phones and spied and reported on her movements explaining how she was simultaneously involved in an adulterous relationship with a car salesman—surely not. Twas a quintessential English scandal involving a Yorkshireman moving to Mayfair and wooing the King's sweetheart. Apparently the car salesman was a bloody good dancer.

The pressure on the King became too much and on December 10 1936, Edward abdicated standing aside as King and given the opportunity to speak to the people of Britain via BBC radio. The no-longer King was introduced as His Royal Highness, Prince Edward.

Apart from Lady Jane Grey, she of the 9 day reign in 1593, Edward's time as King was the shortest in British history.

His brother Bertie became King George VI and with the coronation date already set, it remained so and preparations went ahead for a far more amenable Monarch.

Shortly after Edward's abdication speech, his brother granted him the title of His Royal Highness the Duke of Windsor and soon thereafter the new Duke departed England for Austria.

The abdication with the former Monarch announcing "true love" the reason for his departure, meant his action gave families a jolly good topic to discuss over their Christmas dinner.

In a French chateau, Edward and his bride married and became the Duke and Duchess of Windsor with none of his family in attendance. As Germany built up its military threatening war, Edward began a relationship with the Nazis. The fascist dictator Hitler smiled and welcomed the former King. Whitehall mandarins spluttered into their elevenses.

In 1939, after war was declared, the Duke was given a role liaising between the French and British armies and many believe his sloppiness aided the Germans. Prime Minister Baldwin reckoned the former King was missing a few brain cells, and later, Prime Minister Churchill threatened the Duke with a court martial. Seriously? Now if that event had gone ahead, British history would have produced an interesting chapter. Former Monarch in Tower charged with treason.

Returning to early 1936, it took time for the Miracle celebrations to settle once Victoria returned to the bosom of her family. Her reaction to the ordeal was remarkable. Her maturity belied her years although her parents worried a so far undiscovered and possibly long-lasting type of damage may have been done; however, so far, so good.

The villagers and station and train staff rejoiced in the grand result. At Liverpool Street station, SM Jack Rogers danced a jig in his office. George reckoned he shook hands with more people in the week after Victoria came home than in the previous 12 months. He was on a high and super keen to throw himself into his work.

The mail arrived with an envelope addressed to him by name. Reading the contents made him feel sick. He showed the letter to his senior porter. Sam Mason wanted to explode.

'Is this true?' asked George.

'I'm afraid it is, Mr Miracle and we all hoped the matter was dead and buried.'

The letter, from the LNER Head Office, asked George to explain his absence from duty on the day the coffin of His Majesty King George V arrived at Wolferton station. The wording looked serious.

Sam explained. 'On that day, I told the officer in charge you were dealing with a possible life and death family emergency but he was having none of it. I signed the form on your behalf.'

'Thank you, Sam. You did exactly the right thing and again I apologize for leaving you at such an important time.'

Sam spoke bluntly telling his boss he definitely didn't need to apologize, and if he wanted a reference from all the porters, he need only ask.

George filed, meaning "buried" the letter and went back to work. He tried to put the whole issue out of his mind but couldn't. His response was required and that night he showed the letter to Louisa.

'I can't believe you're in trouble for trying to save the life of your child. Surely the company can see that.'

'I don't think the company's behind the complaint. Sam Mason told me it's likely from an officer employed in the service of the King.'

'Well it's a pity King George has died. He'd be furious such a complaint was made in the first place.'

George thanked Louisa for her support and did what he'd done most of his life—he spoke before engaging his brain.

'I think it might be time for me to move.'

Shock and disappointment forced Louisa to yell. 'What!?' She quickly dropped her voice. 'George, what's brought this on? You love this station. Every member of staff respects you and they all work their socks off for you. The villagers admire and support you and you couldn't have a better relationship with the Royal Family. What on Earth's happened to make you even think such a thought?'

He hesitated before indicating the letter. 'This worries me.'

Louisa exploded. 'Oh that's fiddlesticks. It's a bumptious underling trying to curry favour with the Royals. Explain what happened and there's an end to it. Besides, you must know your wife and children love this place.'

He replied with a quiet and sombre voice. 'Of course I know but we always knew there might be problems once we inherited all that wealth.' She said nothing knowing he was serious. His soft voice continued. 'My darling, living here we're an easy target for criminals.'

Louisa endured pain recalling their recent wretched experience with Victoria. The kidnapping upset her more than she would admit.

'You and the children are my life, Louisa. But here in this country village we're sitting ducks for more kidnapping attempts.' She knew he spoke the truth. 'In a big city, we'd be surrounded by people, with far more police close by, and we can secure the children.'

She spoke quietly. 'It's unfair, George. We all want to live here.'

'And if the Royal Family hears I disappeared just as King George's coffin arrived, well that's me in big trouble.'

'It was with good reason,' interrupted Louisa snapping her reply.

'How can I look the Royals in the eye when they arrive at the station? Meet George Miracle, the station master who deserted his post.'

Louisa sniffed. 'I thought *I* was the worrying type,' she said. 'You beat me hands down.' She kissed him and squeezed his arm before heading upstairs to bed.

The date of the coronation for King George VI was set for May 12, 1937 but preparations took time. The Abbey needed additional seating and structures to support same, the changed order of service needed to be approved, and tens of thousands of soldiers and police officers were required with plans made for their positioning and training before the big day. The list of invitees with VIP guests from home and the overseas Dominions became a major undertaking.

Companies and government departments needed time to produce all manner of memorabilia. Official items such as a new coin of the realm needed to be designed and manufactured.

Remember King Edward VIII insisted on his hairstyle being shown to the world. There were no such demands from his brother.

There were flags, mugs, cups, plates, tea-towels, etc with plans for street parades and parties in towns and villages up and down the land. Far-flung dominions, a part of the British Empire, planned to create their own items in recognition of the new Monarch.

George took three days to reply to his employer explaining his absence from duty when the coffin of King George V arrived at Wolferton. He was tempted to telephone Lord Carruthers or Kenneth Attwood and seek their advice but contacted no-one being embarrassed such a situation existed. He fumed but being a company man from his bootstraps to his cap, George still reckoned he failed.

He thought about Sir Laurence Pennington, the man who became a sort of mentor. He it was who pushed George's application ensuring his unexpected appointment to Wolferton a dozen years ago.

But Sir Laurence could not help. He'd retired from the Board of the LNER and went one step further and retired from life.

George penned and posted his reply.

As was the usual arrangement, son James came home for the weekend. His ability to walk and talk in his unique style never ceased to impress everyone at the station. His parents wanted him to continue his education and when Kenneth Attwood married, left the priesthood and settled with his divorced wife in Cambridge, it seemed a wonderful idea to have James move to Hamilton-Weir House, live with his grandmother and continue his education under the tuition of the former Rector. It became a win-win situation.

James wasn't told the grim details of his sister's kidnapping. Rowena told him Victoria went missing but was found safe and well. After being greeted by his father at the station, the Miracle males went home to be greeted by the Miracle females.

George went back to work and when Louisa was alone with her son, she told him about his father being in trouble with the company for not being on duty when the King's coffin arrived. Louisa explained why and James became confused and angry at the same time.

Being clever he asked a number of questions wanting to know exactly what happened. One question led to another and soon the mind of James Miracle slipped into gear. He said nothing to his mother but went to his room and worked alone.

Two days later a letter, addressed to the Duke of York, was opened by a member of staff at Buckingham Palace. It should have been addressed to 136 Piccadilly and eventually found its way to the Duke. The letter was written by James Miracle and explained the situation in which his father found himself when not being on duty when the coffin of the King arrived at Wolferton. The reason for the absence was stated in plain but persuasive language.

The Duke of York, a person like James with difficulty in speaking in a clear and uninterrupted voice, read the contents.

Later that week, an LNER envelope arrived at Wolferton again addressed to the station master by name.

George found breathing tricky. A jumble of thoughts buzzed in his head. This was the response to his response to the company letter demanding an explanation of his behaviour, his absence from duty. Would he be fined, officially reprimanded, demoted or horror, even dismissed? His hands shook as he opened the envelope.

His fears were trashed. It was another of those letters where what you saw and what you thought you saw were on different planes.

In short, his employer wished to pass on the thanks of His Royal Highness the Duke of York for the splendid service he, station master George Miracle, provided to the Royal Family over many years of dedicated service at Wolferton.

Talk about a hectic heart rate. George read and re-read the letter. He couldn't imagine how it came to be written. There was no mention of one James Miracle. Sam Mason dropped in and stopped when he saw the expression on his boss's face. George said nothing simply handed the letter to the porter.

'I wrote to the company about my absence and this is their reply. Did you have anything to do with this?' asked George.

Sam read the contents and laughed. 'Hardly, sir; as you know I'm in charge of the milk churns.' George shook his head, relieved but perplexed. Sam summed up the situation. 'I think that's the last you'll hear from that jumped-up pipsqueak in charge of the coffin-bearers,' he said handing back the letter. It was.

With Victoria Miracle rescued and George's possible reprimand dismissed and forgotten, Christmas 1936 proved a much happier time at Wolferton. Friends and family arrived, stayed and departed. Rowena came for a fortnight, George's family including his nephews landed on Boxing Day and the New Year saw Lord and Lady Carruthers and their two children, now strapping youngsters, help the Miracles see in 1937.

George's godson, also George, developed a strong bond with his godfather. The others took pleasure in seeing the man and boy going for walks in the village and beyond; between trains of course.

That evening, after the others retired, Georges 1 and 2 went limping to share their hopes and fears. Mind you George 1 didn't fancy long strolls despite being fairly mobile with his prosthetic leg.

'Valerie and I were not at all surprised to learn Victoria was rescued by her famous father,' said the London-based Carruthers.

'Luck played her part, my Lord,' replied the station master. 'If one of my drivers hadn't spotted that tiny light, we would never have gone to that farm.'

'You have too much modesty, George. Now tell me about your boy. Is it true Kenneth Attwood is preparing him to sit for a Cambridge entrance exam?'

'So the former Rector tells me and I have no idea where James gets his brains from but it certainly isn't me.'

Carruthers laughed. 'What did I just say about too much modesty?'

George 2 grunted. 'What did you hear about the abdication?'

'No more than you, old chap. The former King was on a hiding to nothing and everyone I've spoken to reckons King George VI will make a splendid Monarch.'

'He's been most kind to the Miracle family.' They stopped outside the station with the moonlight giving its sturdy architecture a sense of security and safety. In the silence of a cold January night, the stationmaster worried about the future.

'And George, what's happening in Germany with all these reports about re-arming and the rise of the Nazis. Will we have another war?'

'If we do, you and I and our families will be well out of it. You can ride it out here in this beautiful Norfolk countryside.'

George Miracle didn't speak and so piqued the interest of his friend. When the SM did reply, he shocked the Lord.

'I'm thinking of moving, George.'

'Moving? From Wolferton? But why?'

'You know our money situation better than anyone. We don't flaunt it but people talk. Victoria was kidnapped because we're wealthy. We were ever so lucky to get her back unscathed. The men involved were desperate. And just because the first attempt failed, doesn't mean other criminals won't try.'

Carruthers could see his friend was serious and couldn't contradict the logic. 'Where will you go?'

'Hopefully I can get a posting back to London where there are millions of people and lots of police.'

'You'll be out of the frying pan,' said the Lord and left it there.

The SM stared at his friend, confused. 'I don't follow.'

'George, if there's another war, London will be the most dangerous place in Britain. The planes and bombs we saw in the last bust-up are toys alongside today's weapons. You're thinking about moving back to London while I'm thinking about moving to the country.'

The men stared at one another. The station master's mind buzzed with confusion.

Chapter 7

1937 saw a return to the Miracle status quo. Young James spent the week at Hamilton-Weir House with his grandmother enjoying his studies under tutor Kenneth Attwood. The former priest lived nearby with his wife who copied Louisa Miracle. Kenneth's in-laws bequeathed their estate to their only child meaning later in life both George and Kenneth married a spouse who inherited money.

Victoria resumed her education in the village being escorted to and from school by her mother or father or at first by both.

George worked hard at his railway duties keeping the Royal Station ticking over handling passengers and freight.

The coronation of George VI drew ever closer and George Miracle made sure he was always on duty ready to serve any dignitary or member of any royal family who passed through Wolferton.

The former King and now Duke of Windsor finally wed Mrs Simpson who became the Duchess of Windsor although without the title Her Royal Highness, a bitter blow to her husband. Their wedding saw not a single Royal from the Duke's family attend. Edward fumed and bore that grudge forever.

An outsider could be forgiven for thinking the Duke disliked his brother the King and wanted to show him and the rest of the world that the Duke and Duchess of Windsor were important people. In Britain, Edward couldn't travel in an open car with his wife giving her a royal tour. But he could do so elsewhere. Against all advice, the Duke and Duchess accepted an invitation to tour Germany.

In 1937, Chancellor Hitler raised eyebrows by the way he controlled Germany and many, including the British worried about a possible war.

Off went the Windsors touring German factories admiring the way employees were being treated. Of course the Nazis put on a show hiding the suffering of many workers. How blind were the Windsors?

The British government instructed its embassy staff in Berlin to have nothing to do with the former Monarch and his wife. Crowds flocked to greet the visitors. Edward was important again.

The Windsors met a number of German politicians and even travelled to the Chancellor's holiday hideaway at Berchtesgaden for afternoon tea with Herr Hitler. Many photos and much film footage of the tour appeared in cinemas and newspapers including images in which the former British Monarch appeared to give the Nazi salute. You can imagine how well that went down in Downing Street.

This was a time when the possibility of war became a regular topic of conversation. There were supporters of the Duke of Windsor who reckoned he could be the ideal peacemaker if push came to shove and the dogs of war were let loose. What few people knew was how the Duke saw himself as the future head of state in Britain once his country was defeated by Germany. Could the former King become a traitor? Surely not.

Having enjoyed their time in Germany, the Windsors planned a second tour this time across the pond to the United States. After all, the Duchess was born in Pennsylvania.

Alas the second tour was scrapped. Labour activists in the US heard about their German comrades being ill-treated by Nazis and objected to the Windsors. The plan to give prominence and importance to the Windsors hit a roadblock. They settled in Paris and were denied the publicity they, or at least the Duke craved.

In 1910 a young George Miracle began his working life as a station lad at Liverpool Street station in London. His uncle, Fred Carmody was the Stationmaster and the Assistant Stationmaster was one Jack Rogers.

Fast forward 27 years and Jack Rogers was now the SM at Liverpool Street but edging ever closer to retirement. He had admired George's late uncle and followed the nephew's career with interest. Jack pushed George into applying for the position at Wolferton.

But now Jack reckoned a new position would suit George Miracle down to the ground.

When the Great War began, more than a hundred railway companies operated in Britain. Squabbling railway operators would never do when troop movements and ammunition and supplies needed the fastest and safest routes available. This meant the government took charge. They formed the REC, the Railway Executive Committee, a body which controlled all the railways in Britain in time of war.

The Great War ended in 1918 and everyone saw how much better the railways operated with only one authority. So rather than go back to masses of individual companies, only four would operate with the LNER, George's new employer, one of those Big Four companies.

George remained at Wolferton. His children kept growing and loving the location. Louisa never wanted to move—ever. Privately George kept his eye on station master vacancies. He no longer discussed a possible move from Wolferton because Louisa and the children loved the place and to raise the matter he knew would upset his family.

Life went on although not without change. The new Rector at St Peter's lacked the charisma, humour and drive of Kenneth Attwood. The new Rector's wife was the power behind the throne. Louisa and Victoria and James, when he was home, regularly went to church on Sunday mornings with George reluctantly joining them whenever his excuse was too feeble not to do so. The once popular late Sunday evening chats with the Rector of St Peter's were no more.

The coronation of King George VI drew nigh and George agreed to have the station festooned to celebrate the occasion. Whenever the Royal Family with the Princesses Elizabeth and Margaret appeared at Wolferton, George was on hand ready to help.

Princess Elizabeth always asked after the Miracle boy with George proud to report how James was living with his grandmother near Cambridge and studying hard hoping one day to go to university.

The older Princess remembered the boy in the wheelchair, struggling to express himself and creating his own railway timetable and later being able to walk and speak in his own unique way. She considered him remarkable.

'But that would be marvellous,' said Princes Elizabeth. 'You must be very proud, Mr Miracle.'

'Thank you, Princess Elizabeth. He is a credit to himself the way he has mastered his speech and mobility and his family are indeed very proud.'

The coronation of King George VI on May the 12th, 1937 was a magnificent occasion. Like everyone, the Miracle family took a great interest in proceedings. Newspaper photographs gave them the chance to see inside Westminster Abbey. The young Princesses were present and being beside their grandmother Queen Mary enjoyed a front-row seat at the coronation of their parents. People celebrated up and down the land and those in cinemas watched footage taken inside the Abbey and in the streets of London.

Manufacturers of memorabilia, many of whom suffered burnt fingers when Edward abdicated, did well with the new Monarch. A smiling Queen Elizabeth and her two delightful daughters gave the British people a family to be proud of. George Miracle found a spring return to his step and his smile revealed more teeth whenever the Royal Family came to Wolferton.

Taking a day off, George went up to London on private business. He needed to visit Crispin Webb regarding financial matters for the Miracle Trust and wanted to privately discuss his railway future with Jack Rogers. He went first to the home of his and Louisa's financial advisor. The meeting went well with positive news of their share portfolio revealing the strength of their investments.

Crispin Webb made a suggestion. 'I think you should consider raising the rent on your property in Eaton Square. It hasn't been changed for the last two years, the French Government can afford a modest increase and, of course, the property continues to appreciate in value.'

'We have always trusted your advice, Mr Webb. My wife and I are happy to leave the finer details in your hands. We will agree to your recommendations.'

The meeting ended and George headed to Liverpool Street. As he travelled across London, he fancied visiting the palatial property Louisa inherited, if only to stand in the street and admire it. The income from leasing the property provided most of the funding to run Hamilton-Weir House in the countryside near Cambridge.

He arrived in Eaton Square and stopped outside the property. It was many years since he was last here. The park in front of the house was lush and peaceful. He entered the area and sat on a bench looking up at the Miracle-owned mansion.

'Excuse me,' said a middle-aged gent. 'This is a private park. It is reserved for residents of properties in the Square.'

'I didn't know that,' replied George with a calm demeanour.

'Well you do now so I must ask you to leave.'

'I didn't catch your name, sir,' said George in his usual polite fashion.

'Anketell-Smith, Major, retired,' snorted George's adversary who grew more agitated the longer their conversation continued with George showing no sign of moving.

'I have an interest in that property, sir,' said George pointing.

Stunned, the Major looked. 'Which one? Number 54?'

'No sir, further along.'

'That's the residence of the French Ambassador.'

'So I believe.'

'But you're English.'

'You are correct, sir, on both counts.' George stood. 'And you have inspired me to visit the occupants of the property I own. Thank you and good day.'

George smiled at the red-faced Major, left the park and crossed the road to his home. His pompous neighbour gawped.

The station master used the knocker. Eventually the door opened and George explained who he was. Much to the Major's chagrin, the visiting Englishman disappeared inside.

Seated in the first sitting-room now with fine French furniture and antiques on display, George waited wondering what on Earth he would say. A superbly-attired gentleman entered.

'Monsieur Miracle?' he enquired. 'Monsieur George Miracle?'

From his time in a French trench while serving in the British Army, George spoke with confidence. 'Oui Monsieur. Bonjour.'

'You and your wife are ze owner of zis magnificent 'ouse?'

'Oui again, Monsieur and please forgive this intrusion.'

'No, no, no, you are most welcome at any time.'

'I was passing and my curiosity drew me to your front door.'

'Please 'ave a seat, Monsieur.' They sat. 'I was told by Monsieur Webb you are in charge of the Royal railway station at Sandringham.'

'It is near Sandringham, Monsieur; at Wolferton.'

'I am new to zis post and 'ope one day to call on their Majesties at Sandringham 'ouse.'

'And when you do I shall be glad to welcome you to Wolferton station.'

Their conversation flowed with George delighted to have made the move to knock on the door. If the snobbish Major hadn't stuck his oar in, the visit probably wouldn't have happened. George knew his wife would have a long list of questions about the interior of their home in Belgravia not to mention its occupants.

George stood to leave but was stopped by the ambassador.

'Please Monsieur, I 'ave for you a confession. Kindly allow me to speak.'

George sat and the ambassador seemed uneasy.

'I 'ave agreed to your brother-in-law living in the basement 'ere in your 'ouse. I 'ope you do not object.'

George needed to think about those words. *Who is my brother-in-law? Emily's husband lives on the Culpepper farm near Whittleton.*

'e told me 'e used to live 'ere all 'is life and as we are not using the basement, I assumed it would be okay. 'e said 'e 'ad cleared the matter with you and your wife.'

The penny dropped. *This is Louisa's brother, half-brother, Enoch Hamilton-Weir.* George had no memory of Louisa's sibling asking him or Louisa about living in the Eaton Square property.

The SM brushed off the matter, thanked the ambassador and took his leave. Outside in the street, he paused and looked at the metal railings, the front fence. There was a gate at one end. He moved to it and looked down. Stairs led to the door of the basement. There was a window covered with curtains.

Without hesitating, George opened the squeaky gate and limped downstairs. His shrapnel-scented hip didn't approve. Platforms were fine, stairs not so. A small knocker clung to the door. George used it.

'You're early,' called a voice. George heard footsteps before the door opened and Enoch Hamilton-Weir produced a unique expression as shock, surprise and fear struggled for room on his face.

'Good day,' said George. 'Am I addressing Mr Enoch Hamilton-Weir?'

'Who are you?' demanded the tenant with an outpouring of false bravado. His uncut hair and whiskers announced his current social status and empty bank account.

'My name is Miracle and I believe I'm your landlord. I've come about the rent, sir.'

Enoch knew immediately. His rent-free hideaway in the heart of fashionable Belgravia was discovered. He'd been rumbled. *This is the bloke who married my half-sister*. Enoch's mind raced. He thought about slamming the door in the caller's face and doing a runner but to go where? He thought about playing the victim, the impoverished child stitched up by his mean-spirited father. Finally he abandoned all hope and surrendered, turned and walked inside mumbling. 'You'd better come in.'

George had never ventured downstairs in the Eaton Square mansion. It was sparsely furnished, dark and cold. He reckoned at 2am in the middle of February it would be a good training base for a polar expedition.

'There's only gin, no tonic.'

'Don't bother, thank you. I'm not staying.'

The tenant faced his visitor. 'Have you come to evict me?'

'Do I look like a bailiff?'

'So why are you here? I can't believe it's to gloat. You've avoided me for more than ten years.'

George took his time. This visit wasn't planned. He possessed no agenda or aim. Enoch, however, came out in hives. His rent free lifestyle was in imminent danger. He panicked becoming obsequious.

'Look, we did the wrong thing and copped what we deserved. Surely my squatting in this ice-box with the odd rat for company is no skin off your nose. If you want me to beg, I'll beg.'

George found the man and the situation fascinating. 'What do you mean, "We did the wrong thing"?'

Enoch would never confess to conspiracy to murder. The twins and their plan to have Louisa killed would never be divulged. That would have him moved to a prison cell, a bit like his present home only smaller. But he would confess to blackmail. He and his sister suffered for their actions and continued to suffer every day.

'We tried to blackmail the old man about his illegitimate daughter; your wife. The dumb plan backfired and we ended up getting peanuts in the will and as you know your missus and her mother got just about everything. My sister lives in a ramshackle cottage on the coast and, as you can see, I'm living high on the hog in fashionable Belgravia.' His sarcasm decorated the room.

'Did you know my wife didn't know who her father was until news of the bequest arrived at our home?'

Enoch's face screamed disbelief and genuine shock. He and Sophronia were sure Louisa was plotting against them. Now, many years later, Enoch discovered Louisa was not even remotely involved. Sister Sophronia will finally explode.

'All we got was the country estate near Cambridge which we had to sell with the money we got gobbled up repaying the hefty mortgage.'

George pondered telling Enoch the identity of the purchaser of said property and its name, Enoch's name, and what the estate had become but said nothing. To do so might push Enoch over the edge.

'I may speak to my wife and our solicitor about your situation.'

Enoch studied his visitor. 'You said you *may* speak.'

'I don't like kicking a man when he's down.'

Enoch breathed easier and, for once, spoke sincerely and with humility. 'Thank you. I'm grateful for any small mercy.'

'But if you want the present situation to continue, I'd keep my nose clean and not give the real tenants any reason to object to their neighbour.'

Enoch gave a poor salute but one without malice or sarcasm. He spoke softly as he followed George to the front door.

'Thank you, sir' he said and meant it. His life today was wretched but any alternative would be worse. He watched the landlord leave.

George struggled up the steps and out onto the footpath. The imperious Major stared at him from behind a tree. George didn't care and set off for his railway alma mater, Liverpool Street station.

Chapter 8

Station master Jack Rogers was under pressure. His wife wanted him to retire. They discussed the likelihood of another war and the need to get as far away from London as possible. Their home in Epping Forest was hardly in the City square mile but a cottage in mid-Wales sounded perfect. His wife grew up in Cardigan. Jack spent time looking at a calendar on his wall on which he'd discreetly placed a dot under the day he would no longer be a railwayman.

Twenty odd years ago George Miracle was well-known at Liverpool Street. Even as a porter he made a name for himself, once as a suspect in a murder investigation and later in catching a fellow porter who turned thief. The highlight, or was that the lowlight of his time at the busy London station was when a murderer pushed him off a platform onto the tracks and hopefully under the wheels of an oncoming train. Needless to say George survived and his fame spread far and wide.

But today's porters didn't know him from Adam. The SM did and when George knocked on his door, Jack Rogers came alive.

The two men discussed so much with Jack wanting to know all about the safe return of young Victoria Miracle. Once they ran out of their news, George started on his plan.

'Jack, I'm thinking about leaving Wolferton.'

The London SM had the same reaction as others when George explained his fear about more possible kidnappings and wanting his family to be safe.

But Jack headed the conversation in another direction. 'I've been thinking about you, George. I've heard rumours from Head Office about the government reforming the REC.'

George looked puzzled. 'I don't know what that is.'

Jack explained. 'The Railway Executive Committee ran the railways during the last war. While you and I were across the Channel dodging German bullets, the government took control of all the railway companies. Rumour is they may do so again.'

'You think there'll be another war?'

'Would you bet against it?' George shook his head. 'Hitler is ignoring the Treaty of Versailles, re-arming and reclaiming parts of Europe for Germany. If he keeps behaving like that, we'll have a war.'

'So tell me about this REC.'

'You would have been a pimply youth when the first REC began in 1912. The government looked at the 120 odd railway companies and knew individually they'd struggle to co-ordinate even one troop train let alone hundreds. They needed a single authority to deal with the War Office. The Railway Executive Committee was formed and did such a good job running the entire network, the Grouping Act came in after the war and you know all about that.'

'Goodbye GER and hello LNER.'

'Exactly and while there's nothing definite, the word is the government will re-create the REC. I reckon they'll take experienced staff from the Big Four companies and add government so-called experts. With someone from the top brass to head the organization, we'll be back to one body running everything and if the balloon goes up, that is where you come in.'

'Me? What can I do?'

'You're young enough to volunteer but with your war injury, you're no chance for any frontline service. But you're ideal with both war and rail experience; an ex-soldier and an SM. If there's a war, the Government will need experts on making decisions about troop and freight transport and the REC will make decisions on whether passenger services will be cut or curtailed, on timetables, public notices even mass movement of people away from cities. You know so much about timetables and passenger and freight movement. And you've had more dealings with the Royal Family than the PM.'

'Not exactly true,' said George whose heartbeat accelerated.

'So if they bring back the REC, may I recommend you?'

George said nothing. His only priority was to keep his family safe.

'Would I have to leave Wolferton?'

'Of course; the REC will be based in London close to Whitehall.'

George hesitated. Jack had pushed him to Wolferton. Now he suggested something new, something which may not even happen.

The older SM changed tack. 'Look my friend, on that idea of bringing your family to London to reduce the kidnap risk, I reckon that's out of the frying pan and into the fire.'

George cringed. George Carruthers had said exactly that. 'How so?' he asked already knowing the answer.

'If this war happens, and it's looking more likely every day, you want your family as far from London as possible. Being kidnapped is terrible but being bombed is the stuff of nightmares.'

George nodded. 'I take your point.'

Jack explained his plan. 'I'm retiring soon and Audrey and I will be heading to mid-Wales.'

'What? Jack Rogers scurries off to hide in the valleys.'

It was a stupid even cruel remark. George endured shame and began to apologize. Jack raised a hand.

'Forget it but don't tell Audrey I'm planning to become a fire-watcher or air-raid warden and will be here if the shooting starts.'

'Now that sounds like the Jack Rogers I know.'

The men continued chatting, shook hands and Jack walked his young colleague onto the platform.

'So will you think about the Railway Executive Committee?'

George paused. 'If they'll have me and think I can help, I'll be honoured to do whatever I can.'

'Good man. I'll have a word with Sir Ralph Wedgwood today.'

Sir Ralph, great-great-grandson of Josiah Wedgewood of pottery fame, was the Chief General Manager of the LNER.

Heading home to Wolferton, George thought about what he would tell his wife. Certainly the Eaton Square visit would feature with the bit about her half-brother freeloading in the Belgravia basement. She would be staggered to hear about Louisa's siblings not knowing their half-sister had no idea of her father's identity until the will was enacted.

But as to the business with the REC, he said nothing, typical of George Miracle hating to cause sadness. If it did happen, his family would have to leave the home, the station and village they loved.

It went without saying that Jack Rogers wrote a glowing reference for his friend before sending it to Sir Ralph Wedgewood.

Chapter 9

For the Miracle family, Christmas 1937 was especially enjoyable. Memories of a kidnapping still remained but to have everyone present and well gave the festive season a real kick.

When the clan Carruthers arrived for New Year, George went for a stroll with his godson. They wandered away from the station with the weather crisp and the light fading. Young George knew the true meaning and role of a godfather and asked the station master questions he was reluctant to ask his parents.

'I need your advice, sir,' said the now strapping young George.

'I hope it's not about sex and romance,' said the godfather.

Young Carruthers laughed. 'No sir although any tips would be most welcome.' He paused. 'I wish to join the Royal Navy.'

The godfather gulped and could hear the boy's mother. "George Miracle, under no circumstances are you to encourage my son to do anything dangerous".

'I see and what do your parents say?'

Good try, SM but the tactic didn't work.

'They don't know which is why I need the wisdom of my godfather. Please sir, how should I approach them?'

'Now I understand but tell me, why the Navy?'

'You must know that. You introduced me to sailing. You gave me those toy yachts for my birthday and at Christmas?'

George senior nodded. 'Mea culpa,' he whispered.

'Father says another war is coming. You and he both served your country with distinction and I want to do the same only at sea.'

The station master stopped and the men looked at one another.

'Going to war at sea sounds frightening to me and I think I'm right in saying that telling your parents might be even harder. But I doubt they could never be more proud of you.'

The young man couldn't speak. Tears welled in his eyes. He gave the smallest of nods. The station master hugged his godson.

'Let me think about how,' he said, 'and I'll give you the best advice I can.' With an arm around one another they walked back to the magnificent Wolferton station master's house.

The Railway Executive Committee re-commenced in September 1938 beginning its re-birth in the basement of Fielden House near London Bridge. Each of the Big Four companies was represented along with the London Passenger Transport Board. Initial meetings were designed to establish their goals, strategies and membership.

Each of the Big Four companies would recommend experienced people within their ranks with George Miracle being one such person. Of course no war meant there would be no need for the REC.

Its task was made all the more difficult because of the poor state of the railways throughout most of Britain. Since the end of the Great War, investment was sadly lacking, sometimes non-existent. Road and air transport began to boom with the railways much the poor relation. Now when another war loomed large, it was down to the railways to lead the charge, to provide most of the crucial support for the country and this at a time when the network had endured years of neglect being under-funded and poorly maintained.

In October 1938 George received a letter and having read it, knew he must have a serious discussion with his wife. After their evening meal and Miss Halfpenny and Victoria retired, George looked at Louisa. She could read him like a book and spoke as she darned a pair of his socks.

'What's happened, George? And please don't tell me you've applied for a station in London.'

He struggled. He hated hurting her but the reality of another war was staring at him, staring everyone in the face, shouting at them.

'My darling, I have been asked to attend an interview with the possibility of joining a government body set up to run the entire British rail network should we go to war.'

Louisa was impressed. 'I'm not surprised. So what does "attend an interview" mean?'

'I guess they want to see if I'm suitable.'

'And when they realize you *are* suitable, which no doubt they will, what happens then?'

Not that George needed reminding of the fact but once again his wife displayed two of her many qualities; her intelligence and her ability to cut to the chase.

He shrugged. 'I'll become a member of the Railway Executive Committee.'

'And all this is connected to another war?'

'Again, Mrs Miracle, you have a complete understanding of the situation.'

'So how many committee meetings will you have to attend and how often will you need to go up to London?'

He said nothing and she knew he hesitated because what he was about to say would hurt her. His hesitation because of his concern for others was another reason why she first loved him and did so even more strongly today. She guessed correctly.

'So you'll be moving to London and a new station master will take over here at Wolferton where he and his family will move into this wonderful home and we will move out.'

He struggled. 'I haven't been accepted yet. They may not want me.'

'I suppose we could move to Maida Vale.' The property had become rented once medical appointments for James ended.

'No,' said George abruptly. 'None of you will be living in London.'

This serious discussion grew darker. Louisa always knew George cared for her and their family but right now his usually hidden feelings appeared. He would do anything to avoid a repeat of the Victoria kidnapping scenario but living in London during a war was even more dangerous. The cottage at Foxton was a possibility but it too was let.

She helped him. 'Of course we could move to Hamilton-Weir House and be with James and Grannie Mac. They'd love that.'

George produced one of his no-teeth smiles. 'That would be an excellent solution but please let's wait until after the interview.'

A week later, George went up to London. His wife was correct. The REC offered him a position. He was excited but concerned. This body, this group of people looked like it would become responsible for every train, time-table and ticket, every crossing, carriage and clock, every signal, siding and stop sign on every railway line in Great Britain and he would play a part, a small but important part in the decision-making.

He accepted the position and going home spent the whole journey thinking about how he could care for his family while he lived in London with his wife and children in the countryside.

He wouldn't start work with the REC until February 1939 and so Christmas 1938 would be at home in Wolferton. Would it be their last in this glorious part of Norfolk?

In London, the Fielden House basement was taken over by the rail supremoes for the REC with government departments and the War Office reasonably close.

But the building proved unsatisfactory, the basement was deemed unsuitable and the hunt began for a different location. An abandoned Underground station in Down Street was proposed and it became the REC HQ with Whitehall a short drive or healthy walk away through Green Park.

Down Street tube station in Mayfair opened in 1907. It was a poor choice and location for London's commuters. It was close to two other Tube stations, in a quiet street as opposed to nearby busy Piccadilly, and in an area where a good proportion of locals were not on their uppers. Many Mayfair residents could afford a cab and were not inclined to descend all those steps to the platforms below.

Due to a lack of passengers, Down Street station closed in 1932. But six years later it offered many advantages as the REC HQ. Being so far underground, if war brought bombs to London, the REC staff, including one George Miracle, could go about their business without fear of being interrupted. Safety was a major consideration but so too were space and facilities. However, this was an ex-Tube station, not an office building and first it needed serious renovations.

Obviously easy access to trains constantly rattling by on the hectic Piccadilly Line was important but its facilities offered nothing for a busy department performing vital government business. No offices, no essential and quality communication equipment not to mention kitchens, additional lavatories and obviously no bedrooms. It was a railway station. Thus began the great Down Street Tube makeover. The station became the base for a national and vital business.

In the pre-dawn hours when London's Underground trains were asleep, workmen began building brick walls along the station platforms giving security and privacy for REC staff. Bricklayers laboured away at 2am. Corridors built for passengers were divided creating rooms for typists and clerks. New telephone lines were installed. Bathrooms appeared as did bedrooms. A large room with a large table was created where decisions could be made affecting people and materials being transported all over Britain. The Railway Executive Committee Mark II found a new home.

Trains continued bouncing past the closed Down Street Station but a narrow opening at the end of the bricked up platform enabled REC staff, by appointment, to hitch a ride in the cab of a Tube train and move around London below ground. Everything was hush hush.

Apart from offices, there was a mess room and bedrooms enabling senior REC staff to be fed, well fed, and grab some shuteye all without leaving their place of work. If World War Two began, the REC was ready for business.

Soon a Miracle family meeting tackled a major topic. George kept Louisa informed of his REC appointment but they agreed not to tell anyone until any move was definite. Louisa gave her mother a heads up just before George broke his news.

Rowena and Miss Halfpenny were called to the family pow-wow.

'I have an announcement for everyone,' said George.

'Oh Daddy, we're not going to leave Wolferton,' begged Victoria. She was rapidly showing she was as intelligent as her older brother if not more so. Despite her terrifying kidnap experience, she loved the village, her school and especially being able to help her mother care for the Royal retirement rooms on the Royal Station.

George's failure to immediately reply sent hopes crashing.

'The Royal Family will not allow you to leave, Dad,' stated James with plenty of sincerity. 'I know the King thinks you are the best station master in the whole of England.'

The parents admired their son's enthusiasm not knowing it was he who wrote to the then Duke when his SM father faced an enquiry over his absence on the day of the Late King's funeral train at Wolferton.

The patriarch finally spoke. 'As you know, I was wounded in the Great War. I am lucky having only a limp. Lord Carruthers lost a leg. Sadly, many people believe there may be another war.'

'We don't know that for certain,' interrupted Louisa not wanting her children to become unnecessarily afraid.

'Your mother is right but the government wants to be prepared and I have been appointed to work on a committee which will take over all the railways in the entire country.'

'See Dad, you *are* the best station master,' boasted James.

'It means I will go to London to live and work but you will all go to live at Hamilton-Weir House.'

James was thrilled and even Victoria showed excitement.

'I can come and visit you on weekends and of course if there is no war, we can all live together again.'

'But will we come back to live here at Wolferton?' asked Victoria.

George paused. 'Probably not,' he said struggling to say no.

Silence settled as the news was absorbed. George smiled and his children smiled back. He looked around the room and Miss Halfpenny was definitely not smiling.

'I think it will be a good time for me to retire, Mr Miracle.'

The others protested.

'There will be room for you in Cambridgeshire, Miss Halfpenny,' said Louisa. 'You are a part of our family.'

'Or you could remain here and serve the new station master and his family,' added George hating to let down anyone and especially those who helped him and his family.

The humble servant said nothing and everyone knew change was coming if not the form it might take. A war meant death and destruction and uprooting families. Happiness was in short supply.

It was hard to celebrate on New Year's Eve. The station master's house at Wolferton lacked any real joy as the children joined their parents in listening to the chimes of Big Ben on the radio.

Where would they be in a year? What would happen in 1939?

Chapter 10

Adolf Hitler served as a German soldier in World War 1 and fought against the Georges Miracle and Carruthers. After the war ended, Herr Hitler began his political career by joining the German Workers Party and was put in charge of propaganda. He hated Germany's political leaders, the men he believed allowed Germany to surrender and sign the Treaty of Versailles.

Hitler recommended his party change its name to the National Socialist German Workers' Party or in short, Nazi. Hitler was in a hurry and in 1921 became its leader.

The party's ideas were above its station when 2,000 members attempted a sort of coup d'état in Munich. Weapons were involved and the police took prisoners including Hitler who was found guilty and sent to jail. The Nazi Party died.

In a cell, he wrote his part autobiography, part political treatise *Mein Kampf*—My Struggle. The authorities regarded him as a crank and released him early. More fool them. He relaunched the Nazi Party and the rest is history.

All this took place in 1925 when George Miracle had recently arrived in Wolferton and Louisa gave birth to their son, James.

There was a general election in Germany in 1930 and the Nazis did well becoming the second largest political party. Paul von Hindenburg served as the President of Germany seemingly forever and the ambitious Hitler wanted to replace him.

In 1932 Adolf the Austrian became a German citizen so he could challenge von Hindenburg and to help achieve that goal became the first politician to campaign by plane. "Hitler over Germany" was the slogan and it worked.

The Nazis held a third of the seats in the Reichstag with Hitler the Chancellor. Now dirty tricks were always the Nazis' raison d'être. Someone set fire to the parliament building and Hitler seized the moment. Denying any involvement, he blamed the communists.

The resultant uproar saw the Fire Decree declared which ended free speech, freedom of the press and allowed police investigations a free hand. All other political parties were banned as were trade unions and strikes. The Nazis moved in on their political opponents paving the way for Hitler the dictator.

Germany withdrew from the League of Nations and Hitler tore up the Treaty of Versailles. He sent his goons to murder dozens of rivals in his own party copying the actions of Stalin. After the Night of the Long Knives, the "official" death toll of 85 was more likely 1,000 meaning Hitler now reigned supreme.

Expressly forbidden under the Treaty of Versailles, the German military expanded and when the President died in 1934, Adolf abolished the title becoming both Reich Chancellor and Führer.

All that made the decision by those Munich authorities in 1922 to release prisoner Hitler early look like the greatest mistake in parole-granting history.

Military conscription was introduced and Hitler's real goal of claiming and reclaiming land became public knowledge.

When he annexed Austria in March 1938, those who objected were shown no mercy. Many were imprisoned. The new right-wing government in Austria supported the Nazis. The streets of Vienna were lined with adoring men, women and children cheering, waving and saluting as they welcomed the goose-stepping soldiers from across the border. In an open-topped car, the Chancellor acknowledged the rapturous crowd and the Austrian Prime Minister delivered a speech expressing delight that Austria was now a part of the new Germany.

Of course the British government knew of these events. They knew about the appalling treatment of Jews under the Nazis leading up to what became known as Kristallnacht. British spies told their superiors in London about the build-up of the German military. The British were worried, deeply so, but they were not ignorant.

Like Hitler, the British looked to beef up their own military but thought too about the safety of their citizens. Save the children. Using local councils throughout the land, the government ordered a stock take of billets away from London and other major cities. Small towns, villages, hamlets and farms were visited and inspected.

'How many spare beds do you have?' was the question. People didn't have a choice in accepting city dwellers but were paid for every extra mouth they fed.

Of course finding the accommodation was one thing, transporting the million plus city dwellers was another and if war was declared, the big shift would happen thanks to the men and women working for the Railway Executive Committee.

The beginning of 1939 saw a big change in the life of the Miracle family. George resigned from his post at Wolferton which upset the porters, signalman, guards and footplate crews on the trains which stopped at the station. He didn't discuss his new posting only to say he would be moving to London.

Miss Halfpenny went back to live with her widowed sister in the village. Louisa and Victoria joined James and Rowena and took over one of the renovated outbuildings at Hamilton-Weir House making it a big change for everyone.

With the renovation work at Down Street complete, George went to London and moved in. There were gas locks on the doors, security was tight and the former Wolferton SM met a number of fellow workers who, like him, were railwaymen with decades of service.

His first day with the REC saw him discover the work to be undertaken if and when war was declared. Wandering the renovated Tube station was an eye-opener.

At his interview he was told in no uncertain terms that any work for the government in time of war was highly secret. Being employed by the REC meant he would be required to sign the Official Secrets' Act. Once offered the job, naturally George complied.

Sir Ralph Wedgwood was not only George's boss at the LNER, he became head of the newly-formed REC. A group of new operatives gathered in the largest room, the executive committee room where Sir Ralph addressed the gathering.

'Our work depends on war being declared and it's looking more likely every passing day. Being prepared is essential. We'll be delighted if we do all manner of work only to find peace wins out and war is not declared. But if we don't prepare now, if we're not in a position to carry out vital tasks and war *is* declared, we will have failed our people and possibly be responsible for the death of thousands.'

George's heart stirred. He loved being a station master. He loved his time at both Whittleton and Wolferton but this was different. In his previous role he exercised control over a modest number of trains, their passengers and freight at relatively small and quiet stations. Of course, the Royal Family and VIP visitors gave Wolferton a special importance but now he was involved with the railways of Britain on a national scale. For him this was huge.

Sir Ralph continued his welcoming speech. 'The executive of the REC will make the overall decisions but the day to day and the night to night running of the railways will be in your hands. Yes, in time of war this business will never close. You will be charged with finding rolling stock, giving clearance to important trains and ensuring the armed forces and the general population receives all the support they need from the railways. There are tasks we know we'll have to perform and there are tasks which will appear without warning. We have to be flexible and must expect the unexpected. The work of the Railway Executive Committee is vital to winning the war we may be fighting any day.' He paused and looked at faces. 'Congratulations on becoming a part of the REC and I wish you much success in your tasks. Now, let's enjoy a cup of tea.'

George wanted to applaud. His excitement meter buzzed. He found a cup of tea and a biscuit and nodded to a chap beside him.

'George Miracle,' he said putting his biscuit in the saucer to shake hands with his colleague.

'Bernard Houghton,' replied the man and they made small talk before opening up on this new venture. Both were reluctant to say anything controversial knowing that all decisions taken within the REC, especially in time of war, were hush-hush. They settled for talking about their backgrounds.

'I've heard about you,' said Bernard. 'Were you the chap in hot water at missing the late King's funeral train?'

George's heart dropped at least a foot. 'Thanks but I don't wish to remember that.'

'Not sure why. Word was a senior Royal intervened and gave you such a glowing testimonial it killed the complaint stone dead.'

George's heart returned to its former position. It would have caught fire if he ever discovered his young son was responsible for the then Duke of York producing such a glowing reference.

The two men discussed their office space and their sleeping and eating quarters. George had enjoyed fine home cooking from his mother, housekeepers and wife his entire life. Well, he did dabble with bully beef on the Somme in 1916. But now he was on his own. Now the women who cooked and cleaned for him were not under the same roof. So what's for supper tonight, George?

As the middle-aged Miracle began his new career, the German leader kept encouraging anti-Semitism. Employment in certain areas became illegal. Jewish dentists, veterinarians and nurses were no longer allowed to practise. The Nazis declared anyone with Jewish parents or grandparents was definitely non-Aryan and mass non-Aryan migration became a stated Nazi goal.

Addressing the Reichstag, Hitler announced that if war began it would be the fault of International Jewry and such a war would result in the annihilation of the Jewish race in Europe.

One could hardly call his rampant hatred and prejudice subtle.

German Jews, if they were able and brave, fled. Many did but international help was at times thin on the ground. One horrendous case saw a ship with a thousand Jews set sail for freedom only to be refused entry in foreign ports and forced to return. Imagine the despair in refugee hearts as the ship steamed back to a German port.

The world knew of these events. Creating concentration camps was difficult to keep secret. Britain knew about appalling activities in Germany. Everyone in the Railway Executive Committee HQ in Down Street was well aware of these atrocities.

George went to see his family on weekends. He'd arrive on Saturday morning and depart late Sunday. These were wonderful times. Tour guides James and Victoria loved showing their father the home and grounds with its hens and donkeys, the latter proving a huge hit with the disabled children. Seeing the charity in full flight delighted George but being with his family gave him the greatest joy.

The evening meal was filled with non-stop chatter. Louisa had told the children their father was working for the government and wasn't allowed to discuss his job. That didn't stop the children.

'Do you wear your station master uniform, Daddy?' asked Victoria.

'Which London station is your base, Dad?' asked James. 'How many platforms are there? More than at Wolferton I bet.'

The parents exchanged glances both thrilled to see their children full of enthusiasm and interest. George turned the tables asking them about their education. Both were thriving. Kenneth Attwood ramped up his attempts to prepare James to sit for a Cambridge assessment and Victoria was excelling at the local school.

In bed with his wife on Saturday night, George was quizzed about his food intake at Down Street. He lied and wasn't sure why. Perhaps he saw the food provided as being covered by the Official Secrets Act. He changed the subject and spoke about colleague Bernard Houghton and how he was separated from his wife.

But these were pre-war days. When the real fighting kicked off George would become one of the REC staff permanently living at Down Street as the Tube trains scurried past his bedroom.

The hugs and kisses when he left on Sunday afternoon were strong and touching. Going home, George knew these visits would not continue, at least not on any regular basis should war be declared.

The borders of European countries were constantly changing having done so for millennia. Once the Nazis hit their stride, they occupied or set up many puppet governments. Between 1939 and 1945 they invaded countries from Greece to Norway, from France to the Soviet Union. The industrious members of the REC saw the possibility of war racing towards them like the *Mallard* under full steam.

Politically, life heated up when Stalin and Hitler signed a deal to share Poland with the Poles having no say. Britain's Prime Minister Chamberlain met with Hitler and other European leaders in Munich. Papers were signed but the saying, "It's not worth the paper it's written on" would apply perfectly to any agreement made with Adolf Hitler. Even smiling Joe Stalin would later discover that fact.

With the situation ever more threatening, the REC staff assumed the certainty of war as it raced past the Impending stage.

Chapter 11

In August 1939, the REC was on a full war footing and George Miracle was a part of the mass migration committee. In a room in the bowels of the former Down Street Tube station, a government official addressed the group.

'Gentlemen, months ago we began preparing to send citizens, particularly children, away from London and other major cities. Today we expect Hitler will first invade his neighbours; France, the Low Countries and Poland. Their defences are not strong. Poland may even use soldiers on horseback and the French army has a surfeit of doddery Generals from the last war. Unless our British Expeditionary Force gives a helping hand, Hitler will soon dip his toe in the Channel preparing to invade our green and pleasant land.'

George and his REC colleagues murmured their disquiet. Bernard Houghton spoke.

'Are you able to tell us, sir, when things will begin to move?'

'Soon and we know London will be a prime target for thousands of German bombs. The ports too but certainly the Luftwaffe will bomb the capital. Our men will fight, our women will take over the jobs our men have left in order to fight, and our children will be helpless.'

That last word sounded ominous and cruel.

'We all know the little ones are our most precious resource but in time of modern war they can do nothing but get killed or wounded. We must get them away from London and other big cities and the best, the quickest and safest way to do that is by train.'

George surprised himself by speaking. 'We're ready to go, sir once you give the go ahead.' Others murmured their agreement.

'Thank you, we know that. The Prime Minister is considering the situation on a daily basis. You can expect the government to order the trains to depart any day now.' He looked at the group of railwaymen charged with the task of mass migration. 'Good luck, gentlemen.'

George and his colleagues looked at one another. Their planning was complete. The trains, the departure stations, the destinations and the routes were set as a result of their planning which began last year. All the REC needed now was the order to move.

This massive transport of children was called *Operation Pied Piper*. Of course the chief motivation was the safety of the children but there was also a political element. If the children remained in London, mothers would be less inclined to work in the factories and other mainly male occupations. If the children were evacuated, mothers would be free to take over the jobs left vacant by the men who joined up to fight.

Under Neville Chamberlain, the government found making the decision to send the children away seriously tough. Removing little ones from their parents seemed cruel even heartless. It was certainly traumatic. Questions arose. Would they be safe and well cared for? When would they return? Would their departure cause panic?

It took a tough Labour councillor, London's Mayor Herbert Morrison, to light the fuse. He entered 10 Downing Street demanding Mr Chamberlain sign the document to kick start the operation. The PM's lackey assured the councillor the matter was being considered.

'Not good enough,' snapped Herbert. 'You tell Neville if he doesn't sign today, I'll give the order meself and tell half of London the PM's a coward.'

Mr Chamberlain signed the order. Mass migration began with many sad stories. On traffic duty, a London Bobby held up vehicles to allow two small children to cross a busy road. Half way across, the kiddies stopped and spoke to the policeman.

'Goodbye Daddy,' they said.

Their father bent, kissed them then sent them on their way before turning his back as tears ran down his cheeks.

Once the PM ordered the mass evacuation to start, the REC officers put their plans into practice and all this before war was declared.

George took comfort knowing his children were far from London and settled with their mother and grandmother in a rural setting.

'How can we be sure the children will be well cared for and find a loving home?' he asked his colleagues.

'George, our job is to move them,' said one. 'Stop trying to save the world, old chap. Councils have sorted the billets. We find the trains and announce the timetables.'

Parents were given notices stipulating these essential items:

- ✓ a change of underclothes
- ✓ night clothes
- ✓ slippers
- ✓ spare stockings or socks
- ✓ toothbrush
- ✓ towel, face cloth, comb, soap
- ✓ handkerchiefs
- ✓ a warm coat

George took himself to London stations to see how the mass migration worked. Talk about emotional. Hundreds of children covered the platforms and swarmed around the carriages. Each child carried a few possessions, usually in a small suitcase, and wore a cardboard tag with their ID details. Over a shoulder hung a cardboard box with string as a strap and containing their gas mask. Coats seemed compulsory and most heads were covered.

Mothers held the hand of their precious offspring. Beaming children saw it as an adventure, a thrilling holiday in the countryside. Terrified youngsters produced copious amounts of tears. Many parents, knowing they must be brave, couldn't stop their own tears.

Older siblings were thrust into the role of parent being told to take care of little sibling Johnny or Jenny. Mothers prayed their children would never be separated.

George saw mothers getting into a carriage with their child. The government agreed to allow a young and only child to be evacuated with one of its parents. Imagine a four-year-old being sent away alone. Of course a babe in arms could never be evacuated without its mother. Pregnant women joined the exodus.

For the parents their greatest worries were the location of their loved one or ones, and the date they were to return. At the beginning of the last war, both sides confidently predicted it would "all be over by Christmas". They were wrong to the tune of several years. Would this war be the same? Worse, would a mother ever see her child again?

Into the carriages they went, children by the thousand. Engine and station master whistles blasted as locomotives hissed and puffed and moved. Adults waved handkerchiefs and children waved hands. Smoke and steam added to the drama when more than a million children left London as the Second World War paused to begin.

Many families with friends or relatives in the country made private arrangements and drove their child to the new location or went with them by bus or train before returning to their city home. The REC event was a mass exodus requiring thousands of volunteers to help with the million plus children fleeing danger, the evacuees.

When a train arrived at its destination, adults were needed to collect, gather even herd the children to a village hall or school or church. Then it was time for the selection routine.

This had the potential to be horrendous. Children were lined up and the new foster parents would inspect then point and say, "I'll take that one" or "him" or "her" or "them".

Imagine you were the last child to be selected. What did waiting and being rejected do for your self-confidence? *Nobody wants me.* And what if the foster parent was rough and made threats about misbehaviour and the child lived with quiet and loving parents back in London? *I want to go home!*

The trains leaving London were full and the REC played a blinder making *Operation Pied Piper* a great success. This was the biggest mass migration in British history.

Germany invaded Poland, the British and French governments demanded they withdraw and when it was obvious Hitler was not for turning, war was officially declared. The REC was officially open.

Poland was a soft touch and with the Soviets invading from the east, it took only a few weeks before the Poles capitulated. Now Germany was ready to head west but inclement weather and wary Generals halted the advance and thus began what became known as the Phoney War. Naval battles took place but on land it was more or less a stand down until the sun shone again.

For the Railway Executive Committee, their major mass migration activity worked well but when the German bombs didn't fall on London, and elsewhere, thanks to the Phoney War, the unthinkable began to happen—some of the evacuated children returned.

George and Bernard discussed the matter.

'There are reports of children catching trains heading back to London,' said the former station master. 'Bernard, some of the kiddies are coming home.'

'There's nothing we can do, George. They're not prisoners and if their parents want them home then that's their right.'

'Yes but we're at war. Hitler could send the Luftwaffe tomorrow and the East End is sure to be a target. Children in those terraced houses with dozens, even hundreds living close together will be in a direct line of fire. There could be hundreds of casualties.'

'Thousands,' replied Bernard in a soft voice.

The REC could only stand back and watch as some evacuated children returned to London. What was going on? Parents were thinking that if there were no bombs, why can't my children return to the safety of their home? Many did.

One of the REC jobs was to promote a *lack* of use of the railways. "Is your journey necessary?" was a question they printed on posters and stuck up on station billboards across Britain.

The idea was to reduce demand for passenger services, save fuel and keep the lines open for troop trains and movement of raw materials for the war effort. Many services were curtailed and some on weekends were cut altogether. Locomotive speeds were reduced. Passengers could no longer reserve a seat, compartment or saloon. Refreshments while travelling disappeared when restaurant cars were removed altogether. Long-distance travelling became less attractive with fewer sleeping car services.

Throughout September, the first month of the war, George stayed in London. He needed to as working on the mass migration activity became a mammoth and ongoing job. He missed his family and in October was given permission to go home for the weekend.

Troop trains were top priority and George worried about catching a train to Cambridge. His job involved encouraging people to stay at home while here he was travelling to see his family.

When he alighted at Cambridge he saw the station sign was missing. This was to confuse the enemy in case of an invasion. Posters were clearly displayed urging people not to travel unless it was essential. The REC was responsible for these activities.

At Hamilton-Weir House, the reunion overwhelmed everyone. His family hugged him with the children not wanting to let go. Their evening meal took forever as the youngsters couldn't stop talking.

When the children were finally abed, George spoke quietly with his wife and mother-in-law. Aware of the Official Secrets Act, he was circumspect but naturally most of the population knew about the mass movement of children from the cities to the countryside.

'Many infirm children have been moved,' he said. 'I saw disabled kiddies being carried onto trains for their trip out of London.'

Rowena spoke plainly. 'We would love to help more, George, but all our rooms are booked and our waiting list continues to grow.'

'I know that,' said George and spoke about his children. 'I can't believe how they've grown in personality as much as in body.'

'We see them all the time but you're right,' said Louisa. 'We've been amazed at how bright and clever James has become despite his cerebral palsy. Kenneth continues to push him and has even brought a young student from Cambridge to give him lessons in physics.'

'What?' gasped George. 'Surely we have to pay these men.'

'The student is a woman and she's the same as Kenneth refusing to take any money.'

George shook his head in disbelief. 'So tell me about Victoria?'

'There's a surprise there,' said Rowena.'

'Oh?'

Louisa explained. 'Your daughter may be smarter than her brother.' George continued to be amazed. 'Her teachers tell us her reading age is way ahead of her classmates and her brother's new tutor, Miss Rawlinson, is teaching Victoria concepts in mathematics that Mummy and I have no understanding of whatsoever.'

'Well it's obvious they get their brains from their father,' said George which produced a scoffing snort and a cushion sailing in his direction.

Chapter 12

Christmas 1939 was like no other experienced by George Miracle. Now living in London, he saw buildings with their windows taped and sandbags stacked high in front of windows, doors and entrances. At night, street lighting didn't exist and taxis and buses crawled along with tiny beams of light from their headlights. In the first month of World War Two, dozens of Londoners died from traffic accidents being run over in the blackout. And still the enemy bombs didn't fall.

George remembered Christmas 1916 in France. He'd been wounded and lay behind the lines in a field hospital thinking about his pal, Paddy Murphy, who died beside him in No Man's Land.

Now George slept in his narrow bed in the renovated Down Street station wondering when the Phoney War would end. George and Valerie Carruthers discovered his new REC job and insisted he come for lunch on Sundays. Again George worried about making what his organization referred to as unnecessary trips. It was just over 4 miles from Down Street to Tudor Court, Hampstead and the station master put his gammy leg to the test and walked. It hurt.

After lunch the two male friends strolled in the massive garden with Lord Carruthers puffing on his pipe while manipulating his prosthetic leg. 'I've got a bone to pick with you, Miracle,' he said.

'Oh yes, here we go again,' replied his friend.

'Your godson tells me he wants to join the Royal Navy.'

The railwayman expected this having advised the young man to be open with his parents. 'I think honesty's the best approach, young man,' said the SM to his godson who took the advice.

The railwayman continued. 'That's brilliant, George, you must be so proud.'

'Well yes and no because at this time of the war with all those ship losses I admit I'm worried and Valerie is terrified.'

'He's copying his old man. I remember our first meeting at Liverpool Street station where you were dressed and ready for war in

1914. Young George Carruthers wanting to join up is down to his father not his godfather.'

'You gave him a yacht for his 6th birthday and the lad spent hours sailing it on the pond in the back garden. When Valerie took the kids onto the Heath, my son always took his yacht and would come home and talk for ages about which pond he sailed in. If Eton had sea cadets back then, he would have been first to join. And now that war's been declared he wants to be Able Seaman Carruthers RN.'

'And I suppose he's talking about deferring his Oxford studies until after the war.'

'That's exactly what he wants to do.'

George Miracle laughed aloud. 'Like father, like son,' he said. 'Well I say good luck to him,' he grinned and slapped his friend's back.

Because of the lack of military action on the ground, the Phoney War continued. Britain and France had declared war against Germany on September 3, 1939, and seven months later little military conflict on land took place involving troops from the United Kingdom.

The British even swapped bombs for leaflets and dropped messages for the Germans hoping they'd call off their warmongering. It's unknown if Herr Hitler obtained or read a copy.

When a German bomber crash-landed in Essex, the locals with help from the Royal Air Force buried the crew in a local cemetery according full military honours to the airmen with whom they were at war. It wasn't so much the Phoney War as the Terribly, Awfully, Jolly, Good, Pass-the-Port Chaps War.

British soldiers in France preparing for the fight of their lives wanted to import hounds to carry out a spot of fox hunting. Tally ho chaps as we wait for the Hun to start the real stuff. It sounded bizarre. But come May 1940, the word *phoney* would no longer apply.

Two significant events unfolded on May 10. Germany started attacking and Britain found itself a new leader. Prime Minister Chamberlain had tried repeatedly to appease the dictator. The Führer appeared reluctant to invade Great Britain but there was no way he would roll over and shake hands with the Brits.

Winston Churchill long opposed Chamberlain's appeasement policies and when it came to the crunch, the PM stepped aside allowing Churchill to become leader. He formed a new coalition with Labour and the Liberals joining his Conservatives and the two main opposing forces, Britain and Germany were now facing off.

The Germans invented Blitzkrieg or lightning war. The plan was simple. Attack with speed, hit hard and move on. None of this World War 1 caper where you lived for years like drowned rats in a trench.

When the phoney war ended on May 10, 1940, Germany invaded Belgium, the Netherlands and France. Deployed in France, the British Expeditionary Force was up for a battle alongside the French. However it soon became a lop-sided contest.

Within a few weeks the Low Countries and France surrended, the British turned for home and finished as sitting ducks on the beach at Dunkirk, while Wehrmacht officers were quaffing wine in cafes on the Champs Elysées. And all this led to another major task for the REC.

The Railway Executive Committee did a splendid job moving more than a million children from British urban areas and delivering them by rail to towns and villages around the country.

The fact that some evacuated children came home because there were no bombs thanks to the phoney war, was no reflection on George Miracle and his colleagues in the Down Street Tube station. For them *Operation Pied Piper* was a great success.

But the next REC mass migration dealt with adults. *Operation Dynamo* was the REC project to transport vast numbers of rescued Allied soldiers who were left to die or be captured after the *Battle of France*. But first they needed the troops back in Blighty.

There were hundreds of thousands of weary, wounded and shell-shocked soldiers scrambling to survive at Dunkirk on the French coast. England was a mere 25 miles away but it might as well have been a thousand because swimming the Channel was never an option.

Why did the German army, far greater in numbers and equipment and fitness not go for the kill at Dunkirk? Why did the Luftwaffe not endlessly strafe the British Expeditionary Force? Why did Hitler not send his troops to finish off the defeated enemy? The answers to those questions would remain debated for decades.

Some reckoned Hitler believed the trapped men would never be rescued and so hesitated. Others claimed Hitler never saw Britain as

Germany's natural enemy as he did the French. After all, not so long ago a former British monarch and his wife took tea with the dictator.

So while Hitler hesitated, Britain acted. Three days was all it took for the daring rescue and the Germans missed a golden opportunity to cripple the Allied forces.

The Royal Navy and a flotilla of small boats sailed across the Channel to rescue the helpless troops. It seems incredible that some 340,000 men were saved and once home, the REC took over, reacting immediately and effectively as they organized a mass evacuation.

This time those transported were not children wearing a name tag and carrying a gas mask. These were desperate men desperate to get home and back to their units stationed all over the country.

May 26, 1940 was the REC's D-Day. George Miracle and his colleagues worked non-stop. Dover and other ports were awash with rescued troops who needed to be moved and quickly and any delay could turn the brilliant rescue from France into a disaster at home.

Thousands of railway carriages were whisked south. Timetables were created in the REC. Men sat on telephones, day and night, giving and receiving orders which changed not by the hour but the minute. By the end of May 1940 more than 2,000 carriages as part of 600 trains arrived at ports and carried more than 300,000 men away from the potential danger of German bombs. The brilliant rescue from Dunkirk beaches was complemented by the brilliant transport of the men once back in England.

The REC was not fussed with the make-up of these troop trains. If a carriage existed, it was collared. If the REC could make up a long train, they did and if required added a second locomotive. If the carriages were not from the same company, sported a different livery, were configured differently, or even sported different bogies then too bad. Find that rolling stock, create those trains and do it now.

Trains left ports crammed with rescued soldiers. The Navy and weekend sailors behaved magnificently in bringing the troops home. The Railway Executive Committee supported the seafaring heroics with superb organization to clear the docks and speed the men on their way.

Chapter 13

By the summer of 1940, the gloves were off. Both Britain and Germany flew sorties with Britain swapping leaflets for bombs. Hermann Göring once boasted that no German city would ever be bombed making Berliners unhappy when parts of their city were hit and Hitler didn't need an incentive to retaliate. He reckoned smashing London and other British cities would crush the spirit of the people. At least that was his plan. For George Miracle, the war was about to come very close to home.

Louisa worried about her husband taking care of himself. She didn't need to worry because for George and his colleagues living in the Down Street station, food was the least of their worries.

Before the war, the big railway companies all owned one or more hotels. Where George joined the railways at Liverpool Street in London in 1910, a large hotel stood at the end of the platforms. As a lad porter, George would often carry a passenger's luggage into the hotel hoping for a penny tip. The Great Eastern Railway owned the hotel. It was railway property and hotels with dining-rooms employed chefs. As the Railway Executive Committee employed many railwaymen from the Big Four companies, it was straightforward to appoint a chef to Down Street and feed the busy workers.

George Miracle ate well. It was advisable to not mention to the citizens above that the REC rations were rather good. In all the letters and phone calls George sent or made to Hamilton-Weir House, he remained silent on the grub he was served as part of his job.

At Down Street, talk amongst the staff concentrated on the invasion.

'What's the betting, George?' asked his mate Bernard. 'When will Hitler send his army across the Channel?'

'Talk is he'll only set sail after he's knocked out the RAF.'

'That'll never happen.'

George didn't respond immediately. Thinking about the Luftwaffe gave him and most of the REC chaps the creeps. They knew Germany possessed more fighters and bombers than the RAF. They knew Britain was recruiting pilots from wherever they could find them and training these novices by cramming flying hours into brave but inexperienced men.

Across the Channel, Hitler contemplated an invasion. His Generals advised caution. Poland was a pushover but the Germans lost men and equipment fighting a weaker opponent. Britain would be no pushover. In charge of the Luftwaffe, Hermann Göring promised his Führer he could destroy the RAF. With control of the skies, the Wehrmacht could invade and defeat Britain. Look at the Channel Islands. They were already under German control.

Lady Valerie Carruthers was distraught. Her son George was adamant. He was of age and determined to enlist and join the Royal Navy. His parents found the subject more than distressing. In desperation, Valerie pleaded with her husband.

'You have to stop him, George. You sacrificed a leg for your country. Surely that's enough. The ships and planes today are far more dangerous. Those German U-boats can sink a warship without being seen. You must persuade him to take a land-based role, please.'

Their marriage was rock solid, like that of George and Louisa Miracle, and His Lordship didn't need to argue his case. Valerie knew it was wrong to stop her son from doing what his father and godfather did and what the boy desperately wanted to do. George spoke quietly.

'I'll take him to the recruitment centre on Friday.'

Valerie wept in silence.

Hitler hoped his victory in the *Battle of France* would bring Britain to the negotiating table. No such luck. So *Operation Sea Lion*, Germany's plan to invade Britain was his response. River barges and landing craft were readied, troops trained and special weapons created. But first, Germany needed to destroy the RAF.

With the likelihood of an invasion, Britain began a series of defence activities. The more simple ones included removing road signs and railway station names. George Miracle was involved in station signs disappearing and all this was in anticipation of a massive German invasion by land. But first the war in the sky.

The reason why *The Battle of Britain* was won by the home side could be summed up in three words—Hurricane and Spitfire. Mind you having the best radar system too was a big plus.

The Battle of Britain raged for months from July 10 until the end of October 1940. When the enemy stopped sending their planes, the number of killed and wounded was staggering with the Luftwaffe losing nearly twice as many planes as the RAF. Germany failed to conquer the skies and consequently *Operation Sea Lion* never happened. Instead a new form of attack began.

President Roosevelt tried to get the warring countries to agree to a ban on bombing civilians; his suggestion being a good example of wishful thinking. Hopes were dashed and total war it was.

Hitler and Göring knew to attack by day was far more risky than night flights. Thus began months of relentless bombing in different parts of Britain with most happening in London. It became known as The Blitz, a name invented by the British press and a shortened version of the German Blitzkrieg. It began in September 1940 a year after war was first declared.

Over by Christmas my arse.

The German air attacks were on three targets—ships and ports, airfields and factories building planes, and finally cities and civilians.

The REC found itself flying by the seat of its pants. German bombs didn't discriminate. Lines, locomotives, rolling stock, bridges and stations were easy targets. Whether targeted or not, the railways were hit. George and his colleagues were running the entire network and with bombs damaging everything to do with the railways, re-routing became a daily, even an hourly activity. If a line was smashed or a bridge destroyed, repairs and re-routing became the norm.

Being deep below street level, the REC workers were safe but not so the trains and equipment for which they were responsible.

Christmas 1940 was like no other. This was the first occasion when the war exploded in British cities. George wanted to go home, was granted a 48 hour pass and squeezed in some Christmas shopping.

Amidst the boarded up shops and barricaded buildings were signs, *Keep Calm and Carry on* and *Britain Never Shall Yield*. The most common sign was scribbled in chalk on walls and pavements and read, *Business as usual.*

With *The Battle of Britain* over, people were proud of their Royal Airforce and impressed by the speeches of their Prime Minister.

Never in the field of human conflict has so much been owed by so many to so few.

The week before Christmas 1940 turned nasty in London. One night hundreds of German bombers attacked.

Incendiary bombs were doubly dangerous causing deadly fires. In 1666 the Great Fire of London devastated large parts of the city. In 1940 there were some 1400 separate fires and people referred to it as The Second Great Fire of London.

Downstairs at Down Street, messages came through about the devastation. George and his colleagues were responsible for railway problems but it was hard to avoid the carnage elsewhere.

In one night attack on the London docks and the East End, 2,000 people were killed or injured—2,000. How many of these were children who moved to the country under *Operation Pied Piper* but then returned to London because of the phoney war?

George took his leave. With so much destruction in London by night, as he took the train from London to Cambridge, he studied the people in his carriage. It was hard to see as everything was blackened. The carriage windows were covered and up front, the cab of the locomotive was wrapped in black. Not so bad in winter but in summer the cab became like a furnace.

George's fellow passengers sat still, grim and quiet. They were rugged up against the cold. In the darkened suburbs of London, giant barrage balloons attached to steel cables forced German bombers to fly higher hopefully thwarting their aim.

When George's train stopped at stations and his door opened, he could make out public notice signs he and his colleagues created at Down Street, and then the absence of the station name. For a former station master, it was strange to see a station without identification.

He arrived at Hamilton-Weir House and loved greeting his family. Living on a country estate they were far from London and safe. The chance of them being bombed was remote. But if a land invasion were to happen, well, George chose not to think about that.

James and Victoria jostled to embrace their father. He clung to both kissing their faces and the tops of their head. His wife and mother-in-law stood back loving the scene awaiting their turn. His degree of enthusiasm decreased ever so slightly as he switched from offspring to spouse to in-law.

The war was more than a year old, the *Battle of France* was lost and the *Battle of Britain* won although the future was anyone's guess.

Last Christmas, restrictions were not so noticeable. No lights on Christmas trees and food restrictions were minimal. Now in 1940 all citizens needed to pull in their belts. Butter and bacon were hard to obtain. For most, the range of presents on offer became heavily restricted. Homemade gifts were all the rage.

On Christmas Day they sat quietly around the wireless and listened as King George VI, the Monarch who put an end to a complaint about George Miracle being absent from duty when the late King George V's coffin arrived at Wolferton, spoke to the nation.

His Majesty spoke in a clear voice pausing from time to time in mid-sentence.

'In days of peace the feast of Christmas is a time when we all gather together in our home.'

The Miracles looked at one another. Victoria sat on the floor resting against her father's knees. Nobody spoke during the broadcast. Afterwards the mood remained sombre until the youngest family member asked her question.

'Why can't you stay here, Daddy? Why can't you be the station master at Cambridge and live here with us?'

'I was about to ask the same question, Father,' said James.

The fact that the young man, soon to be 16, called his pater, Father raised a few eyebrows. The deeper pitch of his voice added to his new persona. James continued to make his case.

'The Reverend Attwood told me you and he used to have late night conversations at Wolferton. You could have them again if you came to live with us.'

'Yes Daddy, say you'll come home,' added Victoria.

Louisa tried to save her husband.

'Now children, you know your father has an important job helping the government. The war may not be over for a while and until it is, he must continue to work in London.'

Sadness oozed from the children.

'But I will try and come home on weekends and special holidays,' added George.

'The next holiday will be Easter,' said Victoria demonstrating the intelligence George heard about. He didn't have the heart to tell his daughter the government wanted public celebrations to be limited, if not cancelled, as the war continued amid ever-increasing threats. Easter visits would be frowned upon.

'We'll see, young lady,' said the former station master who changed the subject. 'Now what is this I hear about you having a special tutor from Cambridge?'

Victoria took the bait and spent an age telling her father about Miss Rawlinson. 'She lives in Girton College which is only for female students but it's about two miles from the university so that the male students are not encouraged to visit.'

George looked at the other adults and realized his children were far older than he was at their age or possibly even right now.

'I see,' he said. His daughter's knowledge and explanation of matters mathematical amazed him. He pretended he understood but knew he failed.

Christmas lunch sported decorations, crackers and party hats but the food was basic. The government yielded and in the week before Christmas doubled the tea ration and allowed citizens to obtain 10 ounces of sugar. Still it was the company that made the event a happy one. Father was home.

Last week, George searched London for Christmas presents. In a secondhand bookshop he found *Our Girls' Brightest* for Victoria and for his son, *A History of Cambridge University* with dozens of black and white photographs. Both children were thrilled and immediately attacked their tome. He gave his wife soap and his mother-in-law seeds for her window boxes.

In return he did well receiving gifts from all. 'Why don't you smoke, George?' asked Rowena. 'I could have given you a pipe, tobacco, cigarettes and lots of smoking bits and bobs.'

'Yes, Father,' added James, 'I could start to smoke and we could enjoy a quiet puff together. It's the sort of thing we men do together.'

The staggered adults exchanged glances at the suggestion from the young man as James had now become.

'James, I'm too busy reading railway timetables and learning about new locomotives to care about smoking,' said George.

His son's eyes shone as he remembered his days in a wheelchair on Wolferton station recording train arrival and departure times.

'I'd like to go back to doing that,' replied James, 'but did you know all the stations no longer have their names on display?'

'I do know that, son, as I helped create the order for it to happen.'

Silence crashed into the room and George silently cursed himself for having, if not broken the Official Secrets Act, at least certainly having said too much.

Louisa saved him. 'I think your father means he's helping the railways work better now that we're at war. Now, who would like a second slice of Grannie's Christmas cake?'

Even George joined the chorus of eager requests with the word *custard* being popular.

Late that night alone in their bedroom, Louisa mentally checked her list of questions for her often absent husband.

'George, I know you're busy but why haven't you replied to Valerie's letter about your godson?'

George panicked. 'What letter? What's happened?'

'Nothing bad but she rang the other day to say she sent you a letter posted to Maida Vale and hasn't received a reply.'

'Why write to Maida Vale? She knows the cottage is rented.'

'Well if you can't give your secret London address you should ask people to write to you here.'

'I will but what's happened to young George?'

'He's joined the Navy and his parents wondered if you could have a word with him.'

'Of course I will but to what purpose?'

'I don't know. Isn't a godfather supposed to take an interest in his charge?'

He fell silent. 'Yes, of course, and I'll ring Valerie in the morning.' He paused. 'It's tricky, my darling. I can't discuss my work and I'm madly busy. Being an SM was a breeze compared to my current job.'

'So tell me about your life in London or is that too covered by the Official Secrets Act?'

He laughed. 'No but I'm safe and eating well.'

'I can see that,' she said patting his stomach. 'And what do you think of your rapidly-changing children and their new personalities?'

'I love them dearly but am glad we only have two.'

'Oh,' gasped Louisa, 'does that mean we're to have no more?'

He hesitated having lost a bit of his teasing and ready wit. The war with its death and destruction removed a little of his spark. When she jabbed him, he understood and they shifted ever closer.

The next morning, Boxing Day, he rang Tudor House and assured George and Valerie he would try and discover any news about his godson the sailor. He told Lord Carruthers what he could about his secretive work and to contact him via Hamilton-Weir House.

'What happened to the humble station master I once knew?' asked Lord Carruthers. The two friends chatted and laughed.

As much as he loved his family and spending time with them, George wanted to return to Down Street and resume his life with the REC. His farewells were strong and moving. Louisa knew he was returning to a place where bombs constantly fell and people died, were injured or became homeless. She worried, hid her concern but showed her feelings in the way she kissed and embraced him. The thought of him being killed sent a shiver through her body.

James insisted on walking to the gate of the property with his father. The boy's restricted movements and speech still existed but his confidence and enthusiasm for life clearly showed. His larger boot dragged and the strength in that leg became ever more powerful.

James hugged his father and spoke. 'I love you, Dad and hope this war will soon be over.'

George delighted in his son's love and the return to his boyish nature. They parted with each having moist eyes. The station master took a night train up to London and a cab to Down Street. It was not only his place of work but also his home.

Chapter 14

Think war and you think bombs, those horrific objects dropped above factories, airports, docks and houses. Bombs race silently towards the ground to destroy people, pets and places. Bombs don't discriminate between military and civilian targets. Bombs have no soul or conscience. They feel no pain but are brilliant at causing it.

In the late 1930s when it was obvious Germany was preparing for war, Britain too needed to do likewise. This was not the Great War when aircraft were smaller, carried fewer and less powerful bombs, and flew low and usually in daylight to be sure of hitting their targets.

When George Miracle joined the Railway Executive Committee, the aircraft were massive by comparison, carrying huge destructive bombs dropping them from vast heights and often at night.

The government knew Britain must fight fire with fire and many bombs would be needed. Make them quickly and safely. But once manufactured, where and how would they be transported?

You couldn't set up a bomb-making factory in London or any urban area. You needed open flat land, away from people, a good water supply and access to the railways.

Trains would deliver the raw materials and the workforce, and then take away the finished bombs and the workers after their shift. One such place was the village of Ruddington in Nottinghamshire.

It had all the essentials; flat rural land, a plentiful water supply, a railway nearby and a village with a supply of workers. They would be on the job around the clock, working three 8 hour shifts, day in day out. Thousands of workers would be needed and Ruddington with a population of about 3000 could only supply half of what was needed. Nearby towns and villages would top up the numbers. And the railways would collect, deliver then remove those faraway workers.

Before Christmas 1940, contractors began work on the rural land outside Ruddington. In the New Year, George's supervisor called him into the boss's office.

'I want you to take a trip up north, George. There's a new facility still being built and will be used for filling shell and bomb casings.'

'Sir?' replied George all ears.

'The MoD have asked for an experienced railwayman to visit their latest construction site in Nottinghamshire and give their railway lines, sidings and platforms the once over.'

George worried; a default position of his for decades. 'I'm no architect or railway planner, sir.'

'There are plenty of those and I've seen the layout but there's nothing like a railwayman seeing the work in progress in person. It's near the village of Ruddington close to Nottingham. They're expecting you first thing tomorrow morning. Now, any questions?'

Flummoxed, George thought hard. 'To whom do I report, sir. I mean once I've inspected the facility?'

'To me, the REC and I'll forward your comments to the MoD.' The supervisor extended his hand and George shook it. 'Here's a letter of introduction. Just don't tread on any toes or especially any bombs.'

George gave his toothless smile and left. He was tidying his desk when Bernard arrived. 'What's up?' asked the colleague.

'A special assignment,' said George filling his briefcase. 'If I knew any more, I wouldn't tell you,' which left his colleague even more curious.

'Very cloak and dagger,' said Bernard. 'Are you able to reveal your ETA back here at Down Street?'

'Couple of days and feel free to pinch my pudding.' George gave a genuine grin and left.

The Blitz was in full swing and getting a train out of London that night was tricky. He did and travelled the 100 or so miles towards Nottingham and onto Ruddington. He needed a bed for the night being ready to report to the site office at 0800 hours in the morning.

He wandered along the High Street, found the pub and went looking for accommodation. The landlord guessed correctly that the railwayman was from out of town.

'Evening, sir? What's your fancy?'

'I'd like a bed for the night please landlord, possibly two nights.'

'Sorry sir, I can't help.'

'Oh,' said the surprised railwayman. 'Are you fully booked?'

'We're not, sir, nowhere near but it's the local regulations. Anyone working at the new Depot is not allowed to stay in any public house. Apparently pubs are deemed to be dangerous places filled with German spies and loose lips sink ships.'

'I see,' replied George. 'But how did you know I was working at the Depot?'

'I didn't until you just confirmed it but you have the cut of an official, sir, and as much as I'd like your custom, if those government fellahs come in and catch you here, there goes my licence.'

George nodded. 'Understood and good night,' he said heading out only to be stopped at the door.

'Mrs Telford at number 49 serves a darn good supper,' said the landlord and pointed.

George grinned and soon knocked gently on the door of the best guest house in Ruddington. Where Mrs Telford found the ingredients for her guests' supper was covered by the Official Secrets Act. George slept well and was up and about well before dawn.

He reached the gate of the new Royal Ordnance Depot to be confronted by a security officer; two actually. The massive operation with about 200 buildings planned was far from complete but the perimeter fencing and guard quarters were well established.

George produced his letter and ID and was led to a building where a chap from the MoD was expecting him. His moustache was a work of art and his speech even more clipped than his facial hair.

'Railways I believe,' he said and led George on a tour of inspection with the visitor staggered by the scale of the complex.

'We've used thousands of men from Ireland building this place. When up and running, we'll have thousands of women working 24 hours a day six even seven days a week.'

They reached a perimeter fence with an opening revealing a new rail spur line. George asked questions which the MoD chap explained although without much detail. Security ruled the lines.

'Look the name says it all—Royal Ordnance Depot. We fill shell casings. We need to bring in raw material and send out the finished product. We've built this spur line and out there we have a new station and sidings. We'll have a narrow-gauge internal railway transporting goods around the Depot using little electric locomotives. What do you know about electric engines?'

George blanched. 'I managed small locos on a light railway but the locos were all steam.'

'Well as you can imagine, sparks in this place are verboten.'

They headed off the property and approached the new railway station. 'We'll operate 24 hours running three shifts with three trains a day for workers. They detrain here when the carriages are then filled with those coming off shift. Comments?'

George relaxed being able to offer advice on something his experience covered. 'You'll need to ensure your waiting passengers stand well back allowing those arriving the space to quickly exit both carriage and platform. Otherwise it'll be a bun fight and the next shift will be late for work.'

'And what about the type of carriage?' he asked.

'Well transporting large numbers over short distances, carriages with a corridor carry fewer passengers than carriages without.'

'And these branch lines and sidings? How do they look to you?'

'Access for freight should be as simple and as close to the wagons as possible. But I should point out my experience is with fruit, vegetables, mail and hampers from Fortnum and Mason. If you're loading and unloading explosive material, you've no doubt made appropriate safety arrangements.'

George's comments went down well although the mustachioed official gave little away. The inspection continued and then it was time for lunch. A canteen was one of the first buildings erected for the labourers and contractors on the job from day one.

After a wholesome lunch, George sat down with his tour guide who laid down the law.

'I understand you REC chaps are running the railway network. Our work here is vital to the war effort. We need to fill shells and get them away to places around the country. If we can't have trains to transport the raw materials in and a clear run once the trains are loaded, we're wasting our time. Have I made myself clear?'

George's no-teeth smile appeared. 'You have indeed, sir. I can give my colleagues in London a detailed explanation of your set-up and how the railways can get your ordnance quickly and safely on its way.'

Major Mustache appeared happy although you'd never know. He may have been related to the official at Wolferton who demanded to see the station master on the day of the Late King's funeral.

In the afternoon, George was given a tour inside one of the ordnance buildings. He shivered thinking about the damage even one of the bombs could make.

'Most of the workers will be women. In the Great War, you knew which women were working in ordnance. Tiny amounts of explosive material stuck to their hands and when they touched their hair, parts of it turned yellow. Those women were known as the "Canary Girls".

It was late afternoon when George shook hands with the man from the MoD. The REC man didn't fancy another night in Ruddington so set off to catch a train and be back in Down Street before midnight.

He waited on the platform with a few other passengers most in uniform. He mentally prepared his report for the REC. The Royal Ordnance Depot at Ruddington needed the highest priority in terms of rolling stock, locomotives and timetable clearance.

It was dark and cold and a raised voice grabbed his attention.

'You must have something smaller,' said a porter.

'I haven't,' replied the passenger. 'And I must be in London tonight for an important meeting.'

George's curiosity piqued. Even if the trains were on time, and during the Blitz this was unlikely, who attended a meeting at around midnight and who would announce that fact in public?

He decided to investigate and en route made eye contact with two squaddies. A nod of his head saw them follow him.

'Can I help?' asked George interrupting the confrontation between porter and passenger.

The passenger, a well-dressed man, about 30 and speaking with an exaggerated Oxbridge voice turned to George.

'Yes. Please explain to this man that all I want to do is buy a train ticket.' George thought his choice of words unusual.

The porter chimed in. 'He pulls out a fifty pound note. I've tried to tell him this is a train station, not a bank and I can't change it.'

'Your meeting in London, sir,' asked George. 'With the trains it's unlikely you'll be there by midnight. May I ask about this meeting?'

The passenger became a tad agitated. 'It is for the London Fire Watchers. I am a member.'

'I know the group. They have rooms in Piccadilly.'

'That's right,' said the now happier traveller although his happiness vanished when George gave an order.

'Grab him, lads.'

The two soldiers seized the protesting passenger.

'Call the police,' ordered George and the porter hopped to it. The businessman complained vociferously.

When the police arrived, George spoke to them in private. 'He sounds English but my guess is he's a German spy. One of their mistakes is offering money in the wrong denomination—he offered fifty quid to buy a single to London—and when I quizzed him on a London address, he made a mistake. I suggest you lock him up and notify Special Branch.' They did and Mr Fifty Quid never made it to the capital.

The trains did get George back to London and his late arrival caused a few tongues to wag. He said nothing about his visit or the incident with a complaining passenger. In the morning, he reported to his supervisor and delivered his detailed report.

'Well done, George. And an SM in Nottingham reported the capture of a German spy thanks to a visiting REC officer. I can't think who that might have been.'

'He gave himself away, sir.'

'Apparently the man was carrying a roll of film with pictures of the new Royal Ordnance Depot. Are you sure you don't wish to join the MoD or Special Branch?'

'No sir, I'm happy where I am, thank you,' said a smiling George.

For the remainder of the war, the REC gave the highest priority to the trains carrying ingredients to be placed in empty shells and to the ordnance filled by thousands of women with yellow tips in their hair. Trains carrying workers to and from the plant were likewise given a clear run. The REC created timetables that kept the "bomb" trains running uninterrupted. George Miracle was intimately involved with the whole operation.

Chapter 15

Having failed by day to destroy the RAF, Hitler switched to bombing by night with innocent civilians in the firing line. The Blitz meant massive bombing raids every night over London for weeks. Mind you bombs rained down on other British cities as well.

The Prime Minister was working underground in the War Office but some thought the area unsafe. In November 1940 when the Blitz was at its worst, he was asked to move to the Down Street Tube station, home of the Railway Executive Committee.

'You'll have a bath, Prime Minster,' an aide said trying to get the premier to move.

'Will there be cigars and brandy?' asked the leader.

'And whisky as well, sir,' came the immediate reply.

And so George Miracle, who had already met the present King and Queen and their family and the previous King and Queen and the former King's mother as well as many ambassadors and non-British royals as part of his job as station master at Wolferton, could now add the name Winston Churchill to his register of VIP introductions.

The Blitz exploded above Down Street every night. During the day, George and colleague Bernard Houghton were sent aloft for a situation report. Giving the REC first hand reports from experienced railwaymen became essential.

They were able to travel safely as the Underground was available to certain REC personnel by prior arrangement. The communication system in Down Street was first class but there was no better way to inform the REC of conditions above ground than by visiting the railway properties bombed the night before.

They visited Kings Cross which suffered serious damage. They saw the work being done during daylight hours to remove wrecked rolling stock, repair tracks and have the station up and running as soon as possible. This was one of the ways Britain fought the war. Never give in and get life's routines back up and running pronto.

The two REC men headed towards George's railway alma mater, Liverpool Street and were dodging massive holes in roads and fallen building debris when Bernard paused.

'George, it's the King and Queen,' he said looking across the road.

The REC colleagues stopped. Men in uniform explained the damaged buildings with their Majesties looking and listening.

The King wore a naval uniform and Her Majesty was dressed in a tailored outfit with matching hat. She showed as much interest in the damaged city as did her husband. What George and Bernard didn't know was in the wee small hours that day Buckingham Palace was hit with at least two massive bombs. The damage outside the gates was frightening but one bomb exploded inside the Palace where the Queen and two pages were nearly killed.

They huddled in a corridor in case of flying glass with the Queen admitting her knees trembled for a minute or two.

Yet despite that shocking experience, here she was with her husband out amongst their people wanting to encourage them, see their situation first hand and share their grief and misfortune. The Queen felt better knowing her home too had suffered bomb damage.

In the early days of the war, government officials wanted the Royal Family to leave Britain and settle in Canada for the duration. The Queen refused point blank although she did send her daughters out of London to Windsor Castle.

The REC men watched from a distance of about 20 yards. The Queen stood with her back to them but turning, she recognized the Wolferton station master. She spoke to her husband who looked up.

'Mr Miracle,' said the King.

George moved carefully through the rubble, stopped and bowed.

'Good morning, Your Majesties,' he said.

'We wondered where you went after Wolferton,' said the Queen. 'Is your family safe and well?'

'Thank you, they are and living in Cambridgeshire.'

'And how is your boy?' asked the King. 'Still collecting engine numbers?'

George smiled sensing pride. 'He's being tutored in science and mathematics and hoping to win a place at Cambridge.'

'How wonderful,' said the King as the Queen too smiled and expressed her delight. George thanked them and bowed allowing them to continue their inspection.

When George returned to Bernard his colleague discreetly made a bow. 'I knew you were SM at the Royal Station old man but not that you and the King and Queen were on first name terms. If I'd known I was working with a member of the nobility, I would've made you a cuppa *every* day.'

George down-played the incident, they continued their inspection, saw that Liverpool Street was operating normally on a war footing situation and returned to Down Street.

Without the railways, Britain would have really struggled. Troops, raw materials, ordnance and equipment constantly needed to be shifted safely and quickly. The REC found rolling stock and created timetables to make the massive seemingly impossible task work.

George Miracle knew what life was like for men on the footplate and in signal boxes.

Coupling a loco which didn't have the strength to haul long trains with heavy loads would never happen in peace time. "It can't be done," would be the response of every driver worth his salt. But needs must and George and his colleagues found trains, created timetables and sent trains on their way.

Of course a small loco punching or rather pulling above its weight took forever to reach its destination meaning the men on the footplate were working 10, 12 even 14 hour shifts. Firemen fell asleep on the job. Bankers, small shunting locomotives, were often employed to help long trains get up and over an incline.

Mind you travelling slow did have advantages. If an unexploded bomb landed beside a track, and many did, vibrations created by the loco might cause the bomb to explode. Many a driver with his heart in his mouth tiptoed past a hole in the ground hardly daring to breathe while half expecting to be killed at any moment.

Communicating in the blackout became an art. Signalmen, hearing about a raid nearby or heading their way or already taking place at a rail centre or port such as Plymouth, used a series of lamps with colours to communicate with drivers in the dark.

Yellow – raiders approaching your train
Blue – enemy overhead
Red – you're in the thick of it

Drivers were glad of a tunnel which became a bomb shelter. Of course if your cargo involved explosives, you became a disaster on wheels waiting to happen. In certain situations you were forbidden from applying brakes to the wagons in case it created sparks. Some drivers lost control and couldn't stop their highly dangerous train. Unable to pull up and heading towards a station, the fireman would continuously blast the whistle, the warning for clearing the tracks.

Back at Down Street, George thought about his godson, George Carruthers, the young man who enlisted in the Royal Navy. His mother was desperate. News of so many convoy ships being sunk filled her with dread. Merchant or Royal Navy it made no difference. She wanted to know where her son was and to be assured he was safe.

George reckoned if he could find a senior naval officer who might know of his godson's situation, at least he could carry out one of his responsibilities as a godfather.

He asked around the REC office and was given a name of an appropriate naval officer. George wrote a basic letter pointing out that he did not wish to break any rules re naval locations but would be grateful for an address where he could contact his godson.

Handwritten letters wouldn't carry the same weight as one which was typewritten. The REC employed a number of women as typists.

George took his scribbled note to the typing pool and smiled at the first woman he saw who was reading a magazine awaiting her next task.

'Hello Miss,' he said pausing trying to remember her name.

'I'm Hetty Tring, Mr Miracle.'

'Forgive me, Miss Tring,' said George, 'but I have a favour to ask.'

Hetty was not your talkative, gossipy woman.

'What is it?' she asked.

'It's not railway related so I'll understand if you don't wish to help.'

'I'm sat here doing nowt, Mr Miracle. How can I help?'

George smiled. 'It's a letter to the Navy about my godson who recently enlisted.'

Hetty held out her hand and George delivered his scribble.

'One copy please, just the original, and thank you so much.'

George returned to his office as Hetty guided a piece of paper into her ROYAL typewriter, stared hard at George's handwriting and began to type.

He returned later finding Hetty back reading her magazine. She put it down, picked up the recently-typed letter offering it to George.

'All done, Mr Miracle,' she said and he thanked her profusely. 'Would you like an envelope typed too? I have a plain one.'

His gratitude overflowed. Later that day he posted the letter using the Hamilton-Weir House address. He rang Louisa explaining his mail and asked her to open any reply and read the contents.

Three days later when she did, he wanted to kick himself. It was a bland reply saying such information was not available. News about ships, especially those of the Royal Navy would never be sent in an ordinary letter to anyone in time of war. George Miracle, the enemy of Britain. *What sort of nincompoop am I?*

'I thought you were doing important work for the government, George,' said his wife. 'Surely you should know about not requesting war information.'

'I wasn't, I didn't,' he struggled to explain, told her he loved her and would telephone on the weekend.

'The children keep asking when you'll be coming to stay again.'

'As soon as I can,' he said, 'and please give them and your mother my love.'

On one of his visits to inspect rail damage in London, he made a detour to a Navy department finding his way to an administration officer, showed his ID card and relevant REC position and confessed.

'I stupidly asked for my godson's posting in a letter but wonder if I could have any information I might pass on to his parents.'

'Mail can be forwarded to a ship but details of where said vessel is now or might be in the future are naturally not available.'

'Of course,' said George. Eventually he discovered details of his godson's training and his chosen role of gunner.

Perish the thought I must tell his parents that bit of news.

He did and was glad he told Lord Carruthers and not his godson's mother. Mind you the young man had told his parents most of what

George discovered. George promised his friend he would write to his godson and tell the boy's parents any news.

Preparing for their night's work, George and Bernard chatted about the latest war news as they walked from the dining room to their posts. Hetty Tring came out of the typing pool and nearly collided with the REC officers.

It was easy to bump into someone in the confined spaces of the re-jigged former Underground station with its small rooms and narrow corridors.

'Oh I do beg your pardon, Mrs Tring,' said Bernard stepping back.

'Thank you, Mr Houghton,' she said and set off for home.

As the men settled at their posts ready for news of tracks, stations and rolling stock being hit by bombs, George asked a question.

'I thought that typist was Miss Tring; at least that's what I called her when she typed a letter for me.'

'She's married George but,' he whispered, 'to a brute of a husband.'

George paused wondering how his colleague came by such information. 'I'm sorry to hear that.'

'Poor woman's often working late so as to keep away from her drunken spouse.'

George's phone rang and the conversation about the typist ended.

As the bombing continued, the REC became ever busier. One of the worst nights in London happened on May 11, 1941 and George's heart began to pound. Reports of destruction were frightening.

'Incendiary bombs on Waterloo,' called one officer. The fires from these bombs meant the damage and destruction went on and on.

'Holborn viaduct destroyed,' called another colleague.

'Destroyed?' asked George. 'Do you mean damaged?'

'No, destroyed. No way through there. All trains to be re-routed.'

'Houses of Parliament have been hit,' cried another operator. 'They've even whacked Big Ben but it's still chiming!'

The mood in the room where REC officers created new routes for trains at a moment's notice and communicated the new destinations to controllers, signalmen and the like, all to keep the trains moving was tense to say the least.

New timetables would be created before needing to be re-done as even more damage was reported. A damaged line meant finding one that was working while always taking into account other trains. Giving priority to troops, weapons and essential war material was but one of the balls in the air for the juggling George Miracle and his colleagues.

Just when they thought the night had done its worst, news came through that both St Pancras and Kings Cross stations, only a short distance apart, were jointly under attack. Wrecked rolling stock, uprooted track, and station roofs blasted to smithereens became a nightmare for those in the REC. Far worse of course was the human toll with railway staff and passengers dead or injured.

These attacks were Hitler's plan to demoralize the nation. Bomb civilians, spread terror and have the British people demand their leaders sue for peace. What Hitler couldn't destroy was the spirit of those people, and their determination to keep calm and carry on.

The bombing stopped an hour before dawn. George was exhausted having been on duty non-stop for 10 hours. Instead of crawling into his bed to sleep, he took himself up to street level and breathed the not-so-fresh air in the pre-dawn darkness.

The air-raid sirens were silent with fire crews everywhere. George watched as men aimed hoses at flames destroying the city of his birth. It was too much to bear. He walked away.

He turned a corner and heard groaning. Stumbling over fallen masonry, George headed towards the voice. He knelt and lifted bricks from the poor wretch on the ground.

'Stay calm, sir,' said George. 'We'll have you free in no time.'

George removed a brick from the man's throat and looked into the face of former station master and friend Jack Rogers.

Chapter 16

Sunrise was an hour away and in this situation it seemed true that it's always darkest before the dawn? For George in a narrow street off Piccadilly, it was tricky to see. But the blood coming from Jack's nose and throat was vivid.

'Jack, it's me, George Miracle.'

The retired railwayman tried to speak but could only gurgle and cough which sent droplets of blood spurting from his mouth. Jack ignored the flying plasma—he'd seen plenty of that in a trench on the Western Front in the Great War—fought to stay calm, to help and save his friend, his mentor.

He yelled as loud as he could into the darkness. 'Help! Help!'

Back to his friend, he lifted Jack's head and placed a brick as a pillow; what a pillow. George grabbed his handkerchief and held it against Jack's mouth. That stopped the blood but breathing through his broken nose was awful. George didn't notice Jack attempt to raise a hand in protest. He lifted the handkerchief and Jack sucked in air.

For the younger man, it was the same experience, the same feeling of helplessness as when he looked in vain for his kidnapped daughter. He desperately wanted to help, to save his friend but had neither the knowledge nor tools to do so. He could leave to find help but refused because of the possibility Jack might die and die alone.

He called once more as he tried doing anything to help. He removed Jack's helmet realizing the man was a fire watcher; so much for moving to Wales. He loosened Jack's tie and continued trying to stop the flow of claret. He was so concentrated on the man's bloodied face he copped a shock when he looked down and saw Jack's right foot was a sodden mess. His sock was soaked. Masonry smashed his head and once he fell, more bricks landed on his lower limbs.

'Hang in there, Jack, help'll be here any minute and we'll get you to hospital.' George wondered if Jack understood or even knew who was speaking as the older man drifted in and out of consciousness.

Out of the darkness, two ambulance crew men approached.

'You need help?' called one.

'Over here!' George stepped back allowing the professionals through. They studied the victim and performed their first aid routine. George's heart pounded. He wanted to help anyone in this situation but Jack was special.

The men stopped their resuscitation.

'Sorry mate,' one said. 'He's gone.'

George couldn't speak. He thought back thirty years to when he was charged with stealing from his employer, the Great Eastern Railway. The one person who went out of his way to investigate the crime, and exonerate the lad porter George Miracle was Mr Jack Rogers. Decades later that same man pushed George into applying for the SM job at Wolferton. On the eve of his wedding to Louisa, Jack and his wife treated George to a grand meal in their cottage in Epping Forest. And his present job, in the REC, this too was all down to the horribly injured fire watcher. No-one was a better friend to George Miracle than the war hero and retired station master, one Jack Rogers.

'We'll take him away, mate,' said an ambulance officer. His colleague unfolded a stretcher. They stepped back giving George a moment.

He knelt beside the lifeless body. Jack's frozen eyes stared into the night sky. George placed fingers on the bloody face and closed his friend's eyelids. 'Thanks for everything, Jack. I'll tell your dear wife and see she's all right. You take care now.'

He couldn't say any more as his snot and tears took over.

He went with the body and gave the undertaker Jack's details. He asked if he could advise the widow of Jack's death and if the body could be kept for a possible burial in Wales. He hit a wall of red tape.

George discovered Jack and Mrs Rogers moved to a cottage in Wales. He wanted to tell her in person and asked for a couple of days leave. When he gave the reason, leave was granted. Apart from trips to his family and to Ruddington, George rarely left his post in London.

No-one knew the timetables currently in operation better than George Miracle. He set off first thing, hopped on and off trains on his way to Aberystwyth and from there walked until he hitched a ride with a farmer to a village about a mile from the Rogers' cottage.

Edith was working in her vegetable garden at the side of the house when she heard the front gate squeak. She recognized George and knew immediately why he was there.

She knew he was the sort of man who would not write if he could visit in person. Neither spoke, George wanting her to speak because he too froze. She headed for the cottage.

'I'll put the kettle on,' she said and they entered the kitchen.

As she fussed making tea, George knew he should speak. It was the silence which became loud. 'I'm so sorry, Edith. Jack was the best friend I ever had in the railways.'

She chose to speak of anything other than the death of the man she married 53 years ago.

'You'll stay to lunch. You've had a terrible long journey.'

'Thank you,' said George and struggled to make conversation.

Eventually he opened up and explained how he was with Jack when he died. Edith reached out and squeezed George's hand. That was a small but important comfort. She whispered her thanks.

He was glad when she asked about his work and family and the war particularly in London. They chatted for a good hour and she was happy for the burial to take place in the churchyard in Epping Forest near where Jack and Edith lived for forty years. She hugged him when he left and he promised to write.

Going home, George was free from any German bombs but not the Welsh rain. Most of the train trip up to London was in pitch darkness.

The Reverend Kenneth Attwood sat for his usual luncheon after his lesson tutoring James Miracle at Hamilton-Weir House. Young Victoria was at the local school needing work far more challenging than her peers. James remained in his room researching and writing an essay set by his tutor. Despite his cerebral palsy, his handwriting though slow was legible and consistent.

Kenneth entered the family dining-room where Rowena and Louisa were preparing lunch. He greeted the women, sat and tucked a napkin under his chin. He no longer wore a dog collar.

'You do know, ladies, the only reason I tutor young James is because of your wonderful lunches.'

Rowena placed a sandwich in front of him and his mouth watered. The bread was homemade and the butter came from a neighbouring farm. The tomatoes were picked only an hour earlier.

Louisa put down cups of tea and the ladies joined their guest.

'How is your wife, Mr Attwood?' asked Rowena. 'We see so little of her. You must bring her to tea one Sunday.'

'I'm not hiding her ladies but the woman's the main breadwinner in our family. Since her father's passing, Fletcher and Daughter Solicitors is now Daughter only.'

They enjoyed their ration-teasing sandwich but Kenneth stopped the clock on the wall when next he spoke. 'James is to sit for his Cambridge entrance exam next Monday.'

The women stared at the tutor. 'But I thought you said he must be 18,' exclaimed Louisa.

'As you well know, ladies, there's a war on. The university has many of its lecturing staff away fighting, undergraduates have deferred their studies and rules are being re-written as we speak. I've spoken to the university and they will allow James to sit. But as you know, sitting for the exam does not guarantee you'll pass.'

Silence settled. Obviously the family knew about James being prepared for a Cambridge entrance exam but thought it was a year or more away. Before they could speak, who should appear but the budding undergraduate himself?

'You've made a spelling mistake in the question, Mr Attwood.'

'Excuse me,' interrupted the boy's grandmother. 'When did you lose your manners, Master Miracle?'

James apologized. 'I'm sorry, Grannie and Ma.'

'Spelling mistake?' queried the former priest; 'surely not.'

'Yes sir; you wrote Bolingbroke with two l's'

'Ah, well spotted, young man; your observation skill will impress your lecturers. Of course I made the deliberate mistake as a test.'

The student looked at his teacher for confirmation and grinned when Mr Attwood slipped in a subtle wink.

James joined the others and the mood was bubbling with the exam due to happen next Monday.

'Can we tell Dad about my exam?' asked James. 'I'm sure he'll be tickled pink.'

The three adults exchanged glances at the boy's turn of phrase. James continued talking, one of his many talents.

'Mr Attwood has been an excellent tutor starting all those years ago when we lived at Wolferton.'

'Indeed,' said the former Rector. 'Those were halcyon days.'

Halcyon,' said James. 'I know that word. It means happy times and tranquility.'

'Good lad,' said Kenneth. 'But can you spell it?'

'I T,' responded James with a sparkle in his eye. Kenneth included jokes and puns in his years of tutoring and the others smiled or groaned at yet another telling of the oft-repeated corny joke.

After their light luncheon and plenty of conversation mainly from the youngest person in the room, Attwood stood to leave.

'Thank you ladies for a delightful repast and young man I shall see you on Thursday with your essay complete and error-free.'

James escorted his tutor to the front door where he stood and waved until the priest was out of sight.

If only George Miracle knew what was happening to his boy.

The station master faced other personal problems. Work remained hectic with German bombs wreaking havoc on the railways in Britain. Apart from attending to the funeral of his mentor Jack Rogers, George needed to help his best friends, Lord and Lady Carruthers. Their son, George's godson didn't run away to sea; he joined the navy.

Using a contact at the War Office, George learnt about his godson's training, posting and current situation. It would not be great news for Valerie, worried as she was thinking her son could well be killed at sea, dying a terrible death by drowning.

The railwayman contacted the parents. Alas he had no up-to-date news about the godson who became a gunner.

Lord Carruthers tried to help his wife relax. 'Being a stoker is damn hard work, my dear. Shovelling coal below deck to keep those mighty boilers in steam has men drenched in sweat.'

Valerie was hardly pacified. The one-legged Lord didn't make the point that should the order be given to abandon ship, gunners have a much better chance than those poor devils trapped below deck. The war continued to punish people in many and varied ways.

Chapter 17

Thanks to German bombs, most theatres in London closed. Those which did open staged light, fun entertainment. Troops on leave didn't want morbid drama; they craved music, laughter and pretty girls.

Comedians who performed slapstick could hardly fail and those who could sing well-known songs and tap dance were on a winner. But the real hit occurred when the audience joined in. Sing-a-longs became a highlight.

Chorus girls with long legs high-kicking their way around the stage took people's minds off bombs, death and destruction. George was never much of a theatre man even when living in London.

He finished his evening meal and was told to get a bit of fresh air. Supervisors knew the danger of long shifts in cramped conditions below ground. 'Be back by 10 and sooner if Adolf comes calling.'

It was a cool night; the blackout ruled London and George strolled enjoying his time away from claustrophobic Down Street.

Obviously there were no illuminated signs or lights outside buildings, and crossing roads became dangerous with taxis and buses not being heard or seen until the last moment.

George heard music and people having a good time. He drew closer where, in the dark street, a variety theatre was staging a show.

He bought a ticket and an usherette with a torch showed him an empty seat. He leant back and let the show and the audience reaction wash over him. People smoked and even called out to the performers.

When a comic led the cast and audience in singing a popular song, the railwayman surprised himself by joining in with gusto. His applause at the end was enthusiastic. Let yourself go, George.

The usherette escorted another patron to a seat and again used her torch to guide him. The torch lit up a couple in front and to one side of George. He gasped.

A man and a woman were kissing. He didn't find that surprising. Knowing the war brought massive change to people's lives, he saw couples being romantic even in the street. People in love or desperate for company could be buried alive or blown to bits tomorrow, even tonight. Grab your chance at romance while you can.

In this case he gasped because he recognized the couple. The man was his colleague at Down Street, Bernard Houghton and the woman, also from Down Street, the typist Hetty Tring. There was none of this peck on the cheek or holding hands routine. This couple needed to find themselves a bedsit as their osculation turned serious.

Being a bit of a prude, George didn't go in for public displays of a romantic nature but wasn't seriously concerned about their carrying on. There were others in the theatre doing pretty much the same thing. No, George became uncomfortable because Bernard had told him Mrs Tring, not Miss Tring, was married to a brute of a husband.

Adultery was none of George's business but if Mr Tring discovered his wife's extra-marital activity, would he do for Bernard as apparently he did for her? Could Bernard work well or at all for the REC with busted ribs and a few missing teeth?

As soon as the next act, a juggling gymnast finished and bounced off to wild applause, George slipped out and away. He walked back to Down Street thinking what, if anything, he should say or do.

It's none of your business, George.

He was soon hard at work creating a workable timetable for freight trains coming south from the coal fields of Durham having their normal route blocked by a serious derailment in the Midlands.

'Evening, George,' said Bernard sitting. 'Busy night?'

George saw bright red lipstick on Bernard's collar. He thought. *Should I say anything?*

'Have you cut yourself?' asked George causing Bernard to investigate his neck. It was tricky to tell so he slipped away to the lavatory and when he returned the lipstick was barely there.

Despite the war, the University of Cambridge maintained a solid base of students when the government decided not to order conscription for men under 20 years of age in 1939 and 40. They continued to offer places for the medically unfit and conscientious objectors.

Kenneth Attwood, a graduate of said university, kept abreast of current entrance exam regulations and was thrilled to have his student allowed to sit for the exam.

Back in the 19th century, this special exam rewarded students who could regurgitate facts. The successful students were those with excellent memories. The questions to be answered by James Miracle would be more a test of his grasp of different subjects.

After their last lesson on Thursday, Kenneth informed James he would be collected at 8am on the day of the exam. The young man was excited, his mother and grandmother more so.

All three assumed the tutor would arrive in his small car and drive the five miles into the city. Because of the war and the scarcity of petrol, Attwood always rode his bicycle to Hamilton-Weir House. But how would the disabled young man travel? In a few months petrol for private cars would move from rationed to restricted to forbidden.

What did the former priest plan to use to transport his protégé? A bus from the nearest village would still involve a fair old walk. Kenneth arrived and to everyone's surprise and delight, his bicycle now sported an attachment; a small one-seated two-wheeled buggy, a sort of sidecar but in the rear.

'Is that for me?' asked James unable to stop grinning.

'Your carriage awaits, my Lord,' said Attwood with an even bigger smile.

Friendly residents helped the student settle with the roof offering shelter from any rain. With satchel on his lap, James waved to his family and a few Hamilton-Weir House residents who gathered to inspect the "carriage" as Kenneth Attwood stood on the pedals and drove the contraption down the drive.

They passed through two villages and anyone on the high street stopped and stared. James thought he was royalty.

In Cambridge, Kenneth stopped at the gate of his former college where the porter remembered the old boy—he remembered everyone—admired the vehicle and happily allowed it to be parked behind his office.

James and his tutor set off for the library. Initially meeting James, some people were taken aback by his method of walking and speech. He didn't give it a moment's thought. Kenneth escorted his charge into the library and spotted a lecturer who helped James find a seat.

'Good luck, young man,' said Kenneth as he gently squeezed the shoulder of the boy wearing splints and with one of his boots a bit bulkier than the other. 'I'll meet you outside when you've finished.'

James momentarily forgot to say thank you and goodbye as his heartbeat accelerated. Being in the magnificent library building set his heart aflame and the thought that all his hard work might finally pay off caused his hands to shake. Just being there was an achievement.

The REC ran the rail network for all of Britain. In March 1941 the Luftwaffe attacked the Clydebank area of Scotland. Over two nights, German bombs brought devastation and death to the shipbuilding and munitions town. Over a thousand people were killed while many more were injured and made homeless. Of approximately 12,000 houses in the town, 8 were undamaged—8. The nearby oil tanks caught fire which raged for a month.

As with Britons down south in London, the spirit of the people in Scotland was never broken by the Luftwaffe terror raids.

George Miracle and colleagues were faced with a major task. The close proximity of the houses, factories and oil depot in Clydebank, meant the railway in and out of the town needed a massive reconstruction. The Railway Executive Committee got stuck in.

Kenneth Attwood received the results of the entrance exam for his student, James Miracle. As the boy's teacher and as the student studied at home rather than in a school due to his disability, the tutor requested the results be sent to him.

Attwood opened the envelope, studied the results and suffered a sharp pain in his chest. Telling the young man in person would be the right thing to do so he collected his bicycle, sans passenger attachment, and pedalled the five miles to Hamilton-Weir House.

He arrived unannounced and when James discovered his tutor had appeared, he hurried as best he could to the parlour.

'Have you any news, Mr Attwood?' he asked breathing quickly.

'Manners,' said his grandmother and James understood.

'Good day, Mr Attwood. I hope you are well,' said the youth.

'And good day to you, Mr Miracle,' said the visitor. Kenneth dropped the Master Miracle and began addressing the young man as an adult. 'I do have news and it is not what I expected.'

James' heart took a whack. His mother and grandmother endured pain. He desperately wanted to do well, not only to enter university but because his family and especially his father would be so proud.

Victoria was home from school with a cold and she and her mother and grandmother waited saying nothing.

Kenneth removed the envelope with James' exam result. 'I was sure you would pass, James but you have done more than pass, you have been awarded top marks the equivalent of honours.'

The room lost a fair amount of oxygen as every member of the Miracle family gasped. The hugging and kissing from relatives and a pumping handshake from the tutor began in earnest. James drifted off towards a seventh heaven.

When the celebrations eased a tad, the added bonus set hearts pounding when the tutor explained.

'You have been offered a place at Cambridge, James. You will need to choose a faculty and decide if you wish to live in halls and I need to point out my homemade taxi is not up to a daily service.' The others laughed. 'The Michaelmas term begins in September.' The others buzzed.

James finally spoke. 'I cannot thank you enough, Mr Attwood. I would never have achieved this result without your patience and brilliance. I will never forget your kindness, sir.'

The males embraced one another and the women welled up.

James turned to his mother. 'Ma, how can I contact Dad?'

When George Miracle was eventually told the news by telegram, he found it hard to speak. His throat froze. For years his son couldn't speak instead only making unintelligible sounds. He lived in a push chair then later a wheelchair. But he conquered his disabilities and learnt to walk and talk albeit in a unique way. Now shy of 18, he won a place to one of the world's oldest and most respected universities and all that despite having cerebral palsy from which he would never be cured.

George telephoned his boy. Both struggled and both wished they could meet face to face and express their love and pride.

'I'll come home as soon as I can, son. Once again, you are a credit to yourself and have made your mother and sister and me the proudest family in the land.'

George wanted to tell the entire population at Down Street—what parent wouldn't?—and he did tell many although in typical George Miracle style, without any fanfare or boasting.

He took the afternoon off and called on his friends in Hampstead. George and Valerie were always delighted to see their best man and were overcome with the news of James and his university success.

'That is the most wonderful news, George,' said Lady Carruthers. 'What you and Louisa have done for your boy and his disability is nothing short of miraculous.'

'Here here,' added His Lordship.

The railwayman loved discussing the news about his son but knew their boy was serving at sea with his life continually in danger.

'What news of young George?' asked his godfather and the worry in the faces and voices of the parents reinforced what George knew already. The Carruthers struggled with their son fighting a war where ships were constantly called into action and regularly sunk.

The Royal Navy owned many types of ships built for the defence of the Realm but not all its vessels were built by Britain. During the early years of World War Two, the RN once stole a German merchant ship, *Hannover* which carried bananas from the West Indies to Germany. An Allied cruiser and destroyer intercepted the *Hannover* ordering it to stop. With only bananas as weapons the merchant ship was soon captured.

The *Hannover* became *Sinbad*—an appropriate name as she was kidnapped at sea—and sailed back to the Clyde where she was re-fitted becoming an escort carrier. These were small aircraft carriers the Americans called a baby flattop. Scottish locals couldn't understand why the superstructure of a perfectly good ship was being scrapped. They didn't know the full story. Aircraft carriers, no matter how small, needed a flat surface for their planes to land and take off while steaming across the oceans of the world.

Eventually *Sinbad* became HMS *Audacity* and her task was to escort Atlantic convoys bringing vital supplies to Britain. All this detail about a ship carrying bananas for Germany before becoming a small aircraft carrier for the Royal Navy has relevance because a gunner on board said ship was George Carruthers, godson of the railwayman currently working for the Railway Executive Committee.

The convoys to Britain were vital and the ability of German U-boats to send thousands of merchant ships to the sea bed was tragic in terms of lives and cargo lost. HMS *Audacity* with its 8 fighter planes, all Martlets, (a mythical bird without feet) was given the task of escorting convoys across the Atlantic. All wartime tasks were dangerous but at sea, at night even the RN vessels were in dire peril.

It was no use sending planes aloft in the dark, they were fighters and not spotters, and the first you knew a torpedo was heading your way was when your ship exploded. HMS *Audacity* lived a short life protecting only four convoys.

In December 1941 she and her convoy were attacked by 12 U-boats about 500 miles from Spain. The *Audacity* captain chose to leave the convoy to hunt for submarines. That decision, leaving your convoy, would later be banned by the Royal Navy.

Gunner George Carruthers manned one of the *Audacity's* 10 guns and did so for hours. Only four of her aircraft were serviceable. Shooting at submerged U-boats proved tricky if not impossible. Where are they? It made no difference as the first torpedo struck the *Audacity's* engine room and she began to sink. Two more torpedoes seemed to be overkill as they caused the aviation fuel supply to explode blowing off the baby carrier's bow. The German banana boat turned British aircraft carrier was no more. Abandon ship! Its crew was in the Atlantic, dead or desperate. 73 of the ship's company died.

Chapter 18

The government procrastinated when announcing bad news. In September 1940, 600 civilians were sheltering in the basement of a school in London's East End. A German bomb scored a direct hit and the adults and children were buried alive. One argument stated because the school was several storeys high it was mistaken for a factory. Okay but try telling that to the families of the dead.

The war cabinet placed a news embargo fearing a collapse in morale and a propaganda boost for Hitler. When the British press finally reported the incident, the death total was 77 not 600. It was decades before the true story was told.

Such was the thinking of politicians at the time. When convoys were sunk along with Royal Navy ships lost at sea, no-one rushed to announce the deadly news. Lord and Lady Carruthers were constantly thinking of their son and when news of the sinking of HMS *Audacity* finally became public, their hearts shattered.

Valerie collapsed. All her fears, her dreaded expectations came true. George cradled his desolate wife telling her their son was not necessarily dead. Yes, dozens of the carrier's crew were confirmed dead or missing but a few were rescued by other vessels in the area.

'We must believe, Valerie. Please darling, let us not give up hope for George's sake if not our own.' Her tears were unstoppable.

What a contrast between the two families as Christmas 1941 drew close. The Miracles were celebrating their son's first term at Cambridge where James made a brilliant start to his studies impressing all he met. At Tudor House, the fate of Gunner George Carruthers RN remained unknown. He may well be dead, trapped in the sunken hull of his ship. The contrast in mood between the two families could not have been greater.

If you could ask for the best Christmas present ever, you would ask for the safe return of your child and the Carruthers' wish came true.

Gunner Carruthers was rescued. His hearing was shot, his shoulder smashed and one side of his face scarred but he was alive.

His parents kept repeating the words, "He is alive". They spoke aloud and in their minds. Valerie knew about greeting a wounded loved one as her husband, then her fiancée, lost a leg in the Great War.

The Miracles rejoiced when the news arrived in Cambridgeshire. George and Louisa hoped the godson would recuperate and knew he would be spoilt rotten with his parents and sister at home in Hampstead. Godfather Miracle promised a visit as soon as possible.

James lived in halls at Cambridge. They gave him a room with the easiest of access. It didn't take long for fellow students and his lecturers to take to the young man. His disability was obvious but so too was his determination and brilliant mind. They teased him with love and he gave as good as he got.

To start he went home to Hamilton-Weir House on weekends. There was a bus to the nearest village and Cecil the gardener took a horse and cart to the bus stop and collected the undergraduate.

His father came home on the odd weekend and the conversation flowed like an excited stream after the melting of snow in spring. Victoria became a bookaholic and was often seen in a corner of the rambling country house with her face buried in a tome.

People change. 'Ma, I won't be home this weekend,' said James when he telephoned his mother. 'There's a chess tournament with Peterhouse and I've been picked for my college.'

Louisa told George when he rang to check on his family. 'If you weren't sure your family was growing up, George, you might need to revise your opinion.'

'What's happened now?' asked the worried railwayman.

'Your son has found other interests and will not be joining us this weekend.'

The London Blitz ended not so much with a bang but a whimper. There were isolated raids but that constant massive bombing of the capital night after night and elsewhere ended. This was partly because Britain showed no signs of suing for peace and partly because in May 1941, Hitler threw his forces east invading Russia. He ignored Napoleon's similar venture and paid the same price.

But George and the REC were hardly short of work. With the war continuing and on different fronts, more troop movements, more equipment and munitions and more raw materials were needed up and down the country. Locomotives, trucks, carriages and flexible timetables were constantly in demand. George lived on the telephone getting reports of damage, derailments and deaths.

When not flat out tackling emergencies, talk amongst the staff began to concentrate on the possibility of an invasion; not the Germans storming Britain, that plan was dead and buried, but rather a plan in which Britain and her allies crossed the Channel. Once the Americans joined the war, rumours of an Allied invasion ran around pubs, barracks and the REC at Down Street like wildfire.

'If that happens,' said George to colleague Bernard Houghton, 'we'll be run off our feet. How many men will be part of any invasion?'

'Millions and we'll be moving them and their pop-guns by train.'

Hitler didn't neglect his bombing of Britain but changed tactics. Instead of the ports and the capital, he attacked the cultural centres of the island nation. This was revenge; tit-for-tat air raids. There was once a talking point that Hitler refused to bomb Oxford and Cambridge in the hope Britain would never bomb the university city of Heidelberg. Whether such a point of view was true or not, the Germans made no exception with other British icons.

In 1827 Herr Verlag Baedeker created a publishing business producing travel guides with maps of countries which included notes about special buildings. He gave venues a 1, 2 or 3 star rating. A century later German pilots used these travel guides to set their bomb sights on British treasures.

The RAF bombed the German towns of Lubeck and Rostock and Goebbels wrote in his diary, "Like the British, we must attack centres of culture".

And so using the Baedeker Guides, the so-called Baedeker Raids saw German bombs fall on Exeter, Canterbury, Bath, Lincoln and York. Reports flooded into the REC. George's heart hurt when news arrived about the City Station in Norwich copping a pasting. He worked as a porter in that fine city boarding with the SM and the housekeeper Daisy Woods even helping find her long-lost son.

April proved a deadly month for the so-called Baedeker Blitz. York station suffered devastating damage. One German bomb left a vast crater on the main line which caused a massive disruption.

In Bath when the air raid sirens sounded, people ignored them. Being so used to hearing about Bristol being bombed they assumed it was yet another raid on that city only a few miles down the line. What a deadly mistake. The Germans flew back to France, refueled and returned even strafing terrified residents in the streets. Hundreds of Bath residents were killed and thousands injured. Buildings were destroyed and rail services thrown into chaos.

Such raids continued throughout the summer. On the August bank holiday, Middlesborough station suffered horrendous damage with the roof collapsing on a passenger train. In York, LNER A4 Class locomotive *Sir Ralph Wedgewood*, named after George's boss, was hit by a German bomb and had to be scrapped.

The REC worked around the clock diverting trains as people on the ground worked tirelessly to remove the rubble, restore the lines and get the trains running again. In Middlesborough, it took only two days for normal services to be resumed.

Like the first, this war was definitely not over by Christmas and George Miracle wondered when peace would return, if ever, and what he would do when it did arrive.

Chapter 19

Christmas 1942 at Hamilton-Weir House was full of delighted guests with the longest waiting-list ever. Of course the family Miracle was a fixture. On Christmas Eve, the family Carruthers arrived. Years ago they would have motored down from London in a fancy and expensive vehicle. That was no longer possible as by now the civilian petrol ration was abolished.

Lord and Lady Carruthers with their children, George and Annie, arrived in Cambridge by train. They followed instructions and caught a bus to the nearest village. Railwayman Miracle met them with Cecil the gardener and his horse and cart. Piling their luggage and bodies aboard, the visitors set off in not the usual conveyance for His Lordship and family. They were lucky as neither rain nor snow fell.

Many months had passed since members of both families last saw one another. In the case of godson George it was years.

He was marked by the war. His shoulder reconstruction was complete but the burnt right side of his face from the explosions aboard HMS *Audacity* would remain a scar forever. His spirits were high and seeing his godfather gave both a surge of happiness.

The families rejoiced in their shared history. The husbands met at Liverpool Street station in 1914. Louisa worked as a nanny for the Carruthers family for a number of years which was how she met the young station master. Louisa's father bequeathed her the greater part of his estate enabling her to establish Hamilton-Weir House.

But life moved on. Daughter Annie Carruthers, once a sickly child, became a shy, retiring young woman. Sharing with the determined Victoria gave the young women a chance to discover what each planned for the future.

The same went for the sons. James with his cerebral palsy and the wounded George Carruthers made an odd couple with much to share and discuss.

Rowena and the children retired and the parents sat quietly, their mood reflecting the fact their country was still at war.

'What's going to happen, George,' asked Valerie of the host. 'When will this damned war be over?'

No-one reacted to Valerie's blunt speech. All four were war-weary.

'If I knew anything, my Lady, I would gladly tell all. Now the Americans are here, one can only wonder when they'll join our lads and invade Europe. But all I know is that trains continue to help the war effort thanks to so many brave drivers, firemen and others.'

'And you,' said his wife.

'Hear hear,' added Lord Carruthers.

They chatted about their children and when the parents became weary, George brought proceedings to a halt.

'I suggest we retire and let Father Christmas do his rounds.'

It was a busy and joyful Christmas lunch thanks to the many diners. Rations ruled the menu with Rowena working tirelessly behind the scenes. She helped Santa dress. The owners and guests joined the huge dining room gathering of all Hamilton-Weir House residents. Seeing disabled children with beaming smiles as Father Christmas distributed presents was a tonic for anyone weighed down with the woes of war. No-one knew Kenneth Attwood was Santa.

After lunch, George 1 and 2 sat in a snug beside a crackling fire.

'I know you've signed the Official Secrets Act my friend,' said Carruthers, 'but please give me good news about this invasion.'

The railwayman chose his words carefully. 'I will tell you all I know, George, and that will take a second. We get visits from the MoD and the War Office but as of today, nothing concrete has been revealed.'

Carruthers changed tack. 'So what will you do when it's finally over? Will you move back to Wolferton?'

George 2 shook his head. 'I suppose I'll go back to being an SM but where I have no idea but I'll be surprised if it's at Wolferton.'

'You could always move into your mansion in Eaton Square and become a gentleman of leisure.'

They laughed and continued to reminisce proving that friendships which have endured often produce a rich vein of happiness.

George Miracle was the first to leave Hamilton-Weir House. He delighted in being with his family and friends but knew his work at Down Street needed his attention. He reckoned something dramatic waited in the wings. He pondered a possible Allied invasion and victory and what he would do once the war ended.

With 20 years before retiring, he knew doing anything other than being an SM would frustrate and sadden him. But where would he go? If the REC disbanded and he returned to the LNER, their stations went from London to Scotland. He could end up anywhere. His children would probably marry or start to earn a living leaving only him and Louisa to find a cottage beside a railway line and grow old together.

But first, another job occupied his thinking; the invasion of Europe.

The first American soldiers arrived in Northern Ireland. There were about 4000 and fate or luck was on their side. They sailed in a convoy from New York to Belfast and in the 11 day/night journey not a single U-boat troubled them. As the months passed, those 4000 US troops in Northern Ireland grew to 300,000 and St Patrick's Day was never the same.

By the time the invasion became imminent; 1.5 million Americans were stationed in or had passed through Britain. These troops were housed from the Orkneys to Cornwall and whenever mass movement was required, trains were used and given clearance by the men of the Railway Executive Committee in Down Street.

Planning for the invasion began a long time before June 1944. Its two major and much debated aspects were when and where. But a third issue bubbled away in the background—secrecy. Maintaining secrecy proved more than tricky. The Allies wanted a total blackout of their decisions while the Germans desperately sought details and spies on both sides were made to earn their money.

Obviously sourcing the men and machines for the invasion took an age as did the study of possible landing sites but any and all planning would be a waste of time, money and lives if the Germans discovered those plans. The Allies tried all sorts of ruses to fool the enemy.

Planning to invade Sicily in early 1943, they dressed a civilian corpse and released the body from a submarine near the coast of

Spain. Fake official papers were placed on the corpse in the hope they would be delivered to the Germans. They were and the Germans sent troops to Greece and Sardinia making the invasion of Sicily "easier".

Prior to June 1944, inflatable tanks and trucks were placed in Kent near the coast in the hope of fooling the Germans into believing the Allies would land at Cherbourg; another ruse which worked.

Secrecy was everything. Arriving when and where the Germans were not expecting the invasion forces could be the difference between success and failure.

Mind you, the Germans under Erwin Rommel used deception as well, and when the American Rangers stormed the vertical cliffs at Pointe du Hoc, the massive guns they were expecting turned out to be telephone poles allowing the nearby and fully-functional, built-in-secret Maisy Battery to inflict massive casualties on Omaha Beach.

The word at Down Street was that someone from the MoD top brass would arrive today to give the REC chaps a briefing.

'Has to be news of the invasion,' said Bernard.

'Could be news of our promotions,' chimed in Alf Reading.

'What about you, George?' asked Bernard. 'What's this bigwig going to tell us?'

'I'm hoping it's news of Hitler's surrender.'

Someone ran a book with odds on what the visitor would discuss. Super-careful Miracle bet a Bob on it being the invasion.

Half an hour later all REC officers gathered in the committee meeting room and a high-ranking MoD gent was introduced. It was deathly quiet apart from those moments when an Underground train clattered past the abandoned Down Street platform.

'Gentlemen, I hope I don't need to remind you of the Official Secrets Act but I will and say again that anything you hear in this room must never leave it.'

He paused and those REC officers who took long odds on the news not being about the invasion knew they'd done their dough.

'The railways have played an invaluable role thus far in this war and on behalf of the Government and the Ministry I again thank you one and all. But the coming months will see you chaps doing even more dangerous, more vitally important work. You don't need to be a genius to work out that with so many of our friends from across the Atlantic here and providing our wives, sisters and sweethearts with chewing gum and nylons, that they will be joining forces with us and our other allies and taking a trip across the Channel to give Herr Hitler one hell of a bloody nose.'

Spontaneous applause broke out with a following buzz.

The hubbub faded. 'There will be specific and out-of-the-way areas where large numbers of troops will be stationed ready for the off. They will travel by rail. We need you chaps to find the trains to carry men and machines from tanks to tommy guns and always, always in secret.' He paused again.

'Now you will see trains even in the night but you must never discuss what's on board or where they're going with anyone. You won't tell your friends or family but you might chat to a driver or station master thinking they'll need to know what's happening. They don't. Say nothing!' He spoke slowly. 'Keep Jerry in the dark.'

This time the pause was the longest of all. His stare, his glare at the listening audience spoke volumes.

He changed and smiled. 'Are there any questions, gentlemen?'

Alf Reading liked the sound of his own voice. 'When and where will all this be happening, sir?'

'That's an excellent question.' Alf glowed. 'I believe the term is "need to know". Men laughed uproariously and Alf stopped glowing.

Documents were given to George and his colleagues. They were to examine them and draw up trains and timetables to transport men and machines. They began work behind the scenes on what would become the largest amphibious landing in history.

Towards the end of 1943, selected villages in the south of England were evacuated. Residents, many of whom were born in and lived their whole life there packed their possessions and left. Troops used the villages as training bases as they prepared for the invasion. Two of those villages would never be occupied again.

December 1943 was the first Christmas George Miracle didn't go home to be with his wife and children. 'I can't get away, darling,' he said on the telephone to Louisa. 'I'll try and be there for New Year.'

George was always in contact with Hamilton-Weir House and took great pride in hearing about the success of his children. Son James did extremely well in his first year at Cambridge and was full of enthusiasm for the new terms. Ask him about his studies and he could prattle for England.

'I have news about your daughter, Mr Miracle.'

George worried. He loved his children with a passion but carried a special torch for Victoria. Being away from home meant he was not there to protect her. Years ago he was working across the road at Wolferton when the youngster was kidnapped. He never stopped being thankful she was found safe and well. Now he lived in London while Victoria was 60 miles away in Cambridgeshire.

'Oh yes,' he said. 'And what's the young lady been up to this time?'

'Kenneth Attwood came to tea last week and told her more about Girton College.'

'And what's so special about that?'

'You know. It's the college at Cambridge exclusively for females.'

George copped a slap. 'She's not going to university?' he gasped.

'She says if her brother can go to Cambridge, why can't she?'

'Blimey, how can a nanny and a station master produce such brainy children?'

She pretended to be offended. 'Are you saying nannies are simple?'

He laughed. 'Not simple, simply divine.'

His flattery still worked. 'Mind you there's another factor at play here. A couple of young lads from the church have been paying her attention.'

'What?' said George with concern. 'She's too young for courting and besides, any interested males must first get my approval.'

This time Louisa laughed. 'Oh my goodness; you might be able to control trains, my dear but you have no chance with love.'

They laughed together although George with less elan and he promised to visit as soon as he could get away.

Chapter 20

The term "friendly fire" is a fine example of a clear but horrible definition. In conflict you aim to hurt your opponent. If you accidentally hurt your team mate, you're hardly helping. If by hurt you mean kill, then horrendous and disaster don't even come close to describing friendly fire.

Wanting to rehearse the invasion, the Americans found Slapton Sands, a beach in Devon similar to a beach in Normandy, France.

Let's get the landing craft we'll use in the invasion, fill them with our troops, head for the beach and rehearse attacking the Germans.

What could go wrong? How about everything?

As the *Titanic* steamed towards icebergs, her radio operator attended to a backlog of personal messages sent by and to passengers. Other ships in the area sent warnings about the icebergs. "Slow down" or even "Stop" were some of the warnings. These were not forwarded to the bridge of the *Titanic* or at least were delayed. As the saying goes, "Hindsight is 20/20'. It's true that many disasters could have been avoided with the Slapton Sands incident a perfect example.

Exercise Tiger was the American rehearsal off the coast of Devon. The Royal Navy assisted with warships patrolling behind the landing craft just in case any speedy German E-boats slipped out of Cherbourg and attacked the rehearsing Americans.

Radio communication was vital between the Allies. They used different frequencies—an unbelievable error. In addition, radio operators were ordered to maintain radio silence during the rehearsal. What? Even if they're under attack by the real enemy?

The Americans planned to use live ammunition to give their 30,000 troops in nine large tank-landing ships a taste of the real thing. Fire *above* the landing craft, you guys. The agreed invasion time was 0730 hours. A problem with one of the landing craft meant a high-ranking officer switched to 0830 with not everyone being told. All the signs of a possible failure began to gather.

With one British destroyer heading off to port for minor repairs and no replacement made available, different radio frequencies, a ban on radio use and different starting times for the exercise, plus German E-boats discovering the flotilla and it being ripe for the picking, the scene was set for a deadly rehearsal.

Forget about Americans being shot by the enemy or by friendly fire which was how some died. No, many simply drowned. Why? They were given little or no training using lifejackets. Troops wore heavy rucksacks and metal helmets as per their planned arrival in France.

Hey you guys, where do I put my lifejacket? It goes around your waist, dummy. No it doesn't! Sorry, too late.

So when the landing craft were torpedoed by desperate Germans on speeding E-boats, men jumped or fell into the sea where the weight of their rucksack tipped them over and they drowned. The lifejackets became useless, some lethal. Others who didn't drown died from pneumonia in the freezing waters of the English Channel.

The investigators disagreed over the number of casualties ranging between 500 and 800. It was less a cock-up and more a disaster. As per usual, a press embargo was placed on the catastrophe.

If you go to war you know the chances of being killed are high but dying from friendly fire or stupidity has to be beyond belief.

All this happened a few weeks before the planned invasion. If you believed in omens, for the Allies this was not good.

The Slapton Sands "event" was another of those tales the authorities were not keen to discuss. Widespread publicity only happened decades later in 1984 when a local chap found a Sherman tank in 60 feet of water off the Devon coast. The whole horror was uncovered.

Once the Normandy beaches were chosen as the landing spot for the invasion, troops and equipment needed to be moved. George and his colleagues didn't know the French destination but were told to find rolling stock and routes for a big shift. A 15 mile swathe of southern England would become home to a massive army.

Individual REC officers were assigned specific tasks. George was to work on a train heading to Droxford in Hampshire. Trains ran through the Meon Valley along what was affectionately known as the "strawberry line". Droxford had charm and beauty to spare but what had this quiet station got to do with the D-Day landings?

George faced his supervisor. 'You'll be looking after Mr Churchill and his War Cabinet, George. The PM will hold meetings near Portsmouth and wants a mobile base which includes a bath.'

George avoided personal comments. 'What train will he use, sir?'

'The Royal Train with an armoured car as part of the unit. Once there, the train may be split as the PM wants to move around and visit troops. The locomotives and all other details are listed in this folder.' It was handed to George. 'Do you have any questions?'

'Yes sir; why Droxford?'

'It's not far from Southwick House near Portsmouth where the invasion planning meetings are being held. Droxford station has long sidings to house the train and there's a deep cutting nearby with cover should any German planes happen to pay a visit.'

'How long will Mr Churchill be at Droxford?'

'Two or three days and I'm told during his stay in Hampshire, this massive invasion will finally be placed under starter's orders.' George looked at his boss. 'This is it, George. The balloon is about to go up.'

Back in his shared office, George sat and read the notes of his latest assignment. Bernard entered.

'What have you got?' he asked.

'Droxford.'

'Droxford? I've never heard of it.'

'It's a quiet station on the Meon Valley line. What about you?'

'Southampton,' said Bernard revelling in the size and thus he reckoned the superior importance of his assignment. 'The docks are literally bulging with invasion craft. The fields outside the city are crammed with allied soldiers under canvas. There are God knows how many tanks stored in factories and elsewhere ready for loading. George, millions of men and hundreds of thousands of vehicles are ready to depart.' He held up his folder. 'This is the main event.'

George spoke in his usual calm manner. 'You've got the workers and I've got the boss.'

Bernard reacted, annoyed. 'What the hell does that mean?'

'I've got the PM and the War Cabinet travelling in the Royal Train.'

Bernard said nothing.

The REC men tackled their vital work working long shifts. The resident Down Street chef prepared them special meals and their beds begged them to come home, collapse and sleep.

George drew up a timetable and went to his supervisor showing his plans for the Royal Train carrying the Prime Minister.

'It's your usual solid planning, George; thank you. I suppose being a friend of the Royals from your days at Wolferton you're curious about which member is to take the Royal Train?'

'No sir, not at all. I've worked for the King and Queen and other members of the Royal Family but I would never call myself their friend; if anything, I am their servant.'

'Good show but I can tell you their Majesties will not be involved. Mind you the King wanted to join the PM aboard HMS *Belfast* and watch the invasion from sea some 8 miles off the French coast.'

'Surely not,' said George in disbelief.

'Surely not indeed. The Monarch and PM torpedoed together would be a catastrophe like no other.'

Bernard Houghton tapped on the supervisor's door.

'Come in, Bernard.'

'Sir, my plans for Southampton ready for your inspection.'

The supervisor perused the paperwork. George and Bernard made eye contact. Each was privately hoping to outdo the other.

'This too is another outstanding job. Both you gents deserve a commendation. I hope the PM gets to hear about your work.'

George and Bernard thanked their superior and left.

'Trust you to be dealing with the top brass,' said Bernard. 'What's it all mean, George?'

'As the PM once said, "Now this is not the end. It is not even the beginning of the end. But it is, perhaps, the end of the beginning." It looks like the invasion they're calling D-Day is about to happen.'

Chapter 21

It was past midnight and George wanted sleep. He rubbed his eyes, closed the folder of his current project, tidied his pencils—once a station master always a station master—and switched off his desk light. He opened the door of his shared office and was about to turn right to his dorm. Movement caught his eye in the corridor to his left.

It was late, he was tired but he stared. In the dim light at the door leading to the Down Street platform where authorized personnel could hail the driver's cab on the Tube train, he saw a leg disappear. Unusual because of the late hour, the last train had gone and more so as it was a woman's leg wearing a stocking with a seam.

Without thinking he shouted, 'Hey!' and took off. His gammy leg, the narrow corridor and dim lighting meant he was seconds away. He flung open the door to a small room and stared at a petrified Hetty Tring.

'Miss Tring,' said George sounding suspicious. He'd forgotten she was Mrs Tring.

'I'm lost, Mr Miracle,' she blurted. 'I've been working such long hours, especially for you.'

The silence was deafening. No trains ran past but something prompted George to open the door to the platform and step out. In the spooky darkness he heard a sound and looked along the tunnel. He thought he could just make out a person walking—you dare not run along a Tube tunnel—towards Hyde Park Corner.

His mind exploded. *What the hell is going on?*

Turning back inside he stared at the woman who typed his reports. He stepped into the corridor and shouted, 'Help! Security! Help!' A colleague appeared. 'Hold this woman!' shouted George and left.

There wasn't time to wait. The person in the tunnel was the target. From the platform, George gingerly dropped onto the track.

If the last train had gone, the power should be switched off. He didn't feel like testing to find out but started after the mysterious person ahead.

Who is he? What's he doing? Was he given something by my typist? My God, the country's in big trouble and worse, so am I.

Thinking about a potential danger, he forgot to be careful, tripped on the track and sprawled forward. He threw out his arms to stop his head smashing against metal. His right hand hit the live rail. His heart accelerated until he realized the power was off.

His target seemed further away. Lying on the ground, George could hear his quarry. It was impossible to move silently in such a confined space underground when the trains were not running.

The railwayman stood and resumed the chase. Having to constantly step over material gave his shrapnel-decorated hip sharp pain. Ignoring it, George pressed on but stopped as if shot when a burst of wind raced along the tunnel.

That's a train!

In the weak light he could make out both sides of the tunnel. Some were wider with a bench along one wall. This tunnel was basic and narrow. He could hear the train but had nowhere to hide. Breathe in.

He thought lying down beneath the electric rail would be his only chance until the penny dropped.

This is an engineering train running on battery power.

These trains came out after midnight to check on the track, wiring and anything else which might be amiss. It kept coming. George took the punt, climbed up and balanced on two rails, faced the oncoming train and started to wave; frantically.

The driver and his mate were chatting about the mate's missus who was about to give birth when the driver swore. The brake was applied with enthusiasm.

George stood there in the blazing light, his feet frozen but kept waving and closed his eyes. He sensed a collision but felt nothing. He opened his eyes and stared at the terrified faces of the night crew behind the windscreen inches from his face.

The driver opened his door and screamed. 'What the bloody hell do you think you're doing?'

George recovered, hopped down and spoke to the crew. His determination and bravery impressed the men.

'I'm from the REC at Down Street. I'm chasing a person I think might be a spy. Can we get after him?' The shock remained. 'Please,' begged the railwayman. 'Millions of lives could be in danger.'

Off they went with George finding this mode of travel infinitely better than limping in the dark. He stared into the tunnel as the light on the train revealed all.

'There,' shouted George as the back of the man he was chasing appeared in the darkness. The driver drove his vehicle at its top speed which was more tortoise than hare.

'Look out,' screamed George and crouched pulling the driver down with him. The crack of a revolver bounced around the tunnel and a bullet smashed through the cab windscreen. It missed the driver's mate by half an inch with the mate joining his driver and passenger on the floor. It was crowded down there. The train stopped and any doubts about George telling the truth vanished.

'Sorry, mate,' said the crouching driver. 'This is as far as we go.'

'Thanks,' said George and got out. 'I can make it from here.'

'You're mad,' said the driver as George balanced in the tunnel.

'Could you kill the light please,' he asked, 'and can you contact your supervisor?' The driver used a system called *DRICO* standing for *Driver to Control*. It involved pinching two low voltage wires together to get a reaction. George didn't fancy waiting around and so, in the darkness, Miracle of the REC resumed the chase at a walking speed.

Ten minutes ago back at Down Street; George's cry grabbed people's attention. A security guard appeared and ran to George and his typist. Hetty was secured. Wearing pyjamas, Bernard Houghton appeared in the corridor. The woman from the typing pool stood there stunned.

'Hetty!' cried Bernard approaching. 'What are you doing here?'

She lied. 'I heard Mr Miracle call out and came running.'

'George? Why was he yelling? And where is he now?'

The security guard went through the door to the platform. Bernard looked at the woman he loved with a sinking feeling in his stomach.

'Oh Hetty, my darling, what have you done?'

'Get off,' she spat and pushed his hands away. The one word to best describe the look on Bernard's face was terror. He knew he was playing with fire having an affair with a married woman but when he realized she might be involved with matters far more serious, possibly espionage, in a split second his thoughts shifted from embarrassment to a blindfold and firing squad.

The security guard re-appeared. 'No sign of anyone.'

Bernard shoved his now former lover to the guard. 'Arrest her.'

'What?' spluttered the confused guard grabbing the typist. 'What's she done?' Hetty's eyes caught fire.

Dressed in his bland pyjamas and slippers, Bernard pushed past them heading for the platform. 'Do not let her go. That bitch is a spy.'

Hetty let fly with a string of words she never once uttered as part of her pillow talk routine. Bernard was desperate to make amends.

As he stepped down onto the track, he didn't care if the current was still active. His life was probably over. Up ahead, George pressed on and knew the man he chased was armed and willing to shoot.

Making sounds as he travelled, George stopped to listen and thought he could still hear his quarry.

Is he crouched ready to shoot from point blank range?

George kept going and in the distance a glow appeared. He knew this was the next Tube station and the closer he got the brighter the light. Obviously there were no passengers. Squinting, George saw a man hurrying along the platform and yelled.

'Oi! Wait! Stop!'

The man spun around and fired in the one motion. George flattened himself as the echo of the bullet pinged in his ears.

Bernard made good progress reaching the stationary engineering train. He slapped the side of the cab scaring the life out of the crew. They'd been sitting there in the dark wondering if tonight's journey was a dream, a nightmare. First they nearly ploughed into a bloke standing on the tracks and waving his arms. Then their light picked up another bloke who pulled out a gun and shot at them leaving their front window with a hole and a maze of shatter marks. If the driver's mate had been his wife she would have given birth on the spot.

Now the pantomime continued with a geezer dressed ready for bed appearing from nowhere and slapping the side of their loco.

'Have you seen a chap with a gammy leg come along here?' asked Bernard the adulterer.

'Yes and we've been shot at for our trouble,' said the driver who now reckoned joining the army would be less dangerous.'

'Where is he?'

'He set off on a suicide mission, that way.'

'Any chance of a lift?' asked the desperate Bernard.

'There's not a hope in hell, mate. We're employed to check on possible faults, not be killed by a lunatic.'

'What about your comms? How do you report a tunnel incident?'

'Already done,' said the driver. 'Now stand back or you'll get yourself squashed.'

Bernard didn't wait. He wanted to find his mate alive and well.

The gunman fled. He wanted to be out of the Tube, into the darkened streets of London and away. George guessed the man would have followed a plan. Sneak along the quiet tunnel to Down Street, meet his fellow traitor at an agreed time and then be on his toes with the information he collected.

But what information and how can I fix this? Oh my God! Hetty Tring typed top secret plans I gave her.

George hoped like hell the driver in the train had been able to report the incident to the authorities.

From the Hyde Park Corner platform, exhausted and with a throbbing hip, George climbed the stairs. He waited by the locked entrance with help arriving thanks to the *DRICO* report. George wasn't as nimble as the gunman who knew a way out when rehearsing his scheme. A fellow spy working at the station was part of the plan.

Help arrived. In a car with Special Branch detectives as they headed to Down Street, George was quizzed. 'This typist woman, what was she working on?'

George's brain wanted to explode. 'She typed my report on the Royal Train heading to Droxford. There was ...'

'Head office,' snapped a detective and the car changed direction dangerously driving through the dark and empty London streets.

Bernard finally made it back to Down Street in night attire he later turned into dusters.

The Abwehr, the German Intelligence Unit, ran spies for the Third Reich. They sent English-speaking agents to England where most were a dead loss being turned by the Brits. The chap George met in Nottinghamshire trying to buy a single ticket with a £50 note was a perfect example. But with all enemy agents, only one needs to be lucky once.

The Irish Republican Army wanted a united Ireland. The Germans didn't care for the IRA but as they shared a similar goal—smash Britain—it was natural for both sides to at least chat and share ideas. These discussions even happened before World War Two began.

Once life turned nasty for Hitler, the IRA lost interest in the Krauts. Why team up with a bunch of losers?

But one thing the IRA did admire in German strategy involved assassination; kill the leader or leaders. Get rid of the King or Prime Minister, create despair among the masses and thus weaken their enemy from the top down.

Hetty Tring didn't have a brute of a husband but a fanatic who hated the British and would do anything to see Britain defeated.

His fanaticism grew ever stronger as his bosses in Belfast continued to disregard him. Darra MacCool wanted to show the top brass he was a brilliant bomber and a loyal IRA man. He persuaded his pretty English common-law wife, with one set of Irish grandparents, to get a job in the British Government which is how she eventually found her way to the typing pool at Down Street using her single name. Darra played safe by not sharing the same flat.

'Find a weak man, m'darlin',' he told his wife who set her sights on the sex-starved Bernard Houghton.

Hetty signed the Official Secrets Act and was searched morning and night as she entered and left the former Tube station. Nothing was found; of course not as Darra and Hetty were not stupid. Hubby's advice was to look for that nugget of information, that one clue on how the IRA could seriously hurt their enemy, the Brits.

The day the MoD representative came to discuss the invasion, Hetty reckoned the stakes were being raised. Mention of the invasion was rife around the offices. She told her husband and he agreed.

'Get as many details as you can and I'll be outside the Down Street platform tonight after the last train.'

When she discovered the news of the VIPs travelling by train to a station in peaceful Hampshire, she'd found the one tip that might, just might smash the enemy; assassination possibilities, plural. She copied the details of the plan drawn up by George Miracle.

Darra had formed his own cell of fellow Irish terrorists who lived quietly on the south coast where there were more troops than you could point a shillelagh at.

When Hetty handed over the Droxford document, hubby fled through the Underground, took a couple of pot shots, escaped and sent word to his cell about the VIPs due to stay in the train at Droxford. The IRA members oiled their weapons.

Hetty finished up at Special Branch. An hour ago beside the Down Street platform, with George and later Bernard demanding she be arrested, she was cooked. Detective Hamish Robertson, a dour Scot with a wily method of entrapping suspects led the interview.

'Good evening, madam, or should I say, good morning?'

'I don't know why I'm here. I've done nothing wrong,' she said.

'I understand but there are questions I would like to ask if you don't mind.' His best weapon was civility; iron fist, velvet glove.

Hetty sighed. 'If you must but I need to get home. My husband will be wondering where I am.'

No, your husband will be wondering if his mates on the south coast have acted on his information.

'Which REC officers give you typing work?'

'There are different ones but mainly Mr Houghton and Mr Miracle.'

'And this work you do involves typing reports on railway matters?'

'Yes although Mr Miracle once asked me to type something personal, I mean not connected to the railways.'

The detective showed no reaction but his mind raced. He kept his tone flat. 'What was the personal matter?'

'He wanted to know details of a Royal Navy ship, where it was berthed and where it was going.' Not exactly true but Hetty needed to shift the heat. She paused looking at the Scot. Her red herring seemed to work. 'May I go now please?'

'Did Mr Miracle explain why he wanted this material typed?'

She shrugged. 'I think he was asking about a friend or a relative.'

'How many copies did you make?'

'Just the original; he insisted on there being no copies.'

'I see.' He paused and just as Hetty hoped she was home and hosed, the detective metaphorically slapped her hard across the face speaking with that same monotone voice. 'I must tell you, madam, we are going to search your flat first.'

She didn't go home that night.

Like Hetty, George found himself at Special Branch. The interview tended towards adversarial annoying George.

I've caught the possible rat in the ranks and risked my life chasing her accomplice along the tunnel. Why am I now a suspect?

Once Hetty revealed George's Royal Navy memo, the boys in suits from Special Branch moved the SM to another category.

'Tell us what happened, Mr Miracle.'

He explained the incident from seeing a woman's leg to "racing" along the tunnel, being shot in the engineering train, to being met at the next station and collected by Special Branch.

'What made you call for Mrs Tring to be arrested?'

George wondered why such a question should be asked.

'It was late and she would have no business being on the platform.'

'What do you know about the woman?'

'Nothing,' he said and kept lying hoping the detectives couldn't tell. 'I mean one hears gossip but I always try to ignore it.'

George reckoned he was never cut out to be a liar. His main aim was to not mention Bernard and Hetty's affair.

The detective changed direction without indicating. 'Have you ever asked Mrs Tring to type non-railway correspondence?'

George gulped. His sick stomach wanted to revolt.

'Yes I have and realized soon after it was a stupid thing to do.'

'What were the contents of the letter?'

'My godson's in the Navy and I promised to help his parents, Lord and Lady Carruthers, try and discover if their son was in good health.'

'So it was nothing to do with the work of the REC?'

George cringed inside. Having risked his life trying to protect the Crown or government or the REC or all three, George wasn't looking for a medal but he certainly didn't enjoy being treated as a criminal.

What have I done to deserve this?

'No, it was a genuine and stupid mistake pointed out to me by both my wife and an officer in the Royal Navy.'

Unlike Hetty, George was allowed to go home that morning.

Chapter 22

The Royal Train set off for Hampshire on Friday June 2, and thanks to George Miracle's planning enjoyed a good run pulling into a siding beside the station at Droxford. The PM's passengers were his personal staff, members of the War Cabinet, Field Marshall Smuts and a group of crack troops as security. General Eisenhower and his fellow Americans reached Hampshire under their own steam and, would you believe, stayed in caravans in Sawyers Wood near Southwick House.

Near Portsmouth, Southwick House was where the invasion was planned in detail and had a war room with a vast map covering an entire wall showing those important Normandy beaches.

The first night, on his train, the PM dined well and better still really enjoyed his hot bath. Before retiring, the Prime Minister wrote to the King dismissing the idea they should both watch the invasion from aboard HMS *Belfast* bobbing about in the English Channel. A dispatch rider delivered the letter to Windsor Castle.

The IRA cell on the south coast needed a plan. Get Churchill; yes but how? They discovered the venue and discussed ideas. 'I've got a contact in Derry who can radio the Germans. We tell 'em the location and have 'em drop a ton of bombs on the feckin' train,' said one.

'No, it'll take forever and anyway the Krauts reckon we're amateurs,' said another.

Ideas kept coming. None seemed practical until one exploded.

'The fat bastard's on the train. Let's just drive it away and crash it.'

What a brilliant idea. You could touch the enthusiasm in the room. The Republicans were about to pull off the greatest anti-British caper ever. Tomorrow night, Churchill's second at Droxford, would be his last. Up in London, Darra was over the moon. This triumph would give him the status he craved with the IRA bosses in Belfast.

The next morning, Churchill was driven to Southwick House where the main, the only topic was the date for the start of the invasion. The leaders chose June 5, the day after tomorrow.

In the afternoon, the PM was driven to Southampton to inspect the embarkations, addressed troops from the 50th Durham Regiment, then boarded a launch and in the Solent inspected landing craft. He returned to Southwick House where he and Eisenhower polished off whatever whisky remained before the PM headed back to Droxford and a slap up meal including a bottle of 1926 champagne.

A phone call ruined the dining when the latest weather forecast was delivered. It put a dampener on June 5 and a 24 hour delay seemed the best bet. So June 6, 1944 it was. *Operation Overlord* was good to go and even General De Gaulle was brought in on the details.

The Royal Train rested with its locomotive quietly in steam. Another bath and the UK premier was ready for bed.

Naturally the army provided men to guard the Royal Train. These professional crack troops knew exactly who they were guarding but were not alone. Another not-so-crack force was in the area. On Saturday night the local Home Guard with their pimply teenage lads, their elderly retired gents and their shared rifles were given the task of guarding the bridge over the River Meon. The Home Guard lads worked two-hour shifts. They didn't know the VIP passengers were parked in the Droxford siding or even if German paratroops had landed in Worlds End in Hampshire and were creeping about ready to take the bridge at Droxford. The residents of Worlds End slept.

As the Royal Train arrived at Droxford, none of the soldiers guarding the PM knew the IRA was active in their area. The warning from Special Branch had arrived half an hour after Darra MacCool gave his IRA pals the order to get Churchill. Now the crack troops knew but they struck a problem. One of their officers had gone AWOL.

Two of the Home Guard chaps spotted him, a Major heading their way and detained him. He explained the situation but following orders, the Home Guard chaps took the "prisoner" to their senior officer. He was a retired Colonel; stone deaf and needing everything explained three times. Boy was he mightily miffed his men were not told about those on board the Royal Train. Sorting out the mess took time and gave the IRA cell the opportunity to make their move.

The officer-in-charge of the professional soldiers guarding the Royal Train was a Major Guthrie Stride. He perfected threats and snarling.

'If I catch anyone even thinking about dozing, I'll have you swimming to France in full battle dress.' His men believed him.

After midnight on Saturday, two IRA men crept along the line from Droxford to London. 'Are you sure they'll go this way?' asked one.

'They'll wanna get back to London and inside one of them Underground stations,' replied his mate.

'Do these trains run on the Underground?'

'Shut up and keep moving.'

They came to a curve where the track sloped sharply down.

'This is perfect.'

They removed a few spikes, checked to see the section of rail was loose, and moved it leaving a gap before heading back. After about two hundred yards they tied a white shirt to a tree before the derailment spot. They reckoned Winston was due a tumble.

The murderous plot thickened.

Back at Droxford, a soldier pointed into the surrounding forest. 'What's that?' he asked.

'That's a fire,' said his mate. 'Are they signalling the Luftwaffe?'

'There's another,' yelled a second soldier pointing elsewhere.

'And another,' cried the first sentry. Panic set in.

In the Droxford darkness, flames leapt skywards in different places fairly close to the Royal Train.

'Fetch the Major,' said a corporal and Stride strode in. He studied the small but growing forest fires.

'What is it, sir?'

'Are they showing the Luftwaffe where the VIPs are housed?'

The Major didn't hesitate. 'Get the train moving. Plan B now!'

The fires, lit using scrounged petrol, oily rags, paper and kerosene took hold with the forest well alight in different places. It was summer and the vegetation dry.

Major Stride sent an NCO to order the footplate crew to move the train as discussed in a previous meeting; their Plan B.

The footplate crew with their armed guard saw the fires and were wide awake having been told they might need to move at a moment's notice. That moment arrived.

The NCO bounded up and shouted. 'Plan B, gentlemen. Get this beauty into the cutting.'

Well in steam, the locomotive hissed, 'And about time,' said the fireman as the driver started the beast. They moved slowly heading back to the mainline and the cutting.

They hadn't gone a hundred yards when three IRA men launched themselves at the footplate. One came from each side and the other appeared on the top of the tender. Apparently many IRA men enjoyed American gangster films and loved the Tommy guns used by mobsters. Their Irish connections in Boston and New York saw to it their brethren in Derry and Belfast were well equipped with a collection of Edward G. Robinson's toys.

The crew was busy with the engine. The guard's bayonet pointed skywards. A bullet smashed into his upper thigh. He slumped against the coal with his weapon clattering to the bouncing metal floor. The driver and fireman threw up their hands not keen to argue.

'Back to London and step on it,' said the leading IRA man, Liam.

Three guns pointing with one weapon already discharged leaving the guard moaning gave the footplate trio little option. With their backs facing the terrorists, the driver and his mate worked while snatching quick glances at one another. *What can we do?*

The regulator shifted and the beast responded.

'Faster!' screamed Liam wanting the death of the PM more than ever. A Tommy gun barrel in his spine encouraged the driver.

The chap in the signal box panicked. 'What's with the speed?' he yelled and frantically checked to see he had switched the points sending the train back onto the mainline.

'Faster!' screamed Liam again jabbing the driver with his gun.

Major Stride went apoplectic. 'What the hell are they doing? Stop that train!' he roared. Shouting didn't work. Onboard the train the security unit at either end of the armoured carriage panicked. They'd been told the destination was the cutting. Now they were accelerating out of the siding and onto the main line.

The senior officer entered the VIP's car to find the PM half awake and a quarter dressed.

'What's happening?' barked Churchill. 'Why are we moving? I'm addressing the troops first thing in the morning.'

'It's just a precautionary move, Prime Minister. Sit tight, sir, if you wouldn't mind.'

The officer made a swift exit to discover what was happening. 'This isn't Plan B,' he shouted to the other guards.

They shrugged. What would they know?

On the footplate, the fireman kept shovelling as one IRA gunman covered the crew while the other two looked into the darkened forest and farmland to find that white shirt indicating their departure point before the derailment site.

Back on the mainline, the Royal Train set off. The regulator copped more nudges and the speed increased. The IRA trio mixed their threats with looking for the warning sign. Jumping was dangerous but far preferable to standing on a rolling, derailing locomotive. The wounded sentry clutched his thigh still trying to stem the bleeding.

He moved causing the nervous lookout behind the fireman to turn and threaten him. The shooter sitting on the coal in the tender screamed at his fellow IRA man. 'Keep watch!' The guard jerked his head back to the passing countryside and panicked because he was sure he saw the white shirt tied to a tree.

'That's it,' he screamed. 'That was the shirt!' He prepared to jump.

The IRA man behind the driver screamed, 'Faster, go faster!' as he scurried across the bouncing footplate and followed his mate into the night. The shooter on the tender slid down and yelled at the footplate crew. 'Congratulations, you British bastards, you've just killed your feckin' PM.'

Throwing his weapon into the night, he grabbed the side of the cab and just as he paused to jump, the wounded guard snatched up his rifle and thrust the bayonet into an IRA backside. Committed to jumping, the Irishman screamed as he vanished.

The fireman raced to help the shot guard while the driver threw on every braking device he could to stop the train.

With this sudden and all-out braking, the PM's last whisky of the night decorated the carpeted floor.

The IRA white shirt stood another 60 yards ahead. The nervous IRA man caught a glimpse of a white sign warning about cattle crossing the line. The three IRA attackers were not the brightest. Each was found with broken bones and the shooter, the last to jump was unable to sit for two months. All three suffered a shattered mindset once they discovered their total failure.

In the daylight, the derailment point was discovered and repaired.

Back in London in his IRA safe house, Darra MacCool exploded with fury once he learnt his scheme utterly failed. He knew this meant the boys back in Belfast would continue to believe he would never be good for anything other than making tea.

In his office, George received a message about the Royal Train leaving Droxford and then returning soon thereafter. This incident happened in the wee small hours so would not have been for the PM to inspect and chat with the troops in the area. He would have been in bed.

George made a discreet enquiry and discovered details about a failed attack on the train by men believed to be from an IRA cell on the south coast. He absorbed the information in stunned silence.

He wanted to ask how the attackers knew about the highly-secret train with its VIP passengers. He didn't have to ask. He was told.

'It must have been a leak at your end. Check your security, mate.'

His heartbeat started jogging and his sweat glands got busy.

Chapter 23

The D in D-Day stands for Day, a sort of Day-Day. It's not exclusive to the invasion on June 6, 1944. It could stand for Departure because it's the day when the event begins and George Miracle and his colleagues at Down Street played a vital role in the success of the largest amphibious invasion in history.

Before the troops went ashore in France, the Allies bombed the Normandy beaches with warships blasting away from out at sea. There were about 150,000 troops in the first set of landing craft. Allied paratroops dropped in Northern France to attack the many Germans expecting the invasion in their area.

All those inflatable tanks in Kent helped confuse the Germans and once the Normandy location was revealed, the enemy failed to respond immediately. Hitler was asleep and no underling was brave enough to wake him resulting in more delay in sending troops south.

To get the troops to the English ports with their massive amount of equipment including tanks, trucks and supplies was a logistical nightmare. The railways were stretched to the limit.

Finding locomotives and rolling stock and getting clearance for the hundreds of trains fell to the Railway Executive Committee. No wonder they worked 12 hour shifts. No wonder they made countless decisions on the run.

News of the first landings filtered through to Down Street. The good news of early successes was tempered by the bloodbath at Omaha Beach where the Americans were said to have thousands of casualties. The shingles at Slapton Sands were like those at Omaha Beach. Both produced calamitous results.

The REC was never so busy. *Operation Pied Piper* and moving the troops rescued from Dunkirk were major operations but D-Day was in a league of its own.

When work slowed a tad, George tapped Bernard on the shoulder and suggested a cup of tea. The poor bloke was terrified constantly worrying about his former lover being arrested.

In the corridor, Bernard looked for an explanation. 'Am I dead?' he whispered holding his breath as George explained his visit to Special Branch and his knowledge of the IRA attack at Droxford. As the tale unfolded, Bernard wanted the floor to open up and swallow him.

'The IRA?' gasped a shell-shocked Bernard. 'Hetty's in the IRA?'

'Not sure about her but I'll bet the hubby certainly is. I chased him through the tunnel after I'm pretty sure she gave him info you or I asked her to type.'

'My godfather,' wheezed Bernard running fingers through his scalp increasing the rate at which he was losing his hair.

George broke the news as quietly as possible. 'It looks as if she wasn't abused by her husband, my friend; she pretended all that so as to win sympathy in the hope of befriending a kindly soul.'

'Oh Christ, what have I done?'

'Avoided pillow talk I hope.'

Bernard panicked. 'What did you tell Special Branch about me?'

'Nothing but I don't know what *she* said or what they knew already.'

A long pause began. Bernard's breathing sounded weird. He blew air with his cheeks expanding as his mind raced. 'If she tells them we were lovers, I could be charged with treason. That's a trip to the Tower, George. What the hell am I going to do?'

'What do the posters all over London say?'

Bernard twigged and joined in as George answered his own question.

'Stay calm and carry on.'

Back in their office, Bernard imitated a nervous wreck.

Hitler continued to help his enemies and handicap his own side. Tactical withdrawals can save a force from slaughter but the dictator was having none of that withdrawal or surrender malarkey. By overruling his Generals in the field, he became his own worst enemy. He gave the same order on the Eastern front when winter arrived and the Russians fought back leaving his troops to freeze to death.

What's the quotation? "Those who cannot remember the past are doomed to repeat it."

By the end of August, three months after the D-Day landings, in many parts of Europe, the Germans were on the run.

As the fierce fighting raged, life went on in Cambridgeshire where the waiting-list at Hamilton-Weir House continued to grow. More families heard about the wonderful respite service for carers or their disabled child or both and people wondered if they could afford such a brilliant solution.

When told the cost they replied in disbelief. 'Are you serious? Is it really free?' No wonder Rowena and Louisa and the staff were working flat out. Their shifts were as long as those of George Miracle and his colleagues, and footplate crews driving British trains.

In the nearby Cambridgeshire village of Grandchester, market day was still on a Wednesday as it had been for centuries. Farmers brought their animals to be sold although in war time, they were sold under strict rules. The Ministry of Food fixed the price of various grades and types of livestock but animals being sold for fattening could go for the highest bid.

The railways brought new people to country towns. They were refugees from war-ravaged countries or Londoners who wanted to escape the war.

On some railway stations, women were loading and unloading parcels, selling and collecting tickets, sweeping platforms and even waving a flag and blowing a whistle. They replaced those men away fighting for their country or busy with their work in the Home Guard.

Rationing was still active and even people producing food on farms needed to queue like the folks in towns and cities. Sacks of grain would be stacked on a lorry which drove to a railhead where the foodstuff was loaded onto a wagon before being transported to all parts of the country by train.

The REC ruled the railways meaning George found trains for troops and war materials as well as vital food supplies for those at home and abroad. Tins of fruit and vegetables were filled in factories where most of the packers were female as were the fillers of bombs.

Saturday nights at Grandchester saw the local dance with foxtrots and waltzes the popular items. Ladies were discouraged from wearing long dresses in case of an emergency exit. Both the local cinemas were open giving folks a choice. Victoria Miracle, growing into a beautiful young woman, the image of her mother, asked for permission to attend one of those summery Saturday night dances.

'I'm afraid the answer is no, my darling,' said Louisa. 'You're too young, Grannie and I are far too busy to be your chaperone, there's no transport and anyway, your father would divorce me if I said yes.'

Victoria was clever. Her academic progress attested to that but in terms of getting her way or making a point, she outsmarted anyone.

'I wouldn't be alone, Ma, as Sally Clarkson and Amanda Reid will both be coming with me and Sally's mother will accompany us there and back on the bus which will drop me near the end of the drive.'

Louisa knew she'd met her match. Having laid out all the reasons why her daughter couldn't go, her daughter precisely removed each objection leaving Mother dear without a leg to stand on.

Rowena heard most of the conversation and smiled. 'I'll think about it,' said Louisa and when she entered the kitchen and saw her mother grinning, Louisa knew her goose was cooked.

'Was I ever like that with you?'

'Of course,' said Rowena, 'and look how you turned out.'

George kept an eye on Bernard as they worked in the same cramped office. His friend dreaded a visit from Special Branch. Starting a romantic relationship with a married woman was fraught with danger but when the cuckolded husband was an enemy of the state and a fanatical IRA supporter, a bit on the side paled into insignificance.

The visit came when Bernard was super busy. His supervisor popped his head into their small office.

'Mr Houghton, you have two visitors.' Bernard's heart missed a beat, his throat went dry and his bladder began yelling. He made it to a small room—they were all small—where two Special Branch gents gave him the evil eye. Bernard panicked as the questions began.

'Did you give typing work to Mrs Hetty Tring?'

'I did.'

'How would you describe her?'

Bernard shrugged. 'Her work was first-class.'

'And what about personally?'

'Personally?' gulped Bernard.

'Yes, did you get to know her away from work?'

'No but she came in one day with bruises on her face and I asked if she was all right and she told me her husband was a brute and knocked her about from time to time.'

'And?' asked the persistent Special Branch officer.

Bernard shrugged again. 'I offered to have a word with him but she insisted I was not to get involved.'

'And did you get involved?'

'No, sir, no, not at all,' lied the desperate-to-stay-calm railwayman.

'Did you know Mr Miracle asked Mrs Tring to type non-railway material?'

Bernard was thrown. 'I didn't, sir, no.'

There was a pause. 'Aren't you curious to know what it was?'

Bernard shook his head. 'No sir, it's none of my business.'

'Not even a little bit curious?'

'George Miracle is a fine railwayman, a returned serviceman from the last war where he was wounded, and he's been recruited to work here at the REC because of his professionalism, his extensive railway knowledge and his dedication to King and country.'

The detectives were given a glowing testimonial about the Tube runner. Why? The detective who led the talking smiled and stood.

'That's all, Mr Houghton; we won't detain you any longer.'

Feeling massive relief, Bernard departed. Alone, the detectives spoke quietly.

'I've never seen a more nervous man, ever.'

'He can't understand why we didn't mention their affair.'

'Something to keep for a rainy day methinks.'

George looked up when Bernard returned. Nothing was said but the look on his colleague's face told George a date for Bernard's execution had yet to be gazetted.

When people first encountered James Miracle they were struck by his awkward gait and speech. When he walked he slightly bent forward from the waist dragging his right leg a tad. He used his arms bent at the elbow and pushed them across his chest to help maintain his balance and as a source of momentum. Under his trousers he still wore calipers and his right shoe or boot retained a built-up sole.

When he spoke his lip movements were exaggerated and his diction suffered as he sounded drunk or rather tipsy. People who got to know him soon understood every word he said.

His sense of fun and cheeky but friendly nature endeared him to most people. His brilliant mind meant fellow students at Cambridge and his tutors and lecturers struggled to put a lid on their admiration. His results were outstanding and in the weeks before the D-Day invasion, James sat for his final exams.

People expected him to graduate but two questions remained. What grades would he get and what would the young Mr Miracle do once his status as an undergraduate changed to that of graduate?

George missed his family—constantly. His mother and sister and her husband and their two sons, his nephews were often in his thinking. But it was his mother-in-law, his wife and his two children who occupied his thinking whenever he slipped into bed at Down Street.

On his bedside table sat a photo of his nearest and dearest. He would kiss the photo in the darkness before his head hit the pillow. With the D-Day landings established, he requested leave and when granted, rang his wife.

'I thought you'd forgotten us, Mr Stationmaster,' said Louisa.

He ignored her teasing remembering it was he who taught her to use that behaviour.

'Are you all well' he asked, 'and will you be at home when I call this coming weekend?'

Louisa couldn't contain her joy. 'I will be here, my lord, although I can't speak for your children.'

George knew this wasn't a joke. 'What's happened?' he asked with genuine concern.

'Your son is awaiting his final results, hopefully about to graduate and has taken up cricket with a local team in Grandchester.'

'Cricket!' exclaimed George unable to imagine his disabled son running anywhere let alone around a cricket field.

'He's the team scorer and with his vast knowledge of mathematics, produces all kinds of facts involving runs scored per so many deliveries and wickets taken for the same thing and everyone loves him.'

'So do I,' said his father speaking sotto voce before speaking louder. 'And how is our beautiful daughter?'

'Now please don't speak, George until I've finished explaining,' said Louisa not wishing to startle her husband.

'Why am I already worried?'

'With two girlfriends and the mother of one of the girls as chaperone, Victoria goes to the Saturday night dance in Grandchester where she has a lovely time.'

'And?' asked George with a slight tremor in his voice. 'What are you *not* telling me?'

'Stop worrying, George. Now when did you say you were coming?' she asked subtly changing the subject.

'I'll be on the noon train on Friday. I hope you'll all be at home when I arrive.'

'Isn't the lunchtime train at two minutes past noon?'

She was correct and the silence covered his annoyance. She continued. 'I'll see if I can persuade your mother-in-law to tear herself away.'

George let her teasing wash over him. 'I miss you my darling girl.'

She didn't respond at first. She reckoned she missed him even more. 'Friday you say? We'll expect you when we see you.' She made a soft kissing sound and hung up.

Her mother appeared. 'Was that the station master?'

Louisa nodded. 'He arrives on Friday,' and both women enjoyed a warm inner glow.

Chapter 24

As soon as Louisa told her children their father was coming next Friday, both determined to be home when the patriarch arrived.

He caught the bus from Cambridge and walked up the drive of Hamilton-Weir House. His family watched knowing Mr Punctual would arrive on time.

Victoria saw him from a front window and ran towards her father. He remembered the times she would run to him when she was a child at Wolferton, the Royal Station. Now the child running to him was a young woman. Their embrace was strong. By the time their greeting ended, James arrived. He too hugged his father and George found his eyes becoming moist. With an arm around each of his children, they walked to the magnificent home. On the verandah stood his wife and her mother where more hugging and kissing ensured.

They settled in the front sitting-room where the kitchenhand, Dolly, despite the luncheon gong limbering up, appeared with a tray of tea and homemade biscuits. George never went into details about the excellent meals he enjoyed at Down Street. Having a former LNER or GER chef in residence meant he and his colleagues enjoyed a much nicer menu than that dished up for most other citizens.

'So tell me your news, please,' said George. 'Let's have age before beauty so over to you, James.'

'I've just received my results, Dad, and I hope you'll be pleased to know I have passed and am now a graduate of Cambridge University.'

'Bravo, my boy, that is simply wonderful,' said his proud-beyond-belief father moving to his seated son and shaking his hand.

'Ma said not to ring but to tell you in person. I hope you can come to my graduation, Dad. It's at the end of the month.'

'Now just a moment, James,' interrupted his mother. 'You haven't told your father the full story.

There was a pause as George looked at his son. 'I received a distinction, Dad and my Professor wants me to start post-graduate studies next term.'

George shook his head as his heart grew larger. He extended his arms and made his son move to him. Their embrace was long and the station master welled up.

'You have made us so proud, my boy, all of us. Both your grannies will tell the world about their brilliant grandson.' The men resumed their seats. 'But what does this post-graduate study involve?'

James explained the possible new subjects with George struggling to understand and express his pride and delight.

'I don't need to ask if you have thanked Mr Attwood for the years of tuition he has provided and all without any payment.'

'He was delighted with my results as was Miss Rawlinson. She's the PhD student who tutored me in physics and has helped Vicky too.'

'Yes, yes, I remember.' Still struggling to comprehend the triumphant results of his son, George turned to his daughter. 'And now it's your turn Miss Miracle. I'm sure your news will be equally as exciting.'

'I wish to apply for university too, Daddy. I think Mummy told you about Girton College at Cambridge which is exclusively for female students.'

'She did and I must admit I am proud beyond belief but it does disturb your dear old father, who left school at the ripe old age of 12, that my two children are in another league when it comes to study and academic results.'

Louisa challenged the SM. 'So speaks the man who became the youngest station master in England, from 100 plus applicants was appointed to the highly-sought after Wolferton station, and who was recruited to the most important Railway Executive Committee due to his extensive expert railway knowledge and experience.'

George was humbled. 'Yes, yes, thank you, my dear.'

'Not forgetting the man who saved a branch line off his own bat,' added Rowena. 'That magnificent station garden and the druid site were all driven by a certain station master by the name of Miracle.'

Victoria moved and knelt beside her father. 'There you are, Daddy, you're the one we all have to thank. Now please tell us, when will this rotten war be over?'

'And when will you be free to tell us what you did to make the D-Day invasion happen when it did?' asked James. 'I'd love to know.'

George eyed his adoring family. At that moment amidst the horror and death of the world war, he luxuriated in pride and gratitude.

He gave a broad description of the railways moving troops, supplies and people before politely changing the subject asking for a tour of the grounds. Both his children were keen to show him the new works and off went the trio as his wife and her mother discussed the returned patriarch. Lunch could wait.

That night in bed, George put his arm around his wife. 'When are you going to tell me the missing bits about Victoria and her sweetheart?'

Louisa gently jabbed him in the ribs. 'You might not have been to university George Miracle but you're still one of the smartest people I know. You remember what you've been told and, more importantly what you haven't.'

'Enough of the flattery, woman and kindly answer the question.'

'Victoria met a young man at the Grandchester dance.'

'She's not even 17. That's far too young.'

'How old was I when we met?'

George ignored the question. 'What does he do? How old is he? Is it serious?'

'That's a lot of questions, Mr Miracle.'

'I worry not being here to help you and the children. The invasion is making slow progress. Once this damn war ends I'll be back here like a shot.' He paused. 'Should I have a word with Victoria?'

'You mean about the birds and the bees?'

George winced in the darkness. The news about his children thrilled him but he despaired not being at home to help as they grew into adults and began careers and relationships.

'I'm not sure what troubles me more; not being here to help or you doing such a brilliant job in raising our children on your own.'

She squeezed him moving even closer. 'I think you *have* been to university, George Miracle.' He didn't understand. 'You have a degree in flattery; an honours degree.'

On Saturday afternoon he took his daughter to watch a local cricket match where the home team's scorer was her brother James. Father and daughter sat on a grassy hill and wallowed in the warmth of a perfect summer's day. The cricketers were either too young or too old for war.

'I know Mummy told you about my young man,' said Victoria not afraid to raise any topic with the father she loved and trusted.

'She may have done,' said George still not being able to speak freely on matters intimate especially with females.

'His name is David; he's 21 and a pilot with the RAF.'

George was immediately impressed. 'I see.'

'He's away on training exercises so we write to one another.'

'I'm very happy for you, Miss Miracle. But will this ... friendship interrupt your university plans?'

'I have to be accepted first.'

'But will it be a waste of time, this going to university?' She looked at her father forcing him to say more. 'I mean one day you'll marry and have a family and all that time at university will be for nothing.'

'That's strange,' replied Victoria. He didn't follow. 'Mummy said you are a man who looks to the future, a person who can see how life's experiences shape who we become.'

George knew he was being reprimanded in the politest of ways; that his old-fashioned attitudes needed serious renovation and that future generations, including his own children, would soon be running the country having replaced him and his peers.

'You haven't told me about David the pilot.'

She hadn't and was afraid to do so. He looked at her saying nothing. She took a deep breath.

'He's from Australia.' George sensed her concern. 'Does that worry you, Daddy?'

'I'm worried about the risks every RAF pilot faces although the fact you could finish up as a farmer's wife on a sheep station on the other side of the world does give me cause to think.'

The sound of ball on willow was heard followed by cries of "Shot sir," and then a voice they both knew well yelling, 'That's his fifty,' interrupted their chat about matters intimate.

For both it was good to clear the air.

George loved being with his family for the weekend and they loved having him at home. He returned to London thinking less of war and railways and more of his children and their futures.

'Family all well?' asked Bernard when George arrived at REC HQ.

'Thank you, they are and my boy is about to graduate from Cambridge having done so with honours.'

'That's brilliant, many congratulations, George, you must be proud beyond words.'

He was, grimaced and nodded. He chose not to speak so as to keep his emotions under control. To have seen his son not only learn to walk and talk but to be accepted as a university student gave his heart and mind an enormous serving of love and pride, and so much so at times he found it impossible to stop tears. To have him graduate with honours was enough to cause his heart to burst. Tricky because part of his philosophy stated it wasn't the done thing for a man to cry.

'So what's news?' he asked changing the subject.

'More gains in France although the fact the Germans have been there for years isn't making life easy.'

'And what about here; trains running well and on time?' asked George.

'Once an old SM, hey George,' laughed Bernard.

'Not so much of the old, thank you,' sniffed George and they resumed their latest tasks.

Two weeks later, George was granted additional leave, 24 hours only to attend his son's graduation. Another heart-bursting occasion made all the more emotional when able to thank Kenneth Attwood and Bernadette Rawlinson in person. George wondered if he could ever be more proud of his son and pondered the value of friendship, love and generosity all the way back to London.

Christmas 1944 turned cold. For Britons, this was Christmas number 6 to be celebrated while at war. Each year they wondered if it would be the last with bombs, rationing, and the "We regret to inform you" telegrams from the War Office being a regular part of everyday life. Now that the Allies had invaded continental Europe, many dared to hope this would be the last Christmas of World War Two.

George was one of the lucky REC officers being granted leave. He went first to call on Lord and Lady Carruthers in Hampstead. Of course they were thrilled to see him. He thought they'd both aged but said nothing on that matter. He followed his mother's dictum about polite conversation. He wondered if they thought the same about him.

The family Carruthers had turned the ground floor of their massive home into a respite hospital, not as a refuge for disabled children and their parents as at Hamilton-Weir House, but rather for wounded soldiers who were in the latter stage of their recovery. Both George and Valerie's adult children were living at home. Daughter Annie helped her mother nursing the visitors and godson George was in charge of the large vegetable plot in the grounds of Tudor House. The once immaculate croquet and tennis court area disappeared to help in the production of food. Young James remained disfigured from his days as a gunner on HMS *Audacity*. Life took sharp turns for many people and particularly so for the family Carruthers. The father lost a leg and the son was badly injured.

Young George greeted his godfather with delight. The railwayman was given a guided tour of the tomatoes and beans in the temporary greenhouse and the potatoes and pumpkin where the tennis court net once stood.

Lord Carruthers walked to the front gate with the visiting George on his way to Cambridge via London. They were the walking wounded; one with a prosthetic leg and the other carrying shrapnel from their days fighting for King and country. They first met 30 years ago and their friendship not only endured but grew stronger.

'I reckon Mr Churchill's speech about the beginning of the end applies today, my friend,' said the Lord. 'Reports suggest we have them if not on the run then certainly heading back to Germany.'

'Let's hope,' said the railwayman.

'And what will the station master do once that bastard Hitler waves the white flag?'

'Get out of London as fast as I can.'

'Do you remember I once suggested you retire to your mansion in Eaton Square and become George Miracle Esquire, gentleman of this parish?'

They both laughed; a rare activity these last few years. Their handshake and embrace lingered.

On the train journey to Cambridge, George turned being pensive into an art form and pondered his life and family. He managed to buy presents although the scarce range of goods made the task tricky. When he arrived, as always, he studied any posters.

Outside the station he caught the bus and on Christmas Eve 1944 walked from the bus stop to Hamilton-Weir House. There was a pedestrian gate beside the large white, two-gate opening at the entrance to the property. It was cold and becoming dark in mid-afternoon. The front garden of the country estate gave visitors a feeling of welcome with the silver birch and oak trees standing peacefully in the expansive lawns. A few garden benches, situated in shady spots for residents in summer, sat empty in the chill air with dormant daffodils underground struggling to keep warm.

The sweeping driveway with poplar trees either side gave it an avenue like presence. As George drew closer to the house and with the light fading, its lamps shone bright. Despite the cold and darkness he expected one or more of his family to open the front door, call to him and head in his direction. Nothing. No-one.

Ten yards from the door his thinking was confused.

They know I'm coming. They know the time the train reached Cambridge. Hello. Your father is home. Merry Christmas everyone.

He became miffed being required to use the large and heavy knocker on the door. As he went to grab it the door opened thanks to his mother-in-law who struggled to smile.

George sensed fear, a foreboding as if he'd arrived at a house where the residents had recently suffered a death in the family.

He was almost right.

Chapter 25

In December 1944, Hitler was down but not out. He planned one final counter-offensive in and around Belgium to reclaim Antwerp. It became known as the Battle of the Bulge because on a map the wedge the Germans made in the Allied lines looked like a bulge.

Years earlier in 1940, German tanks raced through the Ardennes forest, surprised the French and British Expeditionary Force and won a stunning victory. That was in spring. Four years later, in winter, the heavier German tanks tried a similar route and became bogged.

The Battle of the Bulge lasted for weeks. At times the Germans did well attacking the under-prepared Americans. But as in Russia, the weather proved an obstacle.

German tanks ran out of fuel and broke down. Where were the spare parts and supplies? Ground troops included soldiers as young as 15. Starvation swamped the Wehrmacht. Frostbite became a killer and when the skies cleared, Allied bombers could see German targets and their troops were hammered from above. Now it was all roads lead to Berlin with the British, Americans and Russians racing to arrive first.

In Britain, the Home Guard was stood down. These men, too young, too old or medically unfit to fight, existed to protect the local population. With the chances of Germany crossing the Channel or even surviving now obvious, the lads in the Home Guard handed in their rifles and broom sticks and went back to their regular jobs.

But not all went swimmingly. The Belgian transport ship the SS *Leopoldville* left Southampton with British and American troops destined to fight in the Battle of the Bulge. It was a short trip across to France. Tragically it suffered many of the preparation faults of the landing rehearsal at Slapton Sands off the coast of Devon, and when attacked, hundreds of US troops drowned not knowing how to wear a life jacket.

On the SS *Leopoldville* there were not enough lifejackets, many troops didn't pay attention to the drill, and when a U-boat hit the ship with two torpedoes, lives were lost. They were so close to Cherbourg, many on board were expecting a tow. Nearly 800 Americans drowned, and an unknown number of British. Like the Devon disaster, a media blackout and cover-up swiftly followed. Survivors were ordered to say nothing and Americans were even threatened with the loss of their GI pension if they spoke of the catastrophe.

As George arrived to join his family on Christmas Eve, more dreaded V1 rockets fired from the Low Countries landed on Manchester.

The war was not yet over in Europe and would last even longer in the Pacific.

The station master knew nothing of this as he faced Rowena at the front door of Hamilton-Weir House on the final Christmas Eve of World War Two.

'Greetings son-in-law and Merry Christmas,' said Rowena. 'Please come in.'

He kissed her cheek, waited till she closed the door before whispering. 'What's happened? Has someone died?'

His mind raced. *Surely they would have told me if a family member had died; certainly a close family member.*

'I'll let the others tell you. Come and get warm.' She opened the door to the living-room. 'I told you Father Christmas was coming.'

James was on his feet and heading straight for his father. 'Merry Christmas, Dad,' he said as he embraced the station master.

'Merry Christmas, son,' said George and looked at the two women sitting on the same sofa. Louisa looked sad and Victoria's eyes were red and weepy.

His wife stood and moved to him. Their embrace was tinged with sadness. Victoria hesitated but after her mother stepped back, she embraced her father burying her face in his chest and sobbed.

George looked at his family. No-one spoke. He gently lifted his daughter's face to look into her eyes inviting her to speak.

'Oh Daddy, David's been killed.'

The family was seated and the happiness one would expect on a family reunion, and particularly on Christmas Eve, became a sombre, quiet time. Gone were the usual Miracle jokes and teasing. Victoria explained.

'I've received a letter all the way from Australia. David's mother wrote to me because the RAF or War Office sent her a telegram with the news that David's plane was hit by enemy fire over Germany. It crashed and all on board were killed.'

George hugged his girl and kissed the top of her head. 'I'm so sorry my darling.'

'Mummy said he must have told his family about me which is why they sent the letter.'

'You won his heart, Miss Miracle and I'm sorry I didn't get the chance to meet him.' She seemed cheered by his comment. 'Of course any chap who chose my girl would be all right by me.'

That moved the family and especially the grieving daughter who lost it and cried the more.

It was an unusual Christmas. Victoria's sadness meant the mood was subdued and the family dined alone. George went out on a limb claiming that next Christmas the war would be over and they would celebrate with gusto.

'So if the war *is* over, Dad,' said James, 'what will you do?'

The dining-room fell silent with all eyes on the patriarch. He gave one of his restricted smiles.

'The honest answer is I have no idea. There is talk that the Railway Executive Committee will be disbanded and replaced by another government body.'

'Does that mean your beloved LNER will not return?' asked Louisa. 'Or should I have said your beloved Great Eastern Railway?'

The others were not aware of the patriarch's early railway history but hung on his every word.

'I think you should be a station master in London, Dad,' said his son definitely biased in his opinion. 'I suggest you return to Liverpool Street where you began your now magnificent career.'

George grinned with no teeth on show. 'Thank you, James.'

'Could we go back to Wolferton?' asked Victoria and a sudden silence settled with the others remembering the terrifying kidnapping experience she endured while living there as a child.

'As I said, I have no idea. So let's just hope the war ends soon and before that happens, please may I have a second helping of Grannie's outstanding plum pudding?'

'With custard?' asked Rowena.

'That's a silly question, Grannie,' said a mischievious James and everyone laughed as a group for the first time that Christmas.

Back at Down Street, George continued working as the REC continued running the railways of Britain. He delighted in telling his colleagues about his son's brilliant academic success. Alone with Bernard, George heard in hushed tones about the lack of action from Special Branch.

'I reckon we're both in the clear, George,' he said with nervous pleasure and relief.

'And what about your lady friend, what's happened to her?'

'Gone thank God. Can you believe she was an IRA sympathizer?'

'I can, I arrested her. But what treachery did she perform?'

Bernard lost his relieved happiness and whispered even softer. 'There's a rumour that Churchill and War Cabinet officers were on a special train attacked by the IRA. So what you heard must be true.'

'I gave Hetty the plans for the Royal Train to Droxford.'

Bernard stuttered desperate for a way out of the mess. 'Possibly but the attack failed. I mean otherwise we would have heard about it by now; surely.'

George pursed his lips, nodded and whispered in return. 'If it had succeeded we'd both be in a cell,' and went back to work. Bernard didn't sleep well for a week, longer.

By mid-January the Battle of the Bulge was over and German troops, the ones still alive and not captured, were scrambling home hungry, scared and scarred. Britain and her allies took control of the skies and in February the appalling saturation bombing as seen in the Blitz was returned with interest. Dresden, an ancient city of culture with glorious architecture, was obliterated along with 30,000 of its civilians. Hamburg, Germany's second-biggest city became a smoking ruin with civilians cowering in their cellars to escape the bombs, being found cooked alive such was the heat from the incendiaries.

To the east, the Russian bear awoke from its hibernation and headed west. Hitler was in his counting house counting out his money when along came two mighty armies and smashed his evil nose. Prominent Nazis killed their families including their children before committing suicide.

George and others were right. December 1944 was the last Christmas of the dreadful conflict. In May 1945 he was in London when the news came through. The war in Europe was over.

With his colleagues, typists and chefs he celebrated before heading "upstairs". The streets of London and particularly around Piccadilly Circus which was fairly close to Down Street were full of joyful, tipsy, delirious people dancing in the street. Couples in love hugged and kissed as did couples who first met 30 seconds ago.

George rang his wife and once he checked on her and their family, they found little to say. She knew the news. The whole world knew. The war began nearly six years ago. George and Louisa knew people who were killed, disfigured, made homeless, lost everything and bereaved. The Miracle parents considered themselves lucky.

'I'll come home as soon as I can,' he said.

'We'd all love to see you, Mr Stationmaster. And when you do arrive, will you tell us exactly where home is or will or might be now you've finished working in the tunnels of London?'

He paused. 'It's the same answer, my darling, I just don't know.'

An REC staff meeting was called and George and his colleagues were all ears. These men left their previous position in the railways to work for the war effort. It stood to reason that if the war was over, so too would be the Railway Executive Committee. Or was it?'

'Gentleman,' began the supervisor, 'the government wants us, the Railway Executive Committee to continue running the country's railways.'

A weary collective sigh escaped. Not many employees wanted to remain underground. But if the REC was to continue, surely they could do so in a building with windows offering views of the world outside including fellow human beings and trees and birds and trains you could see and most important, allow you to breathe fresh air.

'May one ask for how long, sir?' said a railwayman speaking for the entire workforce.

'If I knew that, gentlemen, my pay grade would be far higher.'

The so-called witty quip fell flat. Many of these men wanted out.

About two months after Germany surrended, the British people went to the polls. Greatly admired for his war-time leadership, Winston Churchill and his fellow conservatives looked forward to being rewarded with another term at the helm. Mr Popular Churchill enjoyed an approval rating of 83%. But as for the Conservatives, the voters thought otherwise. Was it all that unemployment before the war? Whatever, Clement Atlee, the former deputy prime minister in the war-time coalition government and his Labour colleagues swept to power in a landslide victory.

Life began to change. The new government created an overall body to run public transport in Britain. Known as the BTC or British Transport Commission, it included roads, rails, canals but not planes. One part of the BTC was known as British Railways and this body didn't become the motley mix of independent railway companies, certainly not the 100+ companies at the beginning of the century and not even the Big Four which existed before World War Two.

The term *British Railways*, later to become *British Rail*, slipped into the lexicon covering the nation's above-ground railways. Roads and underground railways were also a part of this new BTC. Clement Atlee and his colleagues wanted action, a major shake-up.

State-owned enterprises became flavour of the month and plans were set to nationalize the railways.

George definitely wanted out of the REC. Twenty years ago when only a young man, he became a station master and now wanted to return to doing what he loved. He didn't have grandiose ambitions and nothing fancy appealed. Promotion was not for him.

Just put me back on a platform with trains and passengers and boxes of fish and fruit.

Money would never be an issue for George thanks to his wife's father's generous bequest. Doing the job he loved was all he wanted. He went to see his boss.

'You're not the first REC officer who's come to see me, George. The last few years have been an experience none of us will ever forget. Now please don't surprise me and tell me you want to stay.'

George laughed. He explained how he wanted to again run a station wearing a cap with the word STATIONMASTER sitting above the brim. He wanted to chat with his porters and to the guards and footplate crew, to the man in the signal box and the gatekeeper. He wanted to greet the locals and help farmers move their produce into town. But he was specific in the type of SM role he didn't want. Not for George any busy city or mainline station with a cast and crew of thousands.

'I loved my time on branch lines at Crabbtree and at Wolferton. Surely there must be a station like those available.'

'I'm sure there will be so is there an area you fancy?'

George had been considering that question for months, even years. 'My children are grown and the family is settled in Cambridgeshire so I guess anywhere in that neck of the woods would suit.'

'Leave it with me and you keep an eye out yourself,' said the supervisor and George went back to his small office 122 steps below ground level in the once abandoned Tube station in Down Street.

It took time for the country to get back on its feet. Children evacuated to the country came home although many became used to their rural upbringing. Blackouts were no longer required, ration books were phased out, and returned servicemen, many with memories they never wished to discuss, returned to their families and former jobs. But it was not the same old Britain.

One of the big changes saw far more people own or have access to a motor vehicle.

Of course trains were still needed to carry people and freight. Services once restricted or even cancelled were brought back. Posters with "Is Your Journey Really Necessary?" were redundant and removed. Stations saw their signs returned. George and the REC were still in charge. They kept working and George kept looking for a position.

What he and most of the REC did know was that the general state of the railways in Britain was poor, even terrible. Locomotives and rolling stock were worked to death in war time and missed regular service and maintenance. The same situation applied to tracks and signalling. On many branch lines, passenger numbers were abysmal. Road haulage accelerated its growth. In North America, locomotives using diesel fuel were chugging along what the locals called railroads. Did this suggest the end of steam? Wherever George landed, if he did, there were troubled times ahead. Big changes were in the wings. Line closures bubbled away in the minds of civil servants and politicians. George thought. *After the war may not be a good time to go back on the rail.* But it was all he knew and certainly all he loved.

Approaching Christmas 1945, George was still in the REC. James was still studying at Cambridge but now as a post-graduate student. Victoria decided not to apply to study at Cambridge but instead wanted to become a nurse, a decision which thrilled her mother and both her grandmothers. George too was pleased although found the achievements of his children bewildering. *What will they do next?*

Occupancy at Hamilton-Weir House was full to overflowing and George looked forward to being with his family over the festive season. He saw details of vacancies becoming available and one in particular took his fancy. He applied and was not surprised he was appointed to the position but the speed with which it happened did see him raise his eyebrows.

'Come off it, George,' said Bernard. 'Look at your record; 20 years' experience as an SM, looking after the Royals and running the whole bloody network as part of the REC. They would've appointed you in a heartbeat. So what do you know of the station and the line?'

'I can name every station and halt but I've never travelled on it. Before I go home for Christmas, I'll become a passenger and see for m'self.'

'What, in disguise? George Miracle wearing a beard and glasses is something I'd really like to see.'

George's smile was close to a grin.

Chapter 26

Christmas lunch 1945 was full of happiness. The family chose to dine by themselves and not with the guest residents in the main dining-room. Silly hats were a clear sign the war was over. George arrived mid-morning on Christmas Day and after hugs and kisses and the giving of presents, the family sat down to what could best be described as a sumptuous lunch. The trimmings were back.

Everyone wanted to share their news and George was eager to learn. 'I think I may have a new career, Dad,' said James grinning and eating at the same time.

'Oh yes, and what was your old one?'

'There's a new laboratory in Cambridge looking for a junior research officer and my Professor has recommended me for the post.'

'And what will happen to your post-graduate studies?'

'They say I can combine the two, starting work part-time.'

'I hope this means your board will increase.'

An even bigger grin appeared on the young man's face. 'Oh and if you ever need any extra cash, I can offer a reasonable rate of interest.'

The room exploded with laughter and James' face became a picture. He loved telling jokes and when they set others laughing, he slipped into comedy heaven. George was thrilled to hear of his boy's success and to see his son capturing his father's sense of humour.

Victoria jumped in as the laughter faded. 'And I too have news, Daddy. I'm to start my nursing training at Addenbrooke's Hospital next month.'

George's heart swelled and he saw his wife's serene expression. She was thrilled at his delight. Their children were growing into talented, sensible and caring adults.

George raised his glass. 'I believe congratulations are in order. Here is a toast to the talented Miracle children.'

Everyone joined in, even those being toasted and the clink of glasses with laughter bounced around the room.

'Now what is *your* news, Mr Stationmaster?' asked Rowena.

The room fell silent. All eyes shifted to George. His heart rate increased because of what he was about to say.

'I have been appointed as station master and will start work in the New Year.'

The room caught fire. Absent for years, the patriarch worked in London and despite the safety of his Tube station hideaway, with bombs falling he missed so much of his family life. Now the war was over and the much loved father and husband was back where he belonged doing what he did so well. But where was this station?

Louisa led the chorus. 'That's wonderful news, George but when did you find out?'

'More importantly,' interrupted Rowena, '*where* are you going?'

George was as excited as his family. 'I found out a week ago but only agreed to accept the position after my visit this week.'

'This week!' exclaimed Rowena. 'You went to your new station before you came here?'

'Of course I did. I need to be sure it's perfect.'

'You're going to Cambridge,' said his clever son.

'Almost, it's one stop out of Cambridge on the Mildenhall branch and my final posting is to Barnwell Junction.'

'Final, what's this *final* business?' asked his mother-in-law.

'I plan to see out my days on a quiet branch line, Grannie and you will always be welcome to pay a visit.'

'Oh thank you very much,' she replied with a faux snooty voice.

'You take the bus to Cambridge and the train to Mildenhall always remembering to alight at Barnwell Junction.'

'Where will you live, George?' asked his now worried wife.

'Well I'm hoping with my wife. There's a pleasant two-storey station master's house which if it were any closer to the line, would have the passengers passing through the parlour.'

The buzz in the room became louder and busier.

'And any of my busy family members will be more than welcome to visit and even stay ... for a limited time.'

The loud laughter was followed by a sudden silence in the dining-room at Hamilton-Weir House. The children's news was exciting and special but clearly their father managed to top the lot.

'But in the meantime, I'm on leave and plan to catch up on several years of missing my family and I hope that appeals.'

It most certainly did; did it ever. There were comments, cheers, and requests for more food. It was the best Miracle Christmas ever.

George knew the branch line to Mildenhall was ideal for him. He wanted a gentle pace of life. Forget VIP passengers, vast lost property rooms and staff coming out of his ears, he wanted the basics and nothing more. About halfway along the 19 and a bit mile long line at Fordham, the Mildenhall line crossed the line to Ely. From there trains could reach Norwich or even Kings Lynn, the latter station he knew well from his days at Wolferton. He was in familiar territory.

On his inspection trip, he didn't wear a disguise, hopped out at the terminus at Mildenhall and went for a walk around the nearby village. This was his type of area, his type of railway. Apart from a brief introduction to the SM at Mildenhall, he spoke to no-one.

He studied the timetable and noted the services. Four trains each way at Barnwell Junction with other services linking up down the line. A daily freight service would hardly rush him off his feet.

He returned to London, served out his two weeks' notice and did the rounds thanking all his colleagues. Down Street had been his home for six years. He made good friends, learnt a hell of a lot about the railways of Britain and now looked forward to being back in harness.

Back in London, he rang his wife. She spoke first. 'George, I've been for a trip to Barnwell Junction.'

She floored him. 'You've what?'

'Well if you expect me to move there, George it's only fair I give the place the once over first.'

He worried. 'What happened? Did you upset anyone?'

'Why would you even think such a question? I introduced myself to the current station master who introduced me to his wife and she kindly gave me a tour of the SM's house.'

George worried more. *What if she doesn't like it? I'll be living at the station while my wife lives miles away in the countryside.*

'It's bigger than Whittleton and smaller than Wolferton and is perfect, but George I'm not sure we'll have any boarders.'

He worried about all her comments. Louisa explained.

'Victoria will be living in the nurses' quarters at the hospital and James will still be in halls at Cambridge.'

'And your mother?'

'Oh come on, George, use your brain. Whatever would she do stuck in a house on a branch line with only a few trains a day? Besides she loves being a part of running Hamilton-Weir House.'

He was stuck for words. She wasn't.

'It'll be like the old days, George, when we were first married; you and me and those smelly old locomotives.'

'How dare you!' he exploded with fake rage. 'I'll have you know, woman, a steam locomotive is the nearest thing to a living being.'

She laughed. 'We can discuss the finer details when you deign to return.'

'Deign to return!' he replied with even more faux outrage.

'We're looking for an experienced worker to take over my duties here. If you know of anyone suitable, please do let me know.'

He struggled for an answer. 'I'll think about it.'

'You do and I hope they give you a gold watch. Bye.'

She hung up and he sat there thinking about how lucky he was to have a wife so kind, so organized and with such a lovely sense of humour. He took some credit for the humour.

He packed his meagre belongings, went out to Maida Vale and checked on the mews cottage feeling even more strongly it should be sold. 'But what if the children want to live in London?' argued Louisa.

Wanting to see his friend George Carruthers, he found his way to Tudor House. The parents of these two families first became friends more than 30 years ago. His Lordship was out. Valerie and the children were thrilled to see him.

'Have you finally stopped running the entire British rail network, godfather?' asked godson George with a sparkle in his eye.

The older George admired the young man who would go through life with his face bearing a Royal Navy battle wound.

The SM explained his new posting and his children's news.

With the war over, Tudor House divested itself of recuperating soldiers. Godfather and godson strolled in the enormous garden.

'So young man, what are your plans? Looking at your magnificent vegetable garden, you could easily make a career with your horticultural skills.'

'My parents would like their tennis and croquet courts back and my father is talking to friends in the city. 'He asked me, what about banking, George or insurance? I'm sure I can find you an opening.'

'And?' asked the station master. 'Is that what you want?'

'No it's not, sir. I joined the Navy to serve my country and doing so outdoors. Being in an office doesn't appeal at all. I admire you and your work being outdoors and dealing with ordinary people.'

George Miracle froze. 'Are you serious? Have I understood you? Would you like to go on the rail?'

His godson smiled which wasn't easy with one side of his face permanently scarred. Fire and flesh do not mix well.

'I've been thinking about it for a while. Could you help me? You know I've always appreciated your advice.'

'Help you? I'll appoint you myself.' The railwayman laughed his eyes sparkling, embraced his godson and led him back inside. 'I reckon your father will be chuffed. I'd love to see his face when you tell him.'

Heading back to Hamilton-Weir House, George remembered the times in his life when the saying, it's not what you know but who, proved extremely helpful. Being appointed to Wolferton from a field of more than 100 applicants was a perfect example.

He wondered how he could help his godson. He knew the young man was mature, could apply himself and with his war service record and his father being Lord Carruthers, young Carruthers would be assured of a job. But where would he go? Some far flung rural line might not suit his parents or sister who would rarely see him. But then serving in the Royal Navy kept him away from family. A first railway posting in London would mean he could live at home.

George could hear his wife giving him advice. 'Find out what *he* wants to do, George and don't assume anything.' He smiled and headed to Cambridge.

January 1946 at Hamilton-Weir House was like no other. A grand time but an air of seriousness washed over the family. The children were adults, the war was in the past, new careers were in the wind and the future seemed full of promise. Louisa shared news with her husband.

'We have an offer of free haulage for our bits and bobs, George.' He wanted details. 'I was telling one of our residents, who is here with her son, about us moving to Barnwell Junction and she said her husband is a carrier and would be happy to move our belongings.'

'How kind,' said George. 'Are you sure?'

'George, people who stay here without charge are more than grateful and look for ways to express their gratitude. This is one example.'

'Wonderful. Well I'd better start packing.'

'You haven't *un*packed yet. I spoke with the Barnwell SM and Mr Harris is happy for us to move in next Sunday. They've already moved their furniture to her sister in Ely.'

He looked at Louisa. 'I thought I married you for your beauty but all this taking care of everything is a bonus.'

'What's a bonus?' asked Rowena who came in with a pot of coffee.

'Coffee?' asked George. 'Have you robbed a bank or the grocer?'

'Have you told George about our new manageress?' asked Rowena.

George looked confused. 'I can't keep up with life here. I've never been so redundant in my life.'

The women smiled. 'Never mind, Mr Stationmaster,' said his wife. 'Next week you'll be back as king of your castle.

SM Miracle did have his uses as next week young George Carruthers was appointed as a porter at the busy London terminus, Liverpool Street.

Chapter 27

It was a mystery in 1913 and remains so today. What happened to the passenger on SS *Dresden*, a vessel owned by of all companies the Great Eastern Railway, the original employer of George Miracle? The passenger, an engineer and inventor, boarded the ship in Antwerp sailing for England. He was due to meet people in London to discuss his new invention.

Before retiring he asked for an early morning call at 6.15am.

The steward knocked on the passenger's door and received no reply. Another knock produced the same result.

'Good morning, sir,' called the steward. Hearing nothing he opened the door to discover the cabin empty.

The passenger's bed wasn't slept in, his night clothes were laid out and his watch remained beside his bed but most disturbing, the entry in his diary for yesterday contained a simple drawing of a Christian cross. His overcoat and hat were found elsewhere on the ship. What could this mean? More importantly, where was the passenger?

The ship was searched and the crew questioned with no-one having seen the missing man once he retired. The obvious conclusion being the passenger left the ship at night while in the English Channel but did he jump or was he pushed?

A few days later another ship spotted a decomposing body floating in the English Channel. The sea was rough and while several personal items were recovered and later identified by the passenger's family, the body was left to the vagaries of the ocean.

The passenger was a German, Rudolf Diesel, who invented the engine given his name as well as the fuel it consumed.

Both were significant inventions. Herr Diesel discovered how a great deal of energy was lost in other processes and his engine and fuel would provide a far more efficient alternative. Diesel engines and diesel fuel would come to be used in stationary machines, farming equipment, motor vehicles, ships and boats and railway locomotives.

Ernest Marples was a Lancashire lad born in 1907. He loved his football and when fans poured out of Old Trafford, 14 year-old Ernie would be there with his tray of fags and sweets acting the right little entrepreneur. His dad was a strong Labour man and Ernie took to a number of labouring trades including going down pit.

At some stage along the way his political allegiance changed and when elected to the House of Commons, Ernie was a Tory. Winston Churchill, on his return to the premiership, appointed Marples as a junior minister. His rise continued.

From Postmaster General to Minister for Transport, Marples left his mark on British life and like many politicians at the time, before and since, worked a second "job". He owned shares in a road-building company; the Hammersmith and Chiswick flyovers being examples of their handiwork.

During his time as Minister for Transport, he plucked an executive from the chemical company ICI to become the first chairman of the British Railways Board. At the time the world and its mother knew the railways in Britain suffered major financial problems. 'We must cut costs,' said the politician with a stake in the success of road transport.

After politics, Ernie became a life peer with the title Baron Marples. He reached the pinnacle of his career but when the Inland Revenue, numerous law suits, the police and a drink driving charge came knocking, the Baron did a runner to Monaco.

Five months after the Herr Diesel drowning mystery, a boy was born in Kent. He grew up to become the ICI executive handpicked by Ernest Marples to run an eye over the nation's railways. His name was Richard Beeching and it's unknown if he ever collected engine numbers. Dr Beeching, PhD, physicist and engineer and Rudolf Diesel, inventor, were two men who played a major role in the world of railways.

There was a connection between the overboard passenger and the first chairman of the British Railways Board; their work greatly impacted the professional life of George Miracle, now the station master at Barnwell Junction just up the line from Cambridge.

The missing German invented an engine which largely replaced steam, and the appointed Beeching produced a report which saw the closure of entire railway lines together with their stations and staff. Thanks to Dr Beeching, nearly 70,000 railway workers lost their job.

Between them, Rudy and Dick brought massive change to the railways of Britain.

We know the floating corpse was Diesel because his son identified the personal effects collected from the body. We know his widow opened a bag he left for her back home in Germany and which contained a small fortune. We know his country put pressure on the inventor to allow only Germany to have access to his inventions. We know he was heading to London to meet with British men keen to get their hands on the plans for a diesel engine.

This thriller, this true story in 1913 laid the foundation for the final appointment of station master George Miracle. In 1946 he arrived at Barnwell Junction, a sleepy station on the branch line to Mildenhall.

It wasn't always quiet because the main Cambridge to Ely line lay a few yards from the tracks into Barnwell Junction. Mainline locomotives thundered past on a regular basis.

George and Louisa settled in the SM's house beside or rather a part of the station; you could say semi-detached. Their children lived in Cambridge—in the university and the main hospital. Rowena continued living and working at Hamilton-Weir House. Now alone and together, would George and Louisa turn into Darby and Joan?

In 1946 when George returned to working on a platform, steam locomotives were still the main source of traction power in Britain and would continue so for many years until slowly, the demise of the steel horse continued creeping ever closer to a scrapyard nearby.

Diesel's diesel engine and fuel offered enormous potential. Road transport grew with new roads and a surfeit of trucks no longer required by the armed forces. If George hoped for a relaxed and quiet life in his middle age, he would be disappointed. Change was coming and George was slap bang in the middle of a railway revolution.

It was so easy for Mrs Miracle to bring her husband his elevenses. The walk from her kitchen to the SM's office could be measured not exactly in nanoseconds but you get the idea. His previous postings at Whittleton and Wolferton saw his accommodation close by but

Barnwell won the closest to the pinny prize. She arrived with a tray bearing a pot, a steaming mug of tea and a plate of biscuits.

'Is everything to your satisfaction, sir?' she asked as he inspected the refreshments.

'The brew as usual hits the spot. One of life's pleasures I missed most during the war was my wife's cup of tea.'

'So you missed the tea but not your wife?'

'Oh I missed her,' he said reaching out, grabbing her arm and pulling her gently to him. He kissed her but stopped when porter Montague Rivers stepped in unannounced and coughed.

'Begging your pardon, sir, but Mr Cleverly is here about his cauliflowers and will deal with nobody except the SM.'

Louisa took her leave looking at Montague, pointing at the tray with tea and biscuits and smiling. George went to see the farmer about his vegetables when Louisa reappeared and called.

'Don't forget you have to check on young George Carruthers and his posting at Liverpool Street.' George waved. He rarely forgot.

This was the daily activity the SM loved; dealing with passengers and farmers. He adored running his own station striving to always offer the best service. Montague was older than George, without ambition, content to follow orders and never made suggestions.

George couldn't discuss the future of British Railways with Monty who lived with his elderly, hard of hearing father in the village. Monty brought his loud speaking to work, a hangover from chatting to the old man. Next station at Quy, George befriended SM Redvers Steady.

Redvers known as Ready as in Ready Steady to people on the branch line was passionate about flowers and won prizes for his geraniums. The first time George arrived at Quy, (pronounced Kwai) Ready took the new boy on a tour of the signal box.

George wondered why as they set off across the tracks. Seen one signal box you've seen them all. Not true as Ready used the steps, porch and much of the inside to grow his prize-winning plants. There were so few trains and the threat of using shunting frames meant the horticultural activity thrived uninterrupted.

'Did you know, George,' asked Ready, 'Charles Dickens was a big flower man and his favourite blooms were scarlet geraniums?'

'No I didn't and I must admit you have an outstanding display.'

'Thank you.'

'Have you thought about decorating the platform?'

Ready looked aghast. 'What and have half the village pinch a bloom for their button hole every Wednesday morning?'

George wondered why locals only pinched flowers mid-week but let the matter drop. They discussed the future of their branch.

'The Labour Party has made no secret of their desire to nationalize the whole darn shooting match, George so I would say it's only a matter of when and it may put our jobs and my flowers at risk.'

'I can't see it affecting the stations on our line,' replied George.

'Unless they close us lock, stock and barrel,' replied Ready giving his endless array of idioms a good airing.

George appreciated having a kindred soul nearby to talk railways with even if their lifestyles were miles apart.

He kept an eye on his godson the new porter at Liverpool Street but those he knew in the old LNER days were no longer around; dead or retired.

One thing George discovered in Barnwell was the local bus service. It only ran on weekends and only between Cambridge and Isleham almost to Mildenhall. At the time it didn't seem a threat to the train but George wondered if it was the thin edge of the wedge?

The Miracles' first Christmas at Barnwell proved memorable. The children and Rowena came for lunch and Louisa pulled out all the stops. The stories James and Victoria told about their studies and careers fascinated their family. The laughter was loud and frequent. Train services were few and James followed his father to the platform for each train. It was like the old days at Wolferton when the disabled boy sat in his wheelchair and noted arrival and departure times.

They'd just finished the plum pudding when the phone rang. George answered it, sounded cheerful on such a day, listened and froze. Louisa looked at him and knew something was wrong.

'George,' she said, 'what's happened?'

Now the others looked at the SM. He struggled to speak.

'It's Ma. She's dead.'

George easily and always remembered two days. His father died on George's 12th birthday and his mother died on Jesus' birthday.

Chapter 28

Talk about a dampener on Christmas Day. There were tears and hugs, condolences and questions.

'I can't believe it,' said the shattered station master. We chatted on the phone only two hours ago. She and John were bringing Emily, Bert and the boys here for New Year and now … and now she's gone.'

'Do they know what happened?' asked Rowena.

'John thinks it was a heart attack. Typical Ma not telling me she'd been having chest pains.'

'You must go to Whittleton, George. John and your sister need you. Get a relief SM and go and sort the funeral,' said Louisa.

'I'll come with you, Dad,' said James who loved both his grannies.

George gave his famous half-smile to his son. 'Thank you, son, but I should tackle this job alone.'

'But we'll all come to the funeral,' said James, 'and I want to see the station where you first met Ma.'

Victoria tried to lighten the mood. 'Is that where you first kissed your sweetheart?'

The unexpected question hung in the air with no-one knowing how to react. Rowena gave her granddaughter a mock ticking off. 'Victoria, I told you that in the strictest confidence.'

'As did I you, Mummy,' replied Louisa.

George played along. 'Nobody told me about it and I was there.'

His joke allowed the others to laugh in a restrained way.

George was granted leave and a retired SM in Cambridge arrived allowing Monty to use his megaphone voice to help the new boss.

George's train pulled into Whittleton and to his sorrow, he knew no-one. All the staff who worked here when he left 22 years ago now were elsewhere, retired or deceased. The station garden still looked in fine condition although Horace Gardiner had long since passed away and his housekeeper Daisy Woods lived with her son in Cricklewood.

He introduced himself to the SM explaining the reason for his arrival, before heading to his stepfather's home once he'd stopped to admire the cottage where he once used to live.

At his late mother's home his sister opened the door. Their greeting was powerful with love and sadness shared for a long time. His step-father looked shell-shocked and moved with difficulty.

George could see he needed to take the lead with his offer pleasing the widower, so the SM called on the vicar who helped with the undertaker, and soon all necessary arrangements were in place. George rang Louisa giving her the funeral details.

After lunch, he said his farewells promising to return for the funeral with his family. He wandered to the station and having a photographic memory for timetables, knew the Crabbie was due. He crossed the lines and waited on the island platform as the loco and single carriage arrived. The engine sounded tired and the carriage looked it. He greeted the loco but she ignored him. No-one remembered him. The driver and fireman were strangers. George watched to see how many carriage doors opened; one. There were two passengers he didn't know. They ignored him. The former SM was a stranger to both staff and locals.

He wanted to ask about the branch but the driver and fireman were in a hurry and headed off with barely an acknowledgement.

'Next train's not for a while, sir,' said the fireman who looked like he could have been cleaning engines last week.

George nodded and headed past the signal box towards the manor house, Ripley Hall.

Is there anyone in Whittleton who remembers me?

He wandered up the drive with memories flooding back. This is where he knew he'd lost his heart to the nanny who was caring for his godson. This is where Stephen Fitzsimons, the Lord of the Manor, wanted to woo George's sweetheart. How long since he shook hands with Stephen?

The grounds of the estate looked magnificent. Away to his right he saw people working in the vineyard. It looked healthy. Everything changes and everything remains the same.

He rang the bell beside the huge front door. He could remember train timetables and station names but the name of the family retainer escaped him. *What's his name? Chivers? Johnson?* He remembered. *Mr Fortescue!*

Only it wasn't said gent who opened the door. George stared at a middle-aged woman wearing working garb and gardening gloves and trying to push her unruly hair out of her face by blowing upwards.

She must be the cleaner.

'Good afternoon,' she said in an unusual accent. 'You don't look like the plumber and don't tradesmen knock on the back door?'

George gulped. 'Good afternoon. My name is George Miracle and I used to live in Whittleton and ...

'Not the youngest and best station master in Britain?' Stunned, George gulped again. 'Come in, come in.' He entered and the woman closed the door. 'Stephen's told me all about you. He was only saying the other day, "I wonder what's happened to station master Miracle?" so your timing is exquisite.'

George failed to speak only because he was overcome.

'Oh I do apologize,' she said. 'I'm Dakota, Stephen's wife. I'm so pleased to finally meet you and Stephen will be cock-a-hoop.'

George was pleased to meet a local who knew him, well, of him and taken aback to find Lady Fitzsimons doing what appeared to be domestic work. *What is going on?*

Stephen came running when the stable boy delivered the news. The reunion was, in a word, joyous. Both men delighted in their memories of time spent together and in saving the branch line to Crabbwell. His Lordship introduced his wife, an American, a divorcee and who met and married Stephen during the war.

They bumped into one another in a Tube station while sheltering during the Blitz. George kept thinking of the previous King and his bride from across the ditch. Did Stephen have to give up his title and land?

Lord Fitzsimons was saddened to hear of Connie's passing and George discovered Stephen's mother too had died. The men made plans to catch up as soon as possible. They exchanged a great deal of news and the topic which greatly saddened George concerned the Crabbie.

'I've given them all the business I can, George, but in vintner terms our little branch line is dying on the vine. The war killed any tourism such as it was and we turned the estate over to evacuees. I'll be surprised if the Crabbie survives another year.'

Connie's funeral was well attended with John Beckwith being highly regarded in the village and the church. Parishioners turned out for the widower. George shook hands with people who knew his mother well but who he'd never met or, if so, couldn't remember.

Catching up with Emily, her husband Bert and their sons was one redeeming activity. The "hit" of the gathering after the funeral was James Miracle with his awkward gait and speech. He made himself known to the mourners. 'I'm the son of Stationmaster Miracle,' he would say to those he met. Following his father's advice he said nothing about his brilliant academic achievements leaving it to others. When told later, people were amazed at his success.

Before taking his family home, on his own, George took a final walk around the village. The shops and houses were the same but the people were strangers. Twenty-two years, which included a world war, put an end to the residents he once knew, even loved.

He stopped outside the cottage of a friend, the author Septimus Oldmeadow. They exchanged Christmas cards for years but the war brought an end to many activities. *Is he still alive?* George could hear the man's voice bowling through his cottage performing a limerick.

> *'A station master resplendent*
> *Was known as the perfect attendant*
> *His whistle and cap gave the chap a handclap*
> *And made him so wise and dependent.'*

The front door opened and George's heart caught fire. *He's alive!* 'Timothy!' called a woman with a sergeant-major's voice. A child appeared followed by the army instructor, his mother. She stared at the station master.

'Good afternoon,' said George. 'Is Mr Oldmeadow at home?'

'Never heard of him,' snapped the woman. 'Timothy!' she barked again as the cheeky lad dared to step out of line.

For George, this sad visit to Whittleton ended with a whimper.

Back at Barnwell Junction, the SM resumed his duties. His erstwhile Sunday night chats with the former Rector at Wolferton were replaced by his Sunday night chats with his horticultural colleague, Redvers "Ready" Steady a station down the line at Quy.

The first and third Sundays of the month were at Barnwell and the second and fourth Sundays at Quy.

'A fifth Sunday will be once in a blue moon, George, so we'll give them a miss,' announced Ready spouting yet another idiom.

After the last Up train on Sunday November 2, they met at Barnwell. Steady pulled up on his ancient motorcycle complete with sidecar. He rarely carried a passenger but nearly always at least one geranium. Louisa retired leaving a cake she'd baked in the afternoon.

The station masters greeted one another in quiet voices not because it was after the last train and Mrs Miracle was abed, but because in the last few days not one but two seriously major railway accidents occurred with dozens of passengers killed and hundreds injured. On their quiet branch line, such accidents were unthinkable.

'One such catastrophe is unbelievable, George,' said Ready. 'But two! Apart from the human tragedy, think of our reputation.'

'We can't do anything about human error but equipment failure is when the real cost of non-existent or insufficient maintenance comes home to roost.'

'I like your idiom, George.'

'This is serious. The whole network has been underfunded for decades and politicians get nervous when accidents happen.'

'So what do you reckon is going to happen?'

'I'm no fortune teller but finding funds to radically improve conditions always comes with cutting costs by closing lines.'

'Not us, we run a tight ship with connections to Ely and beyond.'

They argued into the night with George describing the Crabbtree branch. 'It's got a booming set of one crumbling carriage.'

'One, only one?' queried a disbelieving Ready.

'Do you know, sir, how long it takes to prepare a steam locomotive for its first run of the day?' The geranium king reckoned hours. 'In America they are using these new diesel locomotives which require neither coal nor water and can be ready for work in minutes.'

'You're frightening me, George.' Ready didn't like the picture of the future painted by his colleague. 'Is there any more tea in the pot?'

1947 began with flurries of snow. George lived in his SM's coat and needed extra time to reach inside for his watch on a chain in a pocket of his jacket. Passengers often asked the time or when the next Mildenhall or Cambridge train was due. Such questions were meat and drink to SM Miracle. He'd found his forever home.

It was easy to keep in touch with his children and mother-in-law. They were all in Cambridge or at Hamilton-Weir House and they would visit Barnwell Junction on a regular basis while Louisa popped out to see her mother once a week usually on a Wednesday.

Seated in his office, a man approached and said, 'Knock knock.' The visitor surprised and thrilled George.

'Kenneth,' he exclaimed a smile exploding across his face as the former Wolferton Rector appeared. They'd kept in touch due to the tutoring of James and more recently when George's son graduated. But as time moved on and during the war years when George was below ground in Down Street, their meetings were non-existent.

It was the warmest of greetings with Kenneth wanting to know the latest news particularly about James. George told all.

'But what of you, dear fellow?' asked George. 'How is your wife, your job and your health?'

Before Kenneth could explain, the latest Up arrived and George left. The usual smattering of passengers meant the stop was short and when George returned to his visitor he saw a look on Kenneth's face which gave the SM a chill. George was right to worry.

'There's no easy way to say this, my friend,' said the former priest, 'but I've come to say good-bye.' The look on George's face grew worse.

'You're not ill. You can't be you look so well.'

Kenneth grinned. 'Not departing this mortal coil, sir, just this country.' For George that seemed like a death sentence. 'I've taken a teaching job at a boys' school in Sydney Australia. My wife has family there and we leave next week.'

George shook his head. 'James will be shattered. Does he know?'

Kenneth looked embarrassed. 'I'm afraid to tell him. He's given me such joy and pride over the years, and for me to move to the other side of the world away from your boy, it breaks my heart.'

'I've said it before, sir, we can never thank you enough for all you've done and if it were in my power, I would give you a medal.'

They laughed but were interrupted when the SM's wife appeared. She and Kenneth hugged. They'd seen each other weekly during the war years with George away in London and James having lessons.

Louisa spoke. 'I have news for the station master but being so wonderful a friend, sir; you are most welcome to hear it.'

George interrupted. 'Kenneth has news of his own.'

Louise reacted. 'Oh?' She studied the face of the former priest. Like her husband, Louisa knew bad news loomed large.

Kenneth paused not wanting to upset his dear friend.

When he did, Louisa grimaced. 'James will be devastated.'

Trying to lighten the mood, George questioned his wife. 'So what is your news, my dear? Something to cheer us I hope.'

'Your daughter has a young man who wants a chat with her father.'

'Wonderful news,' said Kenneth with the SM shocked into silence. 'But please, I must be off. Will James be at Ham House soon?'

'This weekend,' said Louisa. 'Do come for lunch on Saturday.'

'Thank you, I'll see you all on the weekend.'

He left and the Miracles looked at one another. 'Should we warn James?' asked Louisa.

George shook his head. 'No, it's between teacher and student. Now what's all this business about Victoria and a beau?'

Louisa scoffed. 'And a beau? You're such an old-fashioned man, George Miracle. Bows are ribbons for your hair.'

'All right but why am I only hearing about this now?'

'Don't you want to know about your future son-in-law?'

'Of course but why am I the last to know?'

'Think George. Victoria's last romance ended in tragedy with her young man shot down over Germany. She took an age to get over her loss and is reluctant to fall in love again. Now she's sure of her feelings. So aren't you at least a little bit curious?'

'What do you mean he wants a chat?' Louisa burst out laughing. 'What? What's so funny?'

'Are you thinking about your nervous brother-in-law who asked permission to marry Emily when all he wanted was a sex education?'

George became defensive. 'No I am not.'

'Your future son-in-law, Mr Miracle, won't want any of your scant knowledge about the birds and the bees; he's a doctor.'

Chapter 29

David Worthington was a young doctor working at Addenbrooke's Hospital. He caught the eye of the young nurse, Victoria Miracle, and in the staff canteen he sat at the same table as a group of nurses.

The nurse beside Victoria nudged her and whispered. 'I told you he's keen.'

'Stop it,' hissed Nurse Miracle who became curious and nervous.

Young Dr Worthington became a favourite amongst the nurses. Gossip between the females saw him listed as a Mummy's boy and shy, a chap who would need encouragement. Victoria thought he reminded her of her father. He was unlike several other doctors with whom she worked. A few older and married men made personal comments which made her feel uncomfortable. David or Dr Worthington as she called him treated her with respect.

They bumped into one another in the High Street when both were shopping. After friendly greetings, he invited her to take tea in the café across the road. Her heart was already accelerating when she agreed and her heartbeat kept racing.

They found it easy to be with one another with David keen to know about her family. He seemed blown away by her brother James and his academic success despite his disability. David asked her on a proper date and to the cinema they went.

The Courtneys of Curzon Street was playing and although the film went on for ages, it didn't take as long for the young doctor to kiss the station master's daughter once he returned her safely to her hostel.

Knowing how much teasing they would receive from fellow workers at the hospital, they agreed to keep their romance a secret for now. It bubbled along nicely. Louisa noticed a spring in her daughter's step and her gentle enquiry was politely downplayed.

The romance was exposed when the couple went walking hand in hand beside the river Cam one Sunday afternoon. The next day a blabbermouth nurse challenged Victoria in the nurses' change room and her blushes put an end to the secret.

David no longer hid his affection and decided to pop the question. Victoria's immediate and enthusiastic answer thrilled the young man. Later, Victoria telephoned Barnwell Junction Station, told her mother everything causing the SM's wife to interrupt the meeting between her husband and Kenneth Attwood.

Later that evening with the last train to arrive, George waited in his office going over accounts. An expected visitor knocked on the door with George impressed. Kitted out in his best, his only suit, the young man addressed the SM.

'Good evening, Mr Miracle. I'm David Worthington and wondered if I might have a word with you.'

'Of course,' said George moving forward with hand extended. 'Please, have a seat.' They sat. 'I understand you've been walking out with my daughter.'

The would-be son-in-law's nerves jangled as did those of the would-be father-in-law who wanted so much to help his worried guest. Any man who took such care over his attire, his hair and especially his shoes scored highly in George Miracle's mind.

'Yes sir; we've become close.'

George struggled for his next question. David desperately struggled for an opportunity to ask *his* question. Who would go first?

'My wife tells me you and Victoria work at Addenbrooke's Hospital.'

'We do, sir.' He wanted to say how much he loved the SM's daughter but worried he might say the wrong thing.

'Are your family local to the area?'

This innocent question produced an unexpected answer.

'Originally they were but today they live overseas.' George waited for more details. 'My parents are medical missionaries working for the Church Missionary Society in China.'

'So medicine runs in the family?'

'It does, sir. My brother is a dentist living in Bournemouth.'

George crunched the eggshells under his feet. Did this mean his daughter would move to Mongolia never to be seen again?

'Do you share your parents' interests in medical missionary work?'

David thought it a fair question. He'd taken an immediate liking to the man helped by his girl's high praise for her much-loved Daddy.

'No sir, I'm afraid I'm a disappointment to my parents as I don't share their enthusiasm for religious beliefs.' George's ears pricked and again he paused for further information. 'Have you heard of the scientist Charles Darwin, sir?'

George stopped himself from saying, "I would be delighted if you were to marry my daughter," but instead added a cheeky comment. 'Do you mean the Devil's Chaplin?'

It took a split second for a grin to appear on David's face and the rest of the conversation seemed to be one between old friends. The young man left with heart afire and a spring in his step. George too buzzed with excitement. He'd performed as his wife and daughter would have wished. His future son-in-law presented as a fine young man and being a doctor, could advise the station master on any aches and pains he might develop in his dotage and so all in all, 'twas a most satisfactory meeting.

The final train pulled in and to the five passengers George's smile appeared to be twice its usual size.

He locked up and went next door, home. In the kitchen sat his wife and alongside her their daughter.

He stared at them and they at him. 'Well?' he asked.

Victoria raised her left hand displaying an engagement ring. Much hugging and many tears became the order of the night before their attention was drawn to the subject of wedding plans.

One problem involved the possible lack of relations on the side of the groom. Writing to his parents in far flung rural China was the only method of communication and allowing for the mail to arrive—if it did—and waiting for the reply—if it came—meant the parents of the groom were likely non-starters.

With the date set and the banns being read, the mother of the bride started in on her SM husband. 'Don't tell me you plan on giving away our daughter wearing your station master's uniform.'

'Why not?' he replied with a hint of indignation. 'I think it looks dignified and appropriate. Besides everyone knows me and I'll look odd in my one and only lounge suit. People will point and ask, "Who's the chap with the bride"?'

'The family wedding photo is going to look a bit light on. The bride with her parents beside her while the groom will be an orphan.'

'Can't be helped my dear. What counts is our little girl is marrying a wonderful young man and both of them will be happy.'

Louisa fronted him and held his arms. 'You're an old softie, George Miracle. Underneath all that whistle and flag bluster is Mr Romantic.'

He kissed her and thought about his life. In his 50th year he'd been lucky with family and friends and the people he'd met. His father, mother and uncle used to always look out for him. Now all were gone to God.

How long before it's my turn?

Chapter 30

January 1, 1948 turned out to be a special day. The railways were nationalized. Close to a hundred years ago, the railways of Britain were privately owned and operated by more than 100 different companies. In many cases it resembled a dog's breakfast. Several companies ran on the same lines competing for the same passengers. A number of lines were poorly planned and meant investors were left with burnt fingers. A few lines should never have opened.

Now it all changed. Now only one railway company existed in Britain and it was publically owned. British Railways was born.

George Miracle once worked for the Great Eastern Railway which became a part of the London and North Eastern Railway. Now George worked for the government. His modest branch line from Cambridge to Mildenhall was now owned by the taxpayer.

At their next Sunday night chat, Ready Steady arrived full of excitement about the big change.

'Should have happened from the off, George,' he said. 'We're both old enough to remember the cock-ups and in-fighting between dozens of private companies. Now we can get on with running a proper railway without shareholders kicking up a stink.'

'I don't share your optimism, sir,' replied George still reluctant to call his colleague by what he, George, considered a disrespectful nickname.

'Mind you I reckon inspectors working for the government could be a bad move for the likes of us.'

'Oh?' asked George wanting more details.

'Well take my geraniums. A snooty-nosed inspector might order me to get rid of the lot.' He mimicked a nitpicking official. 'What's all this rubbish doing here in the signal box? It's a safety issue. Government property is not for personal use!'

'He may have a point.'

'Oh come on, George. It's a hobby. It keeps me sane. The locals always ask about how my blooms went in the various flower shows.

Branch lines are the soul of the community. Platform staff, footplate crews, the locals, we're all one big family.'

'I agree,' said George thinking of something else.

'Here's an example. For years the boys driving the Down have tossed out a lump or two of coal for Lenny Priest at Swaffhamprior. His wife suffers from arthritis terrible like and paying for her care and treatment costs a small fortune. Where's the harm in helping the old bloke keeping his fire going through the winter?'

'No harm, none at all.'

'Mind you he wasn't too happy the other week when a solid lump sailed from the footplate, took an off-break turn, smashed into his greenhouse and wrecked two of his prized tomato plants.'

George saw the funny side but laughed with restraint and they continued chatting about how nationalization might impact their quiet branch line.

David Worthington's parents were a no show. But the wedding went ahead as planned and the service and wedding breakfast started well and got even better. Victoria wore a simple yet stunning gown made by her grandmother, and the bride's mother confused many people at the church wondering if she might be the sister of the bride.

George did look resplendent in his station master uniform and the photo with Rowena, George, Louisa and James with the happy couple took pride of place in the family album for generations. Louisa kept her thoughts private but wondered if and when she might become a grandmother.

The reception at Hamilton-Weir House turned out nigh on perfect. The sunshine gave guests the chance to wander in the blooming garden even admiring the pets housed in outbuildings and fields and kept for younger visitors. Parents of residents willingly agreed to help with the catering and many people remarked on it being the best wedding they'd been to—ever.

George's speech so praised his daughter and son-in-law it provided another reason why guests were so enamoured of the event.

The ballroom in the stately home, long in use as a lounge for guests, received a transformation with a local six-piece orchestra allowing guests to try waltzing, fox-trotting and even doing the

Charleston. From the moment he arrived at the church, James wore a sparkling grin and kept it on nearly all day.

Towards the end, Louisa helped her daughter change into her going-away outfit, again "whipped up" by Grannie. Rowena and Louisa, grandmother and mother turned on the waterworks when their little girl with her new husband waved and drove away to start their honeymoon.

It took a while for all the guests to depart but having farewelled them, George turned to his wife. 'I'll be off my dear.'

'What?' snapped his disbelieving spouse.

'Redvers has offered me a ride back to the station in his sidecar. I've missed nearly a whole day and want to be on the job first thing in the morning.'

'Your daughter's just married and all you can think about is the jolly railways.'

He couldn't think of any answer until his thoughtful mother-in-law arrived with a package.

'Here's your breakfast, station master and as well there are two pieces of the wedding cake for your morning tea.'

'Thank you, mother-in-law,' he said and kissed her cheek.

Louisa mimicked him. 'Oh thank you ever so much mother-in-law,' she said and kissed him as well.

Seriously though, it turned out a grand, grand day.

Just because the entire network became government-owned, didn't mean conditions improved. In fact for many lines they were worse. Now the government ran the lot, it wanted value for money. That meant cutting waste and doing away with unproductive lines.

Any railwayman worth their salt knew there were tough times ahead, and George and Ready were two who appreciated the reality of the situation. They chatted at their regular Sunday evening session.

'I tell you, George,' said the horticulturalist SM, 'if we were just starting out working on the rail, I'd be seriously scared for our future.'

'True but I'm confident the Mildenhall Branch will be way down the list when it comes to closing lines.'

'Oh yes and why so?' asked Ready with a cynical voice.

'We have a good history accepting ambulance trains during both world wars, we have a turntable at the end of the line at Mildenhall—

how many branch lines have a turntable?—and although Branwell Junction isn't actually a junction, we do meet up with other lines at Fordham.'

They continued sipping their tea.

'What have you heard about future plans?' asked Ready.

'Nothing but in private companies, directors work for their shareholders while politicians, our new bosses, work for themselves and their re-election.'

'I reckon our biggest threat is the automobile.' George nodded. 'Before the war few people owned a car. Now it's different. Why walk through all weathers to catch a train when you can pop out your front door and climb into the horseless carriage in your garage?'

'I can remember trying to get more freight on my first branch line. The railway companies were forbidden from changing the rates while haulage companies did deals to carry what once always went by rail.'

'Enough,' announced Ready, 'enough of this misery.' He stood to leave. 'So how many years before you retire, George? I reckon I'll be gone pretty soon.'

'I'm only 50,' George replied and left it there.

Ready sat astride his motorbike. 'Well if I owned a country estate like yours, I'd retire tomorrow.'

George said nothing and waved as his colleague rode away.

Victoria's new life thrilled her mother. The new bride glowed with happiness as she and David rented a flat in the city within walking distance of the hospital. George plugged away at Barnwell Junction, Louisa popped out once a week to see her mother at Hamilton-Weir House and James, having completed his post-graduate studies, now worked fulltime as an analyst for a research company in Cambridge. He shared a flat in town with a workmate.

Major changes to the now national rail network were yet to appear. Struggling branch lines were put on life support. Rumours of diesel locomotives kept circulating and footplate crews up and down the land began having trouble sleeping. Would new drivers take over?

Life pottered along at its usual gentle pace especially on the Mildenhall Branch. George worked away on his paperwork between trains when he heard a female scream. He knew who screamed but not why. He rushed next door and found Louisa slumped on a chair beside the telephone.

'My dear,' he said kneeling, holding her hand and waiting for news. She handed him the telephone receiver. 'Hello,' he said.

'Oh Mr Miracle, it's Claudette from Ham House.' Many of the staff now used the shorthand version for the charity.

'What's happened?' he asked his body tensing as he kept looking at his shocked and now teary wife.

'It's your mother-in-law, sir. She collapsed in her bathroom.' George wanted to say the words, "Is she dead?" but couldn't because of Louisa's presence. 'We called an ambulance and they should be here any moment.'

'What did Nurse Jenkins say?'

'She thinks Mrs McClaren's suffered a stroke.'

'Is she breathing?'

'Yes but her mouth is twisted and she can't speak. Oh, the ambulance has just arrived. Can I telephone you with the details once she leaves?'

'Yes, please do. We'll be here by the phone. Goodbye.'

George replaced the receiver and helped Louisa to a chair in the kitchen. He found the brandy and poured a small amount. She swallowed and nodded but struggled to speak.

'Thank you, George. It's such a shock. Her health's been absolutely fine.'

'Once we know where she's been taken, we'll leave immediately.' Louisa looked surprised. 'We? There are still three trains today.' He looked at her part reprimanding, part disbelieving.

A few minutes later the phone rang with George being told Rowena was conscious, unable to speak and being taken to Addenbrooke's Hospital.

He rounded up Julian in the signal-box and Monty, gave them instructions and rang Redvers who offered to ride over but George suggested he only need do so in an emergency. Remembering his "disappearance" on the day King George V's coffin arrived at his previous station, George helped Louisa into the newly-arrived Up and they headed into Cambridge.

Asking for directions at reception in the hospital, they headed to the ward and were bowling along a corridor when their daughter appeared. She recoiled seeing her mother's face.

Once told the news, Victoria guided her parents to the right ward introducing her parents to the doctor in charge.

'Your mother's suffered a stroke,' he said. 'It's too early to know if the damage will be permanent.'

'Will she die?' asked Louisa wanting to have an exact opinion.

The doctor hesitated hating such a question and erring on the side of not giving false hope. 'I think you should prepare yourself.'

He spoke with a gentle voice but his words caused Louisa to freeze and her husband's arm gave her strength. Victoria whispered she would return and left to complete an important task.

When she did, her husband stood by her side. The quartet moved out of the ward and found a quiet place. Victoria sat beside her mother holding and squeezing her hand while the two men stood.

'Can you tell us anything, David?' asked George.

The young doctor grimaced. 'They'll perform more tests but at present they're trying to keep her calm and comfortable.'

'What happened?' croaked Louisa looking up at David.

'A stroke involves a blockage to part of the brain preventing oxygen and nutrients reaching brain tissue. One good thing is your mother is still alive. Some stroke victims die soon after the attack but so far she's a survivor.'

They waited in silence only to be disturbed by a well-known sound. James Miracle came along the corridor with his usual gait. The others looked at him and for once his face didn't wear a smile.

'How is Grannie?' he said with hope in his heart.

'She's still with us, my boy,' said George. 'But how did you know?'

'Vicky rang and I came in a taxi.'

The family waited uncertain of what to do. Louisa took control. 'George, you should go back to work.'

'No,' he said with a definite voice.

'Mummy might linger for hours, days even. James will stay with me and Victoria and David are close by.'

'Yes, Dad,' said James. 'We'll telephone the station if there's any change.'

George kissed his wife and daughter, shook hands with the males and left. He returned to Barnwell Junction in time for the final two trains and where both platforms oozed silence.

Rowena survived. She looked and sounded like a stroke victim with her speech and movements restricted. James tried to cheer up his grandmother.

'I can teach you how to speak, Gran, and what I don't know about learning how to walk is not worth knowing.'

The nurses were amused, the doctors thrilled to have an in-house therapist albeit a highly unusual one and of course Rowena found the young man's approach inspiring. She would have loved to have been able to laugh and thank her grandson. Her eyes spoke volumes and her tear ducts were in good working order.

Three weeks later Louisa arrived at Barnwell Junction having spent another day visiting her mother. Louisa looked exhausted with George fussing and wanting the latest news.

'The doctors want Mummy to tackle more therapy.'

'Brilliant; it means she's going to survive. Surely you feel better.'

'But she'll need fulltime care and who knows for how long.'

'And Hamilton-Weir House is the perfect place. You'll have all sorts of help preparing your mother's dietary and other requirements and willing residents can relieve you of helping her to bathe and dress. One or more helpers can even read to her.'

Louisa looked at her husband and her expression rang alarm bells in George's mind. 'I think she should come here.'

'Here?' said George confused. 'Whatever for?'

'Because I can care for Mummy and keep an eye on you.'

'Oh for pity's sake, Louisa, I can look after m'self. How many times have I told you about my bully beef surprise in the first war? And you know my Welsh rarebit has won prizes.'

She ignored his pathetic attempt at humour. 'I would have to come home to do your washing and clean the house anyway whereas with Mummy here, I could do both without moving.'

He sniffed to cover the fact he knew he'd lost the argument.

'I'll check with the hospital,' she said.

She did and with certain conditions attached, they agreed. Louisa noted what needed to be changed in what would be her mother's room. George copped a flashback remembering his grandmother in London when the family lived in Wood Green. Though infirm, the old lady still had her marbles but needed constant help. This became life imitating life. The only downside he thought would be his wife's health. Would becoming a fulltime carer put a serious strain on her?

He wanted at least to discuss the matter. He came into the kitchen after the last train. 'What's happened?' he asked.

'Victoria telephoned and said Mummy was resting having eaten all her supper including pudding.'

'Great and has Dr James Miracle begun his Grannie therapy yet?'

'Not yet but there's more news from Victoria.' Louisa hesitated leaving her husband on tenterhooks.

'Well, it's good news I hope?'

'I think even you would call it good news. She said we're going to be grandparents.'

Chapter 31

The fortnight following Rowena's stroke proved to be tough for the family Miracle and especially Louisa. Visiting the hospital every day, wondering if her beloved mother would survive and, if she did, wondering what quality of life she would have meant misery for the station master's wife. The patient was a fighter. Stroke patients can become totally dependent on others for almost if not everything, and there are relatives who believe it might have been better if the stroke had killed their loved one; horrible thought though it may be. Rowena's early life experiences and especially how she survived being a single mother meant she wanted her independence.

Now, out of nowhere came good news. Victoria and David were expecting and George and Louisa could ponder other topics. Will it be a boy or girl? When's it due? What names have the parents-to-be chosen? Will grandparents be required for babysitting? In their doom and gloom came a ray of sunshine, a flash of happiness.

George and Louisa embraced. You could feel the relief and joy coursing through and from their bodies. He kissed the top of her head as she quietly wept.

'It would be grand if Mummy could hold her great-granddaughter,' whispered Louisa having her mother's life constantly in mind.

'Oh it's a girl is it?' he replied.

'Of course, women know about these things.'

'You don't say; so what's going to win the St Leger?'

The next day when she went to visit her mother, Louisa caught up with her daughter and son-in-law. There were hugs aplenty.

'I told your father it's a girl so play along with him if he mentions it.' David laughed more than Victoria. 'And Grannie's coming home to Branwell as soon as she's discharged.'

The last statement caused the expectant parents to be concerned, especially Victoria. 'But Mummy, at Ham House you'll have so much help. At the station you'll be on your own.'

'You sound just like your father.'

'Mummy, just because he's the best station master in the world doesn't make him a caring and professional nurse.' She stopped. 'Oh, I get it; it's because you want to be on tap to starch his shirts and cook his supper. This is not Victorian England, Mummy; men are now allowed to tackle domestic tasks and in my opinion should.'

Conflict bobbed up in this dramatic mood change. The daughter, no longer a child and soon to be a parent herself, told her mother to stop spoiling the family patriarch, Victoria's beloved father. The atmosphere crackled until the son-in-law saved the day.

'Let's concentrate on getting Mrs McClaren well enough to leave hospital first before we choose the best place for her to recuperate.'

Louisa saw a lot of her husband in her son-in-law. He was wise, caring and sensible. The women saw their moment of conflict put on hold and all three went to visit Rowena.

George's phone rang in his office at Barnwell Junction. He took delight in recognizing the voice of the caller, Lord Fitzsimons of Ripley Hall, Whittleton. After the usual exchange of news, Stephen explained the reason for his call.

'I'm not sure you want to hear this, George but an inspector type chap came here yesterday looking at the SM's books. He took a trip on the Crabbie and didn't have to stand at any stage of the return journey. I think there were three passengers on the Down and absolutely no-one coming home.'

'It's an unofficial government policy, my friend. Close failing lines.'

'Well if it does go, you and I should take a little satisfaction in knowing we kept it going all those years with the Druid site and my free plonk.'

'Free plonk?' exclaimed George. 'Blimey if you'd told me that before I'd have been over in a flash.'

They both laughed knowing George's teetotal status.

'How are the locals feeling?' asked George.

'Well nothing's official but as you know, since the war ended life is different. People almost expect change. You don't cross the High Street in the village now without looking to see if it's safe to do so.'

'What, you mean cars?'

'I saw three last Saturday.'

They reminisced. George revealed his mother-in-law's health situation and his future grandfather status. Stephen shocked the SM.

'I've beaten you to that role, old man.' Silence from George. 'My dear wife has a daughter from a previous marriage. Cassandra lives across the ditch and has recently given birth to a healthy young boy named Chuck.'

'Congratulations,' said George trying to take in the news and especially the bit about naming a baby boy Chuck. George couldn't erase the thought of the infant vomiting. *Is that* a *Chuck chuck?*

'I think that makes me a step-grandfather and Dakota is over the moon. She wants us to get over to the States as soon as possible.'

'Well bon voyage and please give Dakota our best wishes.'

After the phone call ended, George sat there thinking long and hard. His older relations were dead or dying, babies were being born and the railways of Britain were changing and fast.

The hospital discharged Rowena. They needed her bed, the care she required could be provided elsewhere and her loving family offered to take her and was able to do so. Louisa won any argument and her mother moved to the Barnwell Junction station master's house.

George made up a ground floor bedroom and cleaned the chimney so a fire could be lit in the guest's room. Louisa fussed and made new curtains. She found inspiration pondering her single mother's sacrifices in raising her only child.

One of the heartwarming experiences came when James arrived to fulfill his promise to be Grannie's therapist. She'd been treated in hospital by a professional but Mr Miracle Junior had a middle name of Determination. He tackled her speech. His parents hung around only to be given short shrift although eavesdropping became the rage.

'Now Grannie,' said James on a chair beside Rowena's bed. 'You need to make a kissing motion like this.' He pursed his lips before opening them and saying, "mmm-wah".

Rowena tried and failed.

'Nearly,' said the grandson. 'Try again.' He made the sound over and over and finally she managed to do so after several attempts. The grin on James' face slipped across to his grannie's stiff dial.

Outside in the corridor, the therapist's parents struggled to stop their tears.

Rowena's speaking improved although she began to sound like her grandson. It proved difficult for her to speak but speak she did. To hear the teacher and student chatting, well speaking a few words and slowly became both amusing and heartwarming. George and Louisa even wondered if Rowena was mimicking her grandson even sending him up. After all he was a professional joker so why not return the favour? Whatever happened speech wise, her spirits were clearly on the rise.

Weeks into the lessons, James arrived as usual on the latest Down. George walked along the platform to greet him and worried when he saw his son and the guard struggling with something. Out came a wheelchair.

'Hello Dad, what do you think of her? Isn't she a beauty?'

A confused SM ventured a question. 'Are you unwell?'

James twigged. 'It's not for me, silly, it's for Grannie.'

They and the device crossed the tracks and James pushed the wheelchair along the Up towards the house. George opened the door. Louisa heard them, stepped out of the kitchen and stopped dead having the same thought as her husband.

'Hello Ma, I've bought Grannie a present.'

The patient's face lit up. As a wee lad when James was first diagnosed with cerebral palsy, the one member of his family who spent hours helping the lad whenever she could was Grannie Mac. Now it was payback time.

'Come on Grannie,' said her grandson. 'Pop yourself in here and let's go for a spin.'

Louisa helped her mother out of bed every day to sit in the sun if it appeared. Now Louisa found her heart racing. Her son took the initiative and both his parents wondered if the move would work. They thought it brilliant for the patient but worried for the therapist.

Despite his gait, pushing the wheelchair actually helped James. It gave him rock-solid balance and the duo headed out onto the platform. Along the Up they went with George and Louisa spellbound as their disabled son became his disabled grandmother's carer.

Rowena's speech and movement improved at a glacier-like speed but her smile began to return. Being happy proved a huge plus. The wheelchair lived at the station and soon George and Louisa became adept at treating the patient to a trip along the platform and beyond.

Speech lessons continued and one day after his lesson, James took his grandmother onto the platform. He returned to his childhood, produced a pad and pencil and explained his method of notating train times, arrivals and departures. It seemed a waste of time until the patient joined the world of trainspotting.

'Is the next train on the Up or Down platform, Grannie?' he asked.

'Errr...Up,' she said.

'Excellent and what's the time?'

She looked at her watch and spoke. '3.46 pm.'

'Correct again so we put the arrival time in which column?'

'A,' she said without hesitation. Holding the pencil became a task in itself but she tried. At first James would hold her hand and guide the pencil but after a few days she appeared a tad annoyed.

'I can do it myself,' she spoke slowly, the best words her teacher could have heard. When alone on the platform, he told his father of the progress and the SM found his throat blocked stopping him from speaking. When told, Louisa shook her head and cried.

James declined an invitation to stay for supper and politely excused himself without giving a reason.

'I can understand him not wanting to stay,' said Louisa, 'but he's always told us why before.'

From her wheelchair, Rowena eked out her words. 'I think he's got a girl ... friend.'

The clock in the kitchen stopped. Rowena's speech alone caused a shock but the possible truth of her sentence busted a spring in the timepiece. Mr and Mrs Stationmaster sat there speechless.

Time drifted by, Rowena's slow improvement continued and James' next lesson drew nigh. They were timetabled for every Wednesday afternoon with the odd weekend visit thrown in for good measure.

'James will be here this afternoon, Mummy,' said Louisa as she put a steak and kidney pie in the oven.'

'I know,' said the stroke victim from her wheelchair giving weight to each word. 'Your special baking is a dead give-a-way.'

George tackled a problem with freight in the goods yard—hardly a yard and on the far side of the mainline from Cambridge to Ely—when the Mildenhall Down arrived with the therapist. The SM knew it was due, saw it approach but couldn't leave one of his few and important freight customers.

Once he did, George hurried across the mainline and onto the Down, and a deserted platform. The SM started to cross to his office thinking his boy must be at home with his grandmother when a voice stopped him.

'I'm here, Dad,' called James stepping from the waiting-room. 'I saw you in the goods yard.'

George headed towards him but copped a shock when his son looked back to the waiting-room and offered his hand. A young woman appeared and took hold of James' hand.

Hell's bells, thought George. *Rowena is right. He <u>does</u> have a girlfriend.* The father reached the couple, his son's grin a corker.

'I'm sorry I wasn't here my boy but freight business is important.'

'Dad I'd like you to meet Isabel. Darling this is my father, George Miracle.'

Darling? Is my hearing going? Isabel yes but Darling?

Still in shock, George willingly accepted the young woman's hand and followed the procedure as instructed by his mother way back in ancient times. 'Never shake a woman's hand, George. Hold it briefly and ever so gently squeeze it.'

'How do you do, Mr Miracle,' she said smiling. 'James has told me so much about you.'

'I see,' said the father and soon-to-be grandfather who smiled. The railways of the United Kingdom were changing and fast but nothing could beat the changes in the life of his family.

I need a serious word with my mother-in-law. Is she in on this?

With George's mind racing, they headed off to cross the lines and reach the house. The SM led the way, opened the door and called. 'Visitors arriving on the Up.'

Of course Louisa expected her son but the tone of her husband's voice and his use of the word *visitors*, plural, tickled her brain. She appeared from the kitchen with flour decorating her apron and hands. Receiving visitors in this outfit was definitely unacceptable. There stood her husband in his usual immaculate uniform and her son likewise well attired in slacks, sports jacket, open collar and cravat—much easier for her son to tie—but making up the party appeared a young woman—*who's she?*—dressed with flair.

She was short but not tiny with a mass of red curly hair being controlled by what looked like a man's flat cap. Her face, devoid of make-up apart from a light splash of pink lipstick displayed a friendly smile. Her clothes looked elegant and her shoes particularly so.

'Ma, I'd like you to meet Isabel, my wife.'

Chapter 32

Needless to say, Rowena's speech lesson and trainspotting routine were put on hold. Louisa thought she would faint. Rowena found a new way to smile with the station master never more confused, excited and tempted to swear.

He never told me she was his wife.

As the others sorted out their rapid breathing, James explained. 'Isabel works for the same company although she's in the brainy department.' His wife's expression suggested pain. 'She used to open the heavy door to our building for me and to thank her I took her out to tea. We enjoyed one another's company and when I asked her to marry me, she surprised and delighted me by saying yes.'

Louisa and her mother purred while George struggled with shock. 'But why didn't you tell us. We would have loved to come to your wedding.'

'I told you, Jimmy,' said his wife.

Jimmy!

'I know, I know but we didn't want a religious service and Izzie's parents are not wealthy, are poorly and live in Cornwall so we decided on a registry office with my friend Gareth from work and his wife as the witnesses. I've moved into Izzy's flat in Cambridge and we would like to invite you all to tea on Sunday. There's an hour, Dad after the 3:11 Down.'

The older adults were stunned. Rowena broke the silence.

'Well I think it's wonderful,' she said in her slow drawl. 'And welcome to the family ... Is-a-bel.'

'Thank you, Mrs McClaren. You're most kind which I knew already thanks to Jimmy.'

George and Louisa smiled with enthusiasm still tainted with amazement. 'When did you learn how to keep secrets, son?' asked his mother.

'Who else knows?' asked George. 'Have you told your sister?'

'We didn't want to excite her being so close to having the baby.'

Louisa made tea. The conversation edged closer to normal.

'So what do you do at the company?' asked George expecting his new daughter-in-law to say she worked as a secretary or typist.

'I work in the psychology department studying human behaviour.'

James explained. 'I do the bald data and Izzie translates it into human behaviour traits. She's the brainy one of the family.'

So not a typist, thought George.

'I'm just a poor old BSc (Hons), Dad, but my wife's a PhD and you must never call her Mrs Miracle but *Doctor* Miracle.'

Isabel frowned. The news kept coming in waves, blow after blow.

Louisa wanted more details but worried she'd sound nosy. 'So you first met at your work?' she asked.

'Keep up, Ma,' said her son. 'I've already told you that.'

'Not exactly,' interrupted the new bride. Even James looked shocked. 'I first met or at least became aware of Jimmy at university.'

Jimmy? She's calling James Jimmy and getting away with it!

'I heard him bowling along a corridor when even his most softly spoken speech sounded loud. I saw his unique style of walking and I thought, "Is this man a student at Cambridge?" If so, he must be someone special.'

'You never told me that,' fired back James.

'You never asked and you talk so much I never got the chance.'

A sudden tension erupted. The family worried. Is this woman a bully and controlling their disabled son?

'There you are,' said James to his family. 'My wife fell in love with me even before we met.'

His enormous grin appeared, she smiled, leant in to kiss his cheek and relief flooded the room.

The refreshments played second fiddle to the presence of the visitor and to the fact the son and heir was now a married man.

When the newlyweds left, Louisa picked up the phone in a flash. 'Are you sitting down my darling?' Louisa hated upsetting her heavily pregnant daughter.

'What's happened, Mummy? Has Grannie died?'

'No but wait for it, your brother is married.'

'What?' exclaimed Victoria with a hundred questions to ask.

'He and his wife have just left. Her name's Isabel although he calls her Izzie and she calls him Jimmy. She has a PhD in ... I can't remember, something psychology, they were married in a registry office and have a flat in Cambridge.'

'Is she nice?' asked Victoria.

'Yes but different. We're all still in shock and I think your father helped himself to a swig of brandy.'

'What!' exclaimed Victoria? That last bit of news proved an even bigger shock than her brother's nuptials.

'But how are you?' asked Louisa. 'Any signs of your daughter ready to appear?'

'David thinks I'm going to be early. I'll see Dr Cole tomorrow.'

They chatted away both still having difficulty comprehending James Miracle being a husband having married in secret. Victoria appeared reluctant to ask.

'Mummy, do you know if they had to get married?'

Louisa blanched. Could it possibly be true? Was she about to become a grandmother twice and in rapid succession? Phew. After the phone conversation she went looking for her husband.

On the Down, George spoke to Monty about news of the recently arranged freight. Louisa approached and George sent the porter away waiting for his wife to speak.

'Victoria thinks the baby will come early and she asked me a question which I couldn't answer.' She paused with George hooked.

'Well?'

'She wondered if James and Isabel needed to get married.'

He reacted with stunned silence. To George it seemed highly unlikely. He knew his son, his manners and attitude to others. But if Isabel was pregnant, James wouldn't hesitate to do the right thing.

'I've faced a few tricky situations in my life, my dear but right now I'm beyond confused. Let's move slowly and rejoice in the fact our children are settled and happy.'

She leant in and kissed his cheek watched by four passengers all waiting for the next train.

David Worthington nailed it. His wife did give birth earlier than predicted, and Louisa was so glad she was there with George stuck at work. At the station, a driver on the footplate of the first train to Mildenhall called out to the SM.

'Are you a grandfather yet, Mr Miracle?'

George smiled. 'Not yet but I'm told it's any day now.'

Any day turned out to be today. Mother and baby were well and Louisa celebrated with her daughter and son-in-law. She knew telling her husband was her top priority.

The station master answered his phone. His wife cut to the chase.

'Are you sitting down?'

'What's happened?'

'Congratulations Grandpa, your daughter and grandchild are well and thriving.'

'Does she look like her grandmother?'

'More like you.'

'What?'

'She is a he and you have a grandson.'

George wanted to skip around his office. 'Marvellous,' he purred. 'So what happened to your prediction because "women know about these things"?'

'I haven't finished, Mr Stationmaster.' She milked the pause. 'His name is George.'

There were occasions when George Miracle became both happy and proud. At this particular moment he drifted over the moon.

For weeks Louisa thought about a family photo featuring four generations of females in the family Miracle. Sitting centre would be Rowena nursing the little girl, the great-granddaughter, with herself and Victoria either side. Such a photo was not to be for now. Of course several photos were taken including one with baby George in the seated grandfather George's arms with Dr Worthington standing proudly behind the beaming station master.

This became the start of a new chapter in George Miracle's life. His railway duties didn't change although other types of change came chugging along the line. A hidden timetable promised massive change.

But now a new generation needed care and with his wife and occasionally other family members, George took to babysitting like a duck to water.

With son James now married, the family was constantly busy. Isabel was not with child and those who thought she might have been copped a tickle from their conscience. Life was never so happy and hectic until ...

Months after wee George arrived, his great-grandmother died peacefully in her sleep. Louisa collapsed with grief. As a teenage domestic in a grand country house, her mother became pregnant when tricked or forced into having sex by a wealthy man. The next morning he regretted his actions and decades later, the man's vast wealth, pretty much his entire estate was bequeathed to Rowena and their daughter.

In the days before the funeral, Louisa walked in the fields behind the station thinking about her mother and the sacrifices she made keeping and raising her daughter. Now her Mummy was gone. Louisa's tears were gone; she'd run the well dry. Her heartache remained and she now realized she had become the matriarch of the family. George long ago became the patriarch. He was in his 50s. Did he want to retire? If so, where would they go and what would he do?

George never showed any interest in gardening or making or repairing things in a shed at the bottom of the garden. More grandchildren might encourage him to do so.

A huge crowd attended Rowena's funeral. Hundreds of people had stayed at Hamilton-Weir House to be cared for by Mrs McClaren. Many travelled serious distances to pay their respects.

The Mildenhall Branch kept busy. Not busy enough to wave away fears of closure but as Redvers Steady now started repeating, 'Any branch with a turntable at its terminus will always be well regarded.' Mildenhall was one of few stations, certainly on a branch line with an operating turntable. A few cynics reckoned its main benefit was to give the footplate crew something to do in the lengthy periods between trains. Push gentlemen, push.

George disagreed with Ready. 'I don't think passengers give a hoot if their loco is tender first and nor do officials at British Railways who are only interested in the bottom line.'

Branch lines up and down the country developed a feeling of dread. Closure became a frightening word. George pushed his grandson along the platform. 'Keep him away from locomotives,' said

Louisa, the doting grandmother. 'All that smoke is bad for his health and the sounds will terrify him.'

George became an expert at accepting his wife's instructions while finding a way to do what he wanted. His grandson would become like his Uncle James and fall in love with trains.

Then it happened. The Crabbie was finally put out of its misery. The branch from Whittleton to Crabbwell closed. A pattern developed. British Railways stopped passenger services but kept freight running although when locals weren't looking, the freight too was withdrawn. Why were closures separated? It may have been to quell local protests by not chopping off the line in one fell swoop.

George heard about it from Stephen Fitzsimons and read about it in official correspondence under *Line Closures*. Sadly Crabbwell didn't die alone. Now the whole network was nationalized, the axe began to swing freely and often.

George discovered branch lines were closed at Ashbourne, Woodstock, Canterbury and Whitstable and in London at Crystal Palace, and these closures were only the tip of the iceberg.

The government became serious about the railways. There were voices wanting to be ruthless in closing lines and others who disliked even hated the mess in which the transport system found itself. The optimists won with a decision made to invest using serious money.

George heard rumours of proposed closures. Steam lost its allure. Coal and water were cheap and available but two new goals stood out; replace steam with diesel power and electrify lines up and down the country. George pondered these plans.

'Those changes will never happen on our branch, Redvers,' he said. 'Or if they do, they won't save our line or our livelihood.'

'Now George, since when did you become a paid-up member of the Pessimists' Society? Listening to you anyone would think the railways are heading for extinction.'

It hurt the SM at Barnwell Junction to think like so and to say what he thought but a premonition first encountered years ago had never left him. In fact it grew ever darker and ever more powerful. He believed the railways in Britain were in for a period of upheaval; in fact for George Miracle, terrible times lay just beyond the next bend.

Chapter 33

Diesel locomotives were up and about in the late 19th century with American and mainland European railway companies pioneers in the field. Britain lagged behind but the LMS became one of the first UK companies to use small shunting locomotives powered by a diesel engine. It was a slow process and for many a sad moment, the thin edge of the wedge for nostalgic steam footplate crews and steam train lovers throughout the land. Mind you, diesel lovers rejoiced.

The powers in charge reckoned electrification would be another worthwhile power source and planning for construction of overhead power lines began. In addition to diesel and electric power, renewal of many miles of line plus updated signaling was badly needed. Maintenance had been a low priority for decades and now the chickens were coming home to roost. British Railways had to modernize and repair or see the whole network suffer to the point of bankruptcy.

George thought less of the country's network concentrating on his own little domain and filled his spare moments entertaining his namesake fifty years his junior. He adored his grandson.

One of the staff at Hamilton-Weir House, an expert knitter, made wee George a jumper with a steam loco on its front. Grandpa delighted in taking the boy for walks in his push chair pointing out all manner of sights and sounds.

On babysitting duty, Louisa sat feeding her grandson one day when his mother arrived to collect her son.

'Hello Mummy and how is young George?' Victoria kissed her mother. 'Minding his p's and q's I hope?'

'He's always perfect, just ask your father who's always asking when his grandson is coming and if we could babysit an extra day.'

Victoria laughed. 'Well he might just get his wish, Mummy.' The women looked at one another. 'Dr Cole tells me I'm expecting.'

Holding a full spoon, Louisa stared at an open mouth but quickly stood and kissed her daughter.

'Wonderful, wonderful news my darling,' she said. 'And this time I won't make a prediction if only to avoid your father having bragging rights for a month.'

They laughed only to be interrupted by the station master.

'Laughter ladies; and what pray tell is so amusing?' Neither woman spoke sending George's suspicions into overdrive. 'Why am I suspicious?'

Victoria put him out of his curiosity. 'Can you fit in more babysitting, Grandpa? Little George is going to have a sibling.'

His face exploded with joy as he hugged his daughter and asked. 'Is it just the one?'

Christmas used to always be held at Hamilton-Weir House. Rowena McFarlane, the founder and driving force of the charity became a fixture in the place, and with the patriarch away in London working for the Railway Executive Committee, Louisa and the children settled in the huge house in one of its renovated outbuildings. Nearly a decade later, life had changed in dramatic ways. Sadly Grannie Mac was no longer around and both the Miracle children were married with one grandchild running around and another on the way.

This coming Christmas they agreed to have a smaller family-only get-together with George and Louisa, their children, their son-in-law and daughter-in-law and baby George. Holding it at Barnwell Junction meant the patriarch could remain on duty slipping out whenever a train pulled in.

Louisa insisted on doing all the catering. Victoria was well into her pregnancy and her mother insisted she put her feet up and enjoy the day. The mother-to-be, husband David and wee George were the first to arrive. More presents were added to those already beneath the Christmas tree the station master had set up with Louisa the champion tree-decorator.

David volunteered to be in charge of the drinks and the SM's roaring fire made the room and ground floor of the house ever so cosy. The only absentees were son James and his wife, Isabel.

'James rang to say they would catch the later train and we are not to start without them,' said Louisa.

Grandpa George checked his watch. 'He's due in six minutes.'

His son-in-law made a friendly remark along the lines of him always being a station master.

'Well James or no James, let's enjoy the eggnog,' said Louisa and the tasty beverage appeared for those who were not pregnant, teetotal or a child. That cut out more than half the company.

Victoria teased her father. 'Now Daddy, are you prepared to guess the sex of your second grandchild?'

'I'm no expert, it's your mother who is but if you asked me to say, I can confidently predict it will be a boy ... or a girl.' The pause before the last three words drew a reaction.

More laughter and teasing ensued as the SM stood and excused himself. Inside, the others heard the Down. They watched wee George heading towards the pile of presents beneath the tree and his father stepped in at the last moment to prevent an early raid. The toddler appeared more interested in the wrapping paper than the contents.

They heard the others outside on the platform and the SM entered first but not as expected. He looked shocked, as if he'd witnessed a derailment at his station. The others stared at him and worried.

'George, what's happened?' asked Louisa seeking assurance nothing bad or worse, nothing terrible had happened.

He struggled to speak. 'James and Isabel have brought a guest.'

Immediate relief for Louisa but curiosity took over. Why would they bring a guest and not give the matriarch a warning?

James stepped into the room with his usual ferocious grin arriving first. 'Merry Christmas,' he beamed. 'And may I introduce my family.'

Silence bounced around the room and even the flames in the fireplace dimmed as oxygen was sucked into lungs. Isabel entered pushing a pram.

A what!?

George, having greeted the couple on the Down platform was still recovering. The others sat in full-stunned mode. It's a pram!

James explained. 'We have adopted a baby girl. Her name is Rose and she's three months old tomorrow.'

More stunned silence from the others although baby George made another thwarted journey towards the base of the tree.

'She's asleep,' whispered Isabel, 'but please come and see.'

Louisa looked at her husband who gave a small shrug and his face screamed, "Don't ask me, I'm as much in the dark as you". The grandmother moved to the pram and looked at the latest addition to her family. Grandma melted. She could see a face from the tip of its nose to just above its eyebrows. The cold outside did nothing to little Rose who was as snug as a bug in a rug.

'She's divine,' whispered Louisa.

Victoria took time to lift her swollen body to the vertical where she too inspected the infant then looked at Isabel who smiled and at her brother who naturally grinned.

'Have you two any more surprises?' asked Victoria.

James seized the moment. 'I thought it appropriate to have a baby at Christmas.' His grin expanded.

The family settled and waited for the fine print. James began.

'Izzie and I have been talking about starting a family for a while and after going through all the options we decided to adopt.'

His wife continued. 'The council sent us to a "mother and baby home" run by the Church of England. They asked all sorts of questions.' Isabel stopped as energetic James wanted to speak.

'When Izzie said her name was Dr Lambert, they thought she meant a medical doctor and wanted to give us a baby straightaway.'

'Dr Lambert?' queried Louisa wondering about the surname.

James explained. 'Izzie has not taken my family name and we don't call her Mrs Miracle.' He spoke directly at his mother. 'There will only ever be one of those.'

The rest of the family bit their tongues.

Isabel continued. 'They approved our application and showed us photos of babies. They said we should change the name of the one we chose so it can start a new life with its new parents.'

The new parents paused expecting a torrent of questions. Silence.

James dived in. 'Oh and Rose is not the only new addition to our family.' The others, already in shock, were spellbound afraid of what else would be announced.

'We have a puppy called Archimedes. He's gorgeous.' James added a note of caution. 'He's being cared for by a neighbour but our landlord won't allow pets so we have to move out in the New Year.'

'You're homeless?' gasped Louisa.

'Don't worry, Ma. We'll find a place,' assured James to his now seriously worried mother.

'Well why don't we sit down and eat,' she said. So after more Rose peeking and explaining, the Miracles enjoyed a unique Christmas lunch with no shortage of topics to discuss.

The food proved delicious but the conversation gave certain luncheon guests a side serving of nerves.

Isabel spoke in her usual blunt manner. 'I'd love to learn a few feeding tips,' she said. 'I fibbed when I told the nurse at the adoption agency I'm an old hand at giving a baby its bottle.'

Louisa and her daughter glanced at one another with both offering to help. *Does this adoption have problems written all over it?*

James excelled at inserting his oversized boot in his mouth. 'We waited a while before adopting so as to stop those people who thought we had to get married.' A pang of conscience whacked certain diners. 'Silly old them,' he said grinning at family members.

The SM didn't feel confident in contributing and breathed better when his watch announced the next train. He left the table.

What a Christmas. At night Mr and Mrs Miracle, that's the Missus who took her husband's name, settled down alone after the last train.

'Not your usual Christmas, my dear,' said George.

'I thought I knew our son but he continues to amaze me. And Isabel knows nothing about being a mother. I'm worried George. Do you think she's controlling James?'

He didn't answer. He never claimed any expertise in matters domestic. 'Little Rose is beautiful.'

Louisa agreed without question. 'She's divine.' But as a mother she wondered about the infant's birth mother. 'I wonder where the real mother is right now. Is her heart broken? Will she spend the rest of her life wondering about the daughter she gave away?'

George thought of Annie and her given-away son, Oscar. 'Or had taken away?' They dwelt on the unknown woman's suffering.

The fire faded. George put an arm around his wife. They survived another Christmas, copped a huge surprise and for George, the world of railways seemed to be teetering on a cliff preparing to fall. Would change occur and if so, would it be minor or massive?

'We'll soon have three grandchildren, George Miracle. You might have to retire early to cope with all your babysitting duties.'

In the darkness he smiled, said nothing but thought plenty.

'We must insist on James and Isabel moving into Ham House. There's plenty of room.' In the darkness George nodded.

A week later the phone rang early at Barnwell Junction and Ham House. George took a call but at Ham House, Louisa helped her son, daughter-in-law and their adopted daughter settle. Their much loved puppy, a Jack Russell called Archimedes caused them to move. He needed more attention than baby Rose whose PhD was in sleeping.

'Louisa,' called a member of staff. 'Telephone for you.'

At Barnwell Junction George answered his phone and told the caller his wife was unavailable.

'But you must be so proud, Mr Miracle,' said a woman.

'I am,' he replied not having a clue what she meant.

'It's not every day you are listed in the New Year's Honours List.'

George paused. *What New Year's Honours' List?* He promised to pass on the congratulations, hung up and found the day's paper. He searched and found the right page when the phone rang again. Another former resident at Ham House wanted to congratulate Louisa. By the time he thanked the caller and promised to pass on the message, he'd found the relevant section.

For meritorious service to the community
Mrs Louisa Miracle, BEM
Hamilton-Weir House
Cambridgeshire

He eventually reached his wife but wanted to congratulate her in person. 'Why didn't you tell me?'

'Oh George, I received a letter ages ago when Victoria was struggling with little George and I put it aside and forgot all about it.'

'You forgot about the King congratulating you?'

The SM began directing a mix of praise and criticism at his wonderful, forgetful wife but her pleasure in receiving the award was outstripped by the pleasure it gave the man she loved.

Chapter 34

The government decided to spend, spend and spend. Hundreds of millions of pounds would be made available to "fix" the railways in Britain. The days of the privately-owned railway companies were long gone. The money for this railway makeover would come from the pockets of the taxpayers. After nationalization, the railways were owned and run and would now be fixed by the government.

It's been said governments are often good at spending money because it's not theirs—it's someone else's—yours and mine, and the situation creates a massive potential problem. You usually care about spending money when it's your own but not so much when the taxpayer coughs up the dough.

The great railway modernization scheme began. But would it work? Would this splash the cash set up the whole British network enabling it to roar into the future? Time would tell.

Surely replacing steam with diesel, building better carriages and trucks, improving tracks and signaling and setting up electrification in various places would cut costs, and make the railways much more appealing to passengers and carriers of freight.

Alas not as was hoped because of the lack of co-ordination between various railway bodies, and the growth of motorways.

Just because it became a national railway network didn't mean strategic planners were all on the same page. And while road transport had become a rival as far back as the 1920s now, post-World War Two, lorries which once ducked and dived through towns even villages, would soon be able to accelerate along new motorways making their travel times shorter and give their door to door service an even greater advantage. Why collect goods from a rail yard when the haulage companies could do it all on their own? These burgeoning trucking companies provided a one-stop, door-to-door service.

To further frustrate the railways, petrol rationing disappeared. People wanting to buy or hire a car could top up their tank.

So sadly after their big spend, the bottom line for British Railways was still very much in the red. For all the good the modernization did, financial losses refused to go away. It was time to get serious.

Victoria and David welcomed their second child, a daughter Madeline named after David's favourite Aunt Maddie, a spinster of her parish. The adored little girl was forever known as Maddie.

George and Louisa practised gurgling and even little George gazed in wonder at his baby sister. Cousin Rose, who looked nothing like the couple who adopted her, started life with a dozen or more foster parents as she and her new Mum and Dad settled in at Ham House.

The station master, thrilled with his growing family, spent time reading reports on government investment in railways and hearing from fellow railwaymen about the real situation at the coal face.

And speaking of coal, it was no longer as much in demand. Diesel locomotives increased in number and men working in pits wondered about their future. Surely they won't close the mines!

In London, Ernest Marples, the Tory Minister moved ministries from the Royal Mail to Transport, maintained his financial interest in a road building company and took charge of abolishing the debt the railways continued to accrue. He appointed businessman Dr Richard Beeching to study and report on the state of British Railways. The physicist and engineer began the task.

His terms of reference were short; stop the rot. Despite a massive investment in the railways in Britain in the 1950s, the railways continued to lose money and according to Minister Marples, such a situation became unacceptable. In the new decade of the 1960s, losing £300,000 a day was beyond the pale. Dr Beeching simply must find ways to reduce expenditure.

His study produced damning statistics, e.g. 1/3rd of lines carried 1% of passengers. No wonder the bottom line looked so bad.

His appointment and assignment were not secret. People discussed the possible outcomes. George Miracle and fellow SM Redvers "Ready" Steady continued their late-night Sunday chinwags.

'I've heard stations are to close, even ours,' said Ready.

'We may not have to wait for this chap Dr Beeching's report,' replied George. 'Lines are already being closed. Do you remember the closures of yesteryear?'

'Yes, sadly I do.'

'Companies closed stations and lines as long ago as the 1920s. And ever since I came to Barnwell Junction, the closures have kept coming. Where's the Midland and Great Northern today or the line from Hereford to Ludlow?'

'Gone, disappeared, never to return.'

'As is the branch I ran from Whittleton to Crabbwell.'

'We're the last of the dinosaurs, George. Our line to Mildenhall may become the final branch still running.'

George looked at his colleague. 'Yes but for how long?'

Life for the Miracle family kept on keeping on. George's sister Emily became a grandmother. Her younger son married a local girl who gave birth a few months later. George wondered if the sex education lecture he gave to his brother-in-law, the baby's grandfather, all those years ago in the Whittleton SM's office, had comprehensively failed.

Isabel accepted a research post in London and she and James and baby now toddler Rose headed south to the capital. Louisa worried but admitted the parents were doing a grand job with their daughter. Louisa "encouraged" the tenants in the Maida Vale Mews cottage to leave and James, Isabel and Rose moved into the property which held many fond memories for James as a child. Isabel became the main family breadwinner while James took in pupils for tuition in-between taking his daughter to and from nursery school becoming one of London's stay-at-home fathers.

Dr and Mrs Worthington's two children were a constant joy to their grandparents. Babysitting could never be considered a chore and requests were accepted with enthusiasm. Teaching grandson George about locomotives gave the station master endless happiness.

The SM constantly thought about retirement. There were options. Louisa's mother's cottage in Foxton, currently being rented, could become available. The mansion in Belgravia's Eaton Square provided the income to support Hamilton-Weir House and the service it provided but none of those properties appealed to George.

He explained. 'The basement at Eaton Square is a possibility although it's an ice-box and would mean evicting your half sibling.'

'Don't be ridiculous, George,' said his wife. 'You can't join the aristocracy, you're born into it. Besides we're too old and you would look silly in a top hat at a Buckingham Palace garden party.'

'Oh and you would know being an old hand at doing just that.'

'One, I only went to one,' she said. 'And who had the late King propose a toast at our wedding at *your* station?'

He wanted to look forward. 'We could retire to Ham House. I could become the under gardener.'

She returned to her sewing wanting to avoid the tricky subject of retirement until it became necessary. Instead they discussed their children and grandchildren.

And as the Miracles kept busy, Dr Beeching kept gathering data for his report soon to be revealed. The branch from Cambridge to Mildenhall kept running but now with a mix of diesel and steam.

On a sunny day George stood on the Down platform of his quiet Barnwell Junction Station. You could see a spring in his step as the air exuded warmth such to entice the bees. A kindly artist hopped out of bed before dawn and painted the sky with a fresh coat of blue, and the slightest of breezes gave the station master a feeling between relaxation and happiness. The first mail arrived and George retreated to his office.

He opened an envelope and removed the enclosed letter. Bullseye! It became one of those times when the words are understood but the brain refuses to believe or accept them. He read a simple message.

Your line is to be closed and your station shut.

With a much faster heartbeat he rang his colleague Ready Steady at the next station, Quy.

'I was just about to ring you,' said Ready.

'So it's finally happening. Does your letter state June 16?'

'Yes and the date is a disaster.'

'I'm sorry?' asked George.

'My geraniums will be coming into full bloom. Moving them could be absolutely disastrous.'

George laughed quietly. 'I don't think the government will send in the removalists or demolition team the next day. Did you note the freight will not close at the same time, and there's no mention of when we must vacate the station house?'

'It's retirement for me, George. I need to find a cottage with a greenhouse and a decent garden.'

'What about an allotment?'

Ready lost it. 'An allotment! Are you insane? My geraniums are world-class, man. Some thieving amateur will pinch a cutting and use my blooms to knock me off my perch.' He changed his voice. 'Have to go, George, the 10:46 is here.'

George hung up, girded his loins and went onto the platform to greet the Up fresh from geranium territory at Quy. He waved to the driver and said nothing.

Do the footplate crew and guards know the news? What about the men in signal boxes or working the gates at level crossings?

He said nothing to Monty his porter and went next door. Louisa sat sewing one of the station master's socks. She stopped and looked at him. After nearly 40 years of marriage to G. Miracle Esquire, she could read him like a book.

'Has someone died?' she asked.

'Yes, my career as a railwayman.'

She knew this was serious. 'Is it because of Dr Beechwood?'

'Beech*ing*, my dear and no, it's the government getting in first. The Mildenhall Branch is to close next month.'

She could see his sadness. 'Are you all right?'

He paused and gave his half smile. 'I think retirement will suit us both very nicely.' He looked around. 'Might we have an early lunch my dear?'

Chapter 35

The last passenger train left Mildenhall passing through Barnwell Junction on June 16, 1962. The line remained open to freight until the end of October 1965. But with George's station closed and his 65th birthday hurtling towards him on the latest diesel-hauled express, he retired as a railwayman and with Louisa by his side they packed and prepared to leave forever.

'Are you taking your SM uniform?' she asked as he packed it.

'Of course; they haven't asked for it back and if they do I'll tell them I didn't receive the memo.' He looked at her and fired back. 'Have you kept your wedding dress?'

'Not the same,' she said. 'Maddie or Rose may want to wear it on their wedding day.'

'And their husband-to-be might fancy wearing my SM uniform.'

His nonsensical remark caused both to laugh out loud. It covered their disappointment at leaving a railway property for the last time.

Their immediate port of call was Hamilton-Weir House with Louisa straight back in service once she unpacked. George offered his services to the gardener and began trimming edges and hedges. Retirement for George and Louisa, who never retired, meant constant work at Ham House and frequent visits from their family.

But no longer wearing an SM's cap didn't stop George Miracle being interested in his former employer—apart from a short stint with the British Army—British Railways. All the talk about Dr Richard Beeching and his reports—he produced two—fascinated the former station master. What would happen to his beloved railways?

The retired couple hadn't settled at their new address a week before the Worthingtons paid a visit. David had joined a private practice and drove a car, a Vauxhall Cresta. Young George and sister Maddie fired an arrow of brightness into the hearts of their grandparents. They were all members of a mutual admiration society.

After lunch and with the children being supervised feeding the animals, Victoria handed a plain envelope to her father.

'This is a small gift from us to both of you,' she said. 'We have booked a hotel for you for a fortnight and you leave this weekend.'

George and Louisa were stunned and looked it.

'No excuses, no procrastination,' added David. 'I'll be here at 10 on Saturday morning to drive you to the station.'

Victoria explained. 'It's to the Gleneagles Hotel in Scotland. The one Daddy you wanted to take Mummy to on your honeymoon.'

'How did you know that?' asked Louisa. She looked at her husband who shrugged; his usual response when cornered.

'This is too kind,' said Louisa. 'There's no need.'

'Of course there is,' argued Victoria. 'You've both worked countless hours for others including your family. Now it's time to put your feet up and have someone else run around looking after you.'

'I hope your rail pass is still valid,' said David to his father-in-law.

A silence before the women embraced and the men shook hands.

George never showed any interest in golf with no inclination to start now. The last stop before Mildenhall, Worlington Golf Links Halt, was the closest George ever came to striding along a fairway.

They reached the Gleneagles Hotel and were much impressed, in awe of the building and its surrounds. The dining-room they chose—there were several—and its menu kept upping their appreciation.

In their spacious room with sparkling en suite facilities and a superb view, Louisa tackled her husband as she read a brochure.

'Are you sure you won't have a few golf lessons, George? There are three courses.' He glared at her. 'You would look fabulous in plus fours, a Fair Isle sweater and a Cabbie Hat with a tassel on top.'

'I've retired Mrs Miracle not gone doolally.'

'There's horse-riding, dog-training and even falconry.'

His response saw him enter the en suite and close the door.

She called. 'There are two swimming pools and a gymnasium.'

Their delightful stay included walks through the 850 acre estate, a bus trip to Edinburgh for a tour of historic places and generally doing next to nothing, which for them proved a most unusual activity. Thinking of his youth and his father, the former SM was tempted to try fly fishing but didn't. After breakfast one morning, relaxing in a guest lounge, he reached for the morning paper and saw the headline:

"Disastrous" and "Crime"

On page 1, the article grabbed his attention. It was a review of the report by Dr Richard Beeching, chairman of British Railways.

No-one understood the state of the railways in Britain better than George Miracle. Nothing in this much anticipated report could surprise him. Alas unexpected surprises flattened the holidaying SM.

Staggered best described his response. Dr Beeching proposed the permanent closure of about 2,500 stations and 5,000 miles of track.

What on Earth?

Of course people protested. It was *their* branch line, *their* station on the chopping block. The unions screamed about the loss of 60,000+ jobs. George read how the Minister for Transport, Mr Ernest Marples, the former sweetie seller outside Old Trafford, told the Commons nothing would happen without his approval.

Why do I not feel better having read his statement? thought George. He, in fact everyone had good cause not to trust the politician with a financial interest in road building. Mr Marples went on to say the government warmly welcomed the report and added, 'Certain roads might have to be widened or strengthened to handle the extra traffic once the rail lines have been closed.' Now there's a surprise.

Dressed ready for an outing, Louisa found her husband. 'I thought we might take a train trip today,' she said smiling.

That smile vanished and she couldn't describe the look on her husband's face.

The Miracles returned to Cambridgeshire refreshed. All the way home, George looked out at stations checking to see if they were on the list to be closed. Louisa knew better than to say anything related to Dr Beeching. She was quietly delighted her husband retired before the drastic report became public.

She worried having heard about men who work hard, retire then drop dead. Being an assistant gardener at Hamilton-Weir House would never give George the happiness he received as an SM. What could she suggest to help the man she loved from dying of boredom?

A week later and back at home she received the surprise of her life when George answered a phone call and went to find his wife.

'How would you feel about a railway here at Hamilton-Weir House?' He stopped speaking waiting for her response.

'A railway, here on the estate?' He nodded. 'In Scotland you distinctly told me you hadn't gone doolally. Now I know you lied.'

'It'll be a miniature railway running around the lake.'

'What lake? There isn't a lake.'

'Yet,' he said starting one of his slow-burning grins. 'First we create a lake tapping into the stream running through the plantation, stock the lake with fish, then lay a 7¼ inch track around the lake, set up a home station and maybe a halt, acquire a ride-on steam loco, open carriages and welcome tourists in the summer.'

Louisa's heart pounded, her happiness buzzed. She kept a lid on her emotions and began mocking her husband.

'This is all about you dragging out your SM's uniform, waving a flag and blowing a whistle.'

'True but it'll get me and the grandchildren out from under your feet.' She dropped the half-peeled potato and the knife and hurried to hug him with all the strength she could muster.

'You could be the Queen and cut the ribbon on the first day.'

'George, I won't be here in fifty years.'

'Not fifty, two at the most.'

'But how, I mean where is this railway coming from?'

'I've just received an offer of rolling stock, a station, a signal box and about a mile of track.'

'What?' gasped Louisa. 'Who's made the offer?'

'You remember the chap we met at Gleneagles, Mr Gillespie?'

'The one with the miniature railway in his back yard?'

'No-one in his family is interested and he reckons once he's gone it'll be ripped up a la Beeching. He's coming on Sunday to chat about his gift to Ham House.'

Louisa shook her head. This was the perfect present for a man missing his work. It would be superb for the disabled children and their families and perfect for her grandchildren. She teased him.

'When you say there'll be fish in this new lake, are you serious?'

'Listen woman, you fry the chips and I'll catch the fish.'

Epilogue

Richard Beeching became a life peer, Baron Beeching and died in 1985. Many disagreed with his reports but few of those were lorry and bus drivers and road builders. By 1965 Britain had a Labour government and Mr Marples' replacement did not get on with Dr B who resigned and went back to private industry. His legacy stood out in rotting sleepers, weed-sprouting lines, rusty rolling stock and abandoned, derelict stations.

During the 1964 campaign, Labour promised to stop the rail closures but didn't; how strange, a broken promise from a politician.

One criticism of the Beeching cuts claimed he produced a short-term gain and a long-term loss. His brief to save money did not bring financial prosperity. He saw the railways in monetary terms ignoring the social and public service role trains played. Ironically his task to cut costs sat alongside his salary far greater than that of the PM and all other heads of industry. Unsurprisingly the line to his home in East Grinstead kept running.

Did Beeching fail to consider the future? Did he ever wonder what Britain might be like in 50 years' time? He made a prediction on the future 20 years hence and proved to be hopelessly wrong. No-one owned a crystal ball but if car ownership took off, would the roads become crowded? Did he, did anyone know the meaning of gridlock?

Surely the population would increase and more people would travel producing a greater demand for public transport. Did that notion slip into his thinking? Did Transport Minister Marples give the good doctor a bespoke pair of blinkers?

Beeching was described as arrogant towards transport policy and the politician Tony Benn declared, "Beeching imagined himself as a new de Gaulle, emerging from industry to save the nation". The journalist Matthew Engel stated, "He misread the future very badly".

Hard hit were many seaside resorts. Families spent their summer hols at places with a train into the town. No train, no holidaymakers.

Branch lines were feeders to main lines. Close the branch and the main lines suffered. Worse, Beeching made no recommendation re the land over which closed lines once ran. The government developed a policy disposing of land. Bridges were required by law to be maintained. Close the line and you don't have to spend a penny.

Mind you there were benefits. Beeching pushed for unit trains in which an entire train would carry the one product e.g. cars, or carry products all of which were going to the one destination.

For decades previously if a freight train carried a variety of items heading for a variety of destinations, this would involve much shunting in yards, uncoupling, pushing wagons back and forth and recoupling adding time to the journey thus adding to the expense. Unit trains certainly saved money and still do today.

Beeching recommended fast intercity trains which meant large numbers of passengers could travel quickly without numerous stops. This part of his legacy has continued ever since.

But road transport was not always the first choice as many farmers preferred trains. Too late, they disappeared. Strawberries and flowers carried by a lorry would not take kindly to the bumps and swerves meaning the fruit and blooms were damaged. Not so by train.

Haulage companies preferred delivering to major depots. It was not worth their while to deliver small orders all over the place. So by closing many rural lines, producers copped a double whammy.

Replacement buses took over with many duplicating trains running from closed station to closed station. Plenty of passengers hated buses, refused to use them causing bus routes to be cancelled.

And did Dr Beeching consider the safety factor? More lorries and buses meant more accidents and road fatalities. Trains were safer.

Another major unintentional consequence of the cuts saw the birth of heritage railways. Often only running a short distance, in time these railway societies thrived. They took over an abandoned line, often just a part of it, and saved a slice of British railway history.

Quick thinking individuals formed societies, bought locomotives, rescuing engines from scrap yards and transporting rolling stock vast distances by road to start a new life in a new railway company. The restoration of stations and signal boxes became a sight to behold.

Passengers longing for the halcyon days of steam flocked to these heritage lines and still do today.

When tracks were lifted, certain track beds were covered with tarmac or rolled and turned into walking and cycling paths. No trains but the scenery, bridges, viaducts and culverts remain in situ. Elsewhere miles of closed lines succumbed to Mother Nature.

Many station masters' houses were bought and became private residences. The entire station at the former Royal Station at Wolferton is a private residence and a majestic living museum.

There are instances where a line axed by Beeching has been re-born. The Okehampton to Exeter line is back running and the government has given money to open other closed lines in the Department of Transport's Restoring Your Railways Fund.

Dozens of former stations have been restored and new ones built but other lines will never re-open thanks to planning decisions. With a line closed, developers applied and councils approved meaning an estate or a business park now sits where once a line and stations used to operate. Farmers too snapped up unused railway land.

A new railway did open soon after Dr Beeching's cuts. It came alive in the grounds of a country estate near Cambridge, home to the charity at Hamilton-Weir House. George Miracle became the driving force behind the miniature railway which ran a total of 1 mile and 1 chain around a man-made lake. Everything needed for the railway came from a Scotsman in Perth who decades ago created the line in his back garden. None of his family wanted to take over the running of this private railway and when by chance, George Miracle met Dougal Gillespie at the Gleneagles Hotel, the re-birth was sealed. Known as the Miracle Railway, the transfer did take time. Not the fifty years suggested by Mrs Miracle but just over two years before the first service departed. Louisa Miracle did in fact cut the ribbon.

Dougal's family celebrated seeing the line removed but grumbled when they realized the cost of moving said line and its buildings, rolling stock, signals and more from Perthshire to Cambridgeshire would cost a pretty penny thus depleting the patriarch's funds in his will. Were they related to Sophronia and Enoch Hamilton-Weir?

George contacted a number of his railway friends and nearly all responded with enthusiasm. Retired railwaymen saw an opportunity to get back "on the rail". Ready Steady offered to decorate the station with his prized geraniums. A chap with a bulldozer, a relative of a former resident at Ham House, gave his weekends and his bulldozer to kick start the creation of the lake to be named Loch Gillespie. The benefactor arrived to deposit the first hatchlings in his pond.

A call for retired enginemen to drive the ride-on loco gave George a headache. How could he say no to so many keen retired drivers?

Being a few miles from Cambridge, a modest road appeared at the rear of the estate with a small bus purchased. It left Cambridge station every hour on train days—summer weekends and bank holidays. Families came from near and far and by train with the bus ferrying them to and from the Miracle Railway.

George's sister Emily brought her family including two grandchildren for Christmas 1970, and Grandpa Miracle had the loco fired up exclusively for Ham House residents and his family.

The one disappointment was the absence of son James, his wife Isabel and their daughter Rose.

'But why can't you come?' asked Louisa on the phone a week before December 25. Isabel hesitated. 'James is not well,' is all she said. Naturally Louisa wanted full details. 'He gets tired more easily these days and in the cold, I think he's better off at home.'

Louisa explained the situation to George. They looked at one another worried with both thinking the worst.

'Is this serious?' asked Louisa.

George took his time. 'Possibly,' he said not wanting to distress his wife. 'Remember the doctor who told us James might not reach 20?'

'I'll go to London and find out the truth.'

'We'll both go after New Year.'

They did and were warmly welcomed. Rose had blossomed into a delightful young girl and with two highly educated parents seemed destined for a distinguished life. This time, James was the target of the visit. He maintained his impish grin but sat throughout. Louisa, with heart thumping, wanted the truth.

'How are you, son?' she asked, 'and please tell me everything.' She said "me" and not "us" playing her motherly card.

'I'm fine, Ma, just look at me,' he replied speaking more slowly than usual.

'You're not fine, Daddy,' said Rose scaring her grandparents and even giving James and Isabel a start. 'Tell Grannie and Pop what the doctor told you.'

Another pause and this time the tension moved up two notches.

'What would doctors know?' said the man who grew up with cerebral palsy and still lived with it today.

His mother snapped. 'Please don't insult us, James.' This time she dragged in the son's father using "us".

James surrendered and told all taking his time to pronounce his words. 'Apparently my heart is misbehaving. The specialist thinks it is growing weaker. I am to take life slower and he recommends I use a wheelchair whenever possible.'

George jumped in. 'What can we do to help?'

'Have you obtained a second opinion?' asked Louisa.

James copied his mother calling a spade a spade. 'I'm taking a drug to thin my blood and I have two of the best nurses in the world who do everything for me except wipe my bottom.' He grinned while the others didn't. 'However, I still have that pleasure to look forward to.' Out came a bigger grin.

Emotion spilt onto the lounge-room floor and the farewell from his parents was moving. George kissed his son and told him he needed help with the bookkeeping for the Miracle Railway. James could handle such a task with his eyes closed and it was a sad attempt at trying to get his boy involved in the project.

'Do you want me to go trainspotting like I did at Wolferton?' asked James again with his teeth exposed to the world.

The former SM struggled not to cry. On the train trip back to Cambridge, George and Louisa spent a lot of time thinking and not speaking.

The miniature railway was a godsend. Louisa was certain it kept her husband alive and well. James eventually made it to Ham House with everyone waiting on him hand and foot. His wife and daughter were brilliant in caring for him and his father took much pride in pushing his boy in his wheelchair along the tiny Miracle Railway platform.

Back in London and only two months after his visit to see his parents, James' heart gave up and the man died in his sleep.

It hit his wife and daughter hard but his parents were shattered. They hugged one another for an age and wept without caring.

'Parents do not bury their children,' said Louisa to which George made no reply. The lump in his throat stopped him from speaking.

The funeral was standing room only and the coffin placed on an undertaker's trolley with two of the pallbearers in their wheelchair. They were all former residents at Hamilton-Weir House.

Elsewhere their Lordships Carruthers and Fitzsimons passed away. George Carruthers' son, George Miracle's godson left the railways and became a Gillie in Aberdeenshire. George and Valerie Carruthers' daughter, Annie, once cared for by Nanny Louisa McClaren, married an architect who supervised the renovations to Tudor House in Hampstead.

Stephen Fitzsimons, upon the death of his American wife and inspired by George and Louisa Miracle, left his estate to a charity for injured servicemen and women as a hospice.

Of the trio, George Miracle outlived his two friends. He suffered abdominal pain in silence and after being nagged so much by his wife, finally agreed to having a chat with his son-in-law.

David was spoken to in no uncertain terms by both his wife and mother-in-law about how he should go hard on the old station master. 'No pussyfooting around,' was the order. The next day George was in hospital. His symptoms were those of an older male with prostate cancer.

Tests and more tests provided a prognosis. The cancer had spread elsewhere and surgery was deemed to be ineffective. Family members came from near and far. The doctors told Louisa the possible or rather the likely outcome, and with her daughter and son-in-law by her side remained brave throughout knowing the man she always loved was going to die sooner than she hoped. She told the world he was a typical fighter and would go on forever.

They knew she didn't believe it but not a soul contradicted her.

George was sent home to die. Once he became too ill, he would be sent to a place to receive palliative care. In the meantime, stubborn old fool that he was, and with summer a-comin' in, he insisted on going to work on his railway. Grandson George came for the weekend and was assigned the task of station master's keeper. He pushed his grandfather in the wheelchair once owned by the late James Miracle.

Station staff all knew the boss was poorly and made a point of finding a minute or two to come and have a chat. George loved it.

After the first train of the day pulled out, young George pushed his grandfather to the end of the platform.

'Pop, I want you to be the first to know.'

'Oh you're not getting married,' groaned the SM, hiding his delight. 'Your uncle did and even started a family without telling me or your grandmother.'

The young man smiled. 'Not marriage, Pop, it's a career choice.' The old man stared at his namesake. 'Despite my father urging me to go to university, I've decided to join the railways.'

The retired railwayman sat there speechless.

'I applied for a porter position and have been accepted.'

'But I could have helped you,' almost groaned the former SM. 'Why didn't you ask me?'

'I wanted to make it on my own, Pop, but I did add a note saying my grandfather was retired station master George Miracle.'

The old man still couldn't speak. He opened his arms and the men embraced. For ages, George senior couldn't wipe the smile off his face. Everyone couldn't get over his cheery behaviour which went on for a month. When Louisa was told her husband's end was near, she contacted Isabel and Rose and all his loved ones gathered around his bed. Pain-relief drugs saw the dying station master drift in and out of consciousness. Dabbing eyes became the norm for family members.

Just as everyone thought he'd finally slipped away, he rallied. Louisa was holding his hand.

'What is it, George? Can I get you something?'

He struggled to speak. 'Is James recording the arrival and departure times at Wolferton?'

Looking at her husband, she spoke with a calm confidence.

'Yes my darling and he'll report to you after the last Up.'

There was a smile on the station master's lips; that once-seen never-forgotten half smile which appeared effortlessly, always preparing to break free, as in his 80th year and still in harness, George Miracle pulled in at his final terminus.

The Detective Joanna Best Mysteries

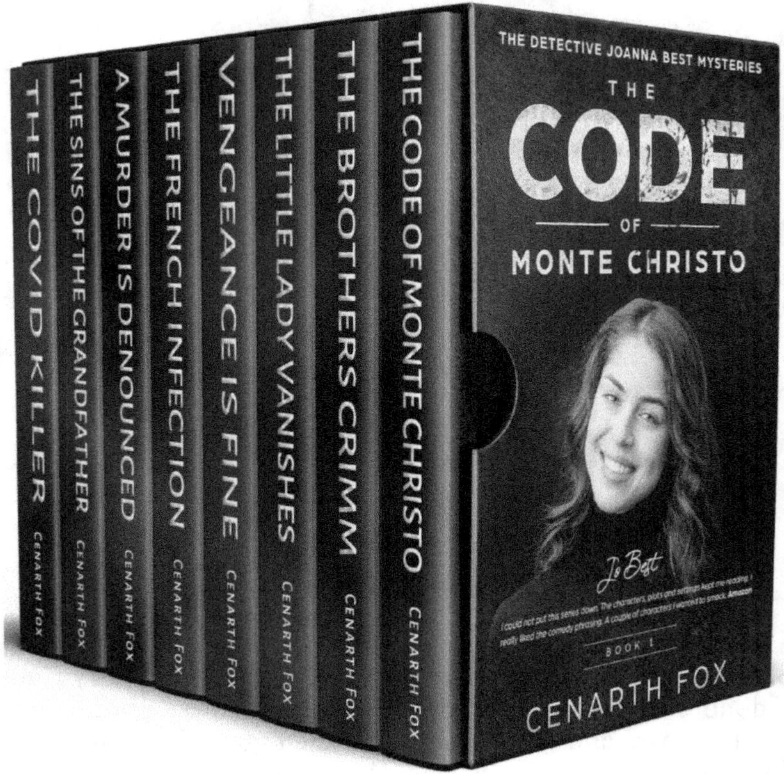

www.cenfoxbooks.com

Joanna Best is the youngest homicide detective in town. Smart, feisty and gorgeous, she's brilliant at cracking cases and rubbing people up the wrong way. Jealous colleagues are desperate to undermine her. Certain criminals want her dead. Juggling a career with Victoria Police, having three men madly in love with her, and a strange family, Jo Best's adventures will drag you in. Her second banana is an Australian born Chinese IT guru who makes computers sing. Her best pal is a female 60ish police surgeon, a forensic genius and chocoholic.

I could not put this series down. The characters, plots, settings, kept me reading. I really liked the word comedy phrasing. A couple of characters I wanted to smack. **Amazon**

Sherlock Holmes

The great man is soon to retire. On his last night at Baker Street, the loyal landlady drops a bombshell. Holmes is staggered. Mrs Hudson has done what!? Sherlock Holmes never panics—until now. Dr Watson arrives and is stunned. It's their greatest challenge. Sir Arthur Conan Doyle is furious. A famous author turned WW1 counter—intelligence spy is on the case. *The Strand Magazine* smells a scoop. Inspector Lestrade from Scotland Yard plans revenge, and at stake is the brilliant reputation of the world's most famous consulting detective. His only hope is to 'play the game'.

www.cenfoxbooks.com

A delightfully imaginative pastiche. Recommended. **Peter Blau BSI**
An extraordinary book, one of the most enjoyable pieces of Holmesian fiction I've read in a long time ... a complex, ingenious and deliciously funny story of intersecting realities, and the conclusion is entirely satisfactory. I love it! **Roger Johnson**
Commissioning Editor: *The Sherlock Holmes Journal*

Three World War Two Thrillers

Louise Beatrice Wellesley, nicknamed Plum by her big brothers, is a brilliant and beautiful English actress studying at Cambridge in 1939. She's recruited as a spy for the Secret Service and soon is on stage in a Parisian nightclub wearing a costume to shock her mother. Sharing a dressing-room with Edith Piaf is never dull. War begins and in Paris, Louise fights Nazis, the French police, part of the Resistance, and a British traitor. Back home at Windsor Castle, she joins a group of actors and stars in *Cinderella* before the Royal Family. When the IRA kidnaps a Royal, the leading lady carries out a Girls-own rescue and so impresses Winston, he demands she join the SOE. Plum plays the role of a nun in Lyon, is captured and tortured by the Gestapo, fights an archbishop, climbs the Pyrenees and, back in London, uncovers a mole in Baker Street thanks to someone who knows Sherlock Holmes. Go girl.

I have read 100's of books on WW2. I can honestly say this trilogy will go down as one of the most enjoyable. All 3 books were riveting. I adored her and can't recommend these books enough. **Amazon 5★**

A Plum Jewel is the third in the series about a beautiful young actress turned spy. In the opinion of this reader it may be the best. Cenarth Fox has loaded this tale with so many twists and obstacles the reader may feel the need to take notes. Mr. Fox's knowledge of the working of wartime Britain and France is remarkable. The reader is right in the middle of the action. I can't recommend this book strongly enough. **Scott Skipper 5 stars**

The Plum Trilogy – www.cenfoxbooks.com

Agatha Christie and the Brontes

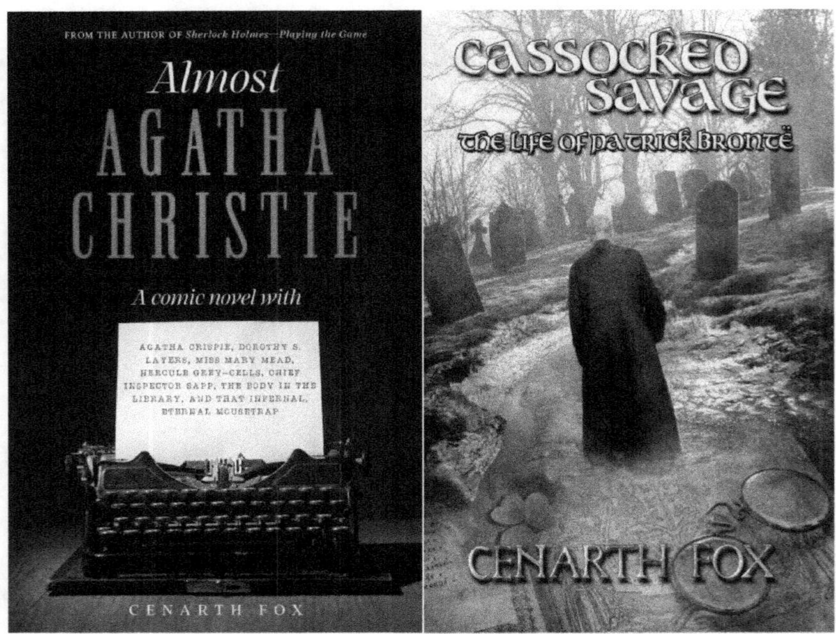

Agatha Crispie is an unheard of novelist living on the south coast writing unheard of tales such as *The Rat Trap* and *Murder on the Oriental Express*. Will they ever be published? There's a body in the library and Agatha vanishes. Miss Mary Mead and Monsieur Grey-Cells find ashes in the grate. Agatha's ashes? If you know the Dame's characters and stories, it's a hoot. There's so much of Agatha Christie in *Almost Agatha Christie*.

Patrick Bronte, father of the famous sisters, lived an amazing life. From poverty in Ireland he graduates from Cambridge University. He buries his wife and 5 of their 6 children. All his children predecease him. Celebrated author Elizabeth Gaskell writes a biography of Patrick's daughter Charlotte and castigates the Anglican priest. He forgives the writer. But others don't and one suggests Patrick should be taken into the garden and shot. Discover the truth in this moving and revealing novel.

www.cenfoxbooks.com

Meet the Author

I always enjoy hearing from readers with their questions and/or comments. I have a free newsletter (Foxy's Follies) with news about my latest books, plays and musicals. If you'd like a copy, please send a request by email. I never share the email address of my subscribers.

cen@cenfoxbooks.com
writer@foxplays.com

And if you'd care to post a review of my books on Amazon, Goodreads or both, I'll be most grateful.

Happy reading

Cenarth Fox
www.cenfoxbooks.com

P.S. The scripts/librettos of my stage shows can be read online at www.foxplays.com